DEMONS RISING
THE STORY OF THE WAYWARD SCOUT

Dutch Van Alstin

Copyright © 2019 Dutch Van Alstin.

All rights reserved. No part of this book may be reproduced, stored, or transmitted by any means—whether auditory, graphic, mechanical, or electronic—without written permission of the author, except in the case of brief excerpts used in critical articles and reviews. Unauthorized reproduction of any part of this work is illegal and is punishable by law.

ISBN: 978-1-6847-0572-6 (sc)
ISBN: 978-1-6847-0573-3 (hc)
ISBN: 978-1-6847-0571-9 (e)

Library of Congress Control Number: 2019907205

Because of the dynamic nature of the Internet, any web addresses or links contained in this book may have changed since publication and may no longer be valid. The views expressed in this work are solely those of the author and do not necessarily reflect the views of the publisher, and the publisher hereby disclaims any responsibility for them.

Any people depicted in stock imagery provided by Getty Images are models, and such images are being used for illustrative purposes only.
Certain stock imagery © Getty Images.

Lulu Publishing Services rev. date: 06/12/2019

ACKNOWLEDGMENTS

I must thank some very special people who have been instrumental to me in my writing, each in their own unique way:

My friend and fellow author, Joseph Gary Crance (author of *The Ryland Creek* series), who showed me why I should take my writing seriously.

Mr. James Omen, teacher and motivator at Corning West High School, who saw something in me many years ago that nobody else did.

Jesse "James" Mullen, owner of the two greatest and most authentic biker bars in the world—Tip Top Tavern and the Ride Hard Saloon in Bradenton, Florida. It's where bikers go to just be bikers.

My future daughter-in-law, Ms. Jacquelyn Denissoff, for her creative design of my book cover, and her courage for marrying into this crazy family.

My friend Cathy Hart whose last name is more than a mere coincidence. She is a writer as well, and her talent is not yet known by all.

A special huzzah to my very patient copy editor and proofreader, Joyce Mochrie (www.one-last-look.com) for her flawless, detail-oriented assessment of this book and her overall kindness to me throughout this process.

To the millions of miles of unfamiliar road that I have covered since 1974 on two wheels.

A special thanks to my dad, who was the first to introduce me to the sensation of bugs in my teeth when he brought me home my first motorcycle when I was nine years old. My dad was the writer in the family. His talent will never be recognized, but I know it's true.

"..you'll shed blood for your family, but you don't need blood to be family"

DEDICATED TO FOUR GREAT MEN

R.C. (Mickey) Fitzwater
Founder: Cobras MC, Steuben, New York

You remind me that loyalty, real loyalty, although extremely rare, doesn't die while you still live. You are the only person—**ever**—who stuck up for me. No more needs to be said; your inspiration to me says it all. I truly love you, my friend and Brother. Thank you! You are the best!
"Just how long do clams last unrefrigerated?"

Charles (Chuck) Max
President: New Breed MC, Rochester, New York

A father, husband, [blood] brother, son, friend, and brother. You made me feel important. You made me remember life is ever growing. I miss you. R.I.P., my friend and Brother.
"Bumbles don't always bounce."

Kenny Hotaling
Founder: Northern Riders MC, Corning, New York

My first mentor in the MC world dating back to the 1980s. There were some rough days and long miles. Thank you for all your wisdom, your trust, your leadership, your support, and your acceptance.
"It wasn't a bear, it was just me snoring."

Rick (Ghost) Ellsworth
Road Vultures MC, Rochester, New York

I cannot thank you enough for all those talks. You are as real and genuine a man as I have ever met. Your graciousness is unmatched, and I have all the respect for you in the world.
"You say that like victory is a bad word."

CHAPTER 1

The Scouts

1995

"Congratulations, Mister Garcia," the chairman said with an extended hand outward.

"Yep. Yep. We worked hard, let me tell you, we worked hard. And, uh . . . uh . . . uh . . . please . . . uh . . . call me *Grant*," Grant replied.

"As you wish," he replied. "How is Digger feeling about it, Grant?"

Grant looked about the room and spied his fifteen-year-old son sitting calmly with his hands folded on his lap. Young, seemingly proud Digger formulated coordinated smiles at congratulators and other parents from the troop who patted him on the back or whispered a kind word. Digger shook his head and mumbled some expression of thanks.

"I think he's proud, too," Grant said. "We put a lot into this, as you know, and he's finally made it to our goal."

"I know it suited Trent well on his college application for Dartmouth, among all the other feats he accomplished in school."

Grant smiled as the chairman continued to hold his hand. "It's our job," the chairman paused. "No, no," he corrected himself with a tinge of histrionics. "It is our *duty* to keep these young men focused on the positive and to maintain their dignity and character to reflect the community as a whole."

Grant nodded his head in tacit agreement.

"You see, Grant, without such organizations like the Boy Scouts, our young men will not learn about loyalty, justice, faith, honor, sacrifice, commitment, pride, and the concept of family. Think about it," the chairman continued, "those values, the morality, and the character they need to keep on the straight and narrow. If not for the Scouts, where would they learn the true meaning of all of those attributes?"

"I couldn't agree more," Grant said. "And on that note, I was wondering if the committee reviewed my application for membership."

"Ah, yes," the chairman said, now clasping both hands around Grant's hand. "We have it, and we are looking at it. However, as you know, this troop has a full membership board right now. But you know, as well as I do, that all your hard work and dedication is greatly appreciated, Grant."

Grant smiled.

"As I was saying before, Grant, who knows what these boys would succumb to if not for the guidance of respectable citizens of this troop such as us. We have a lot to be proud of here, Grant."

"Yes, yes I know that."

The chairman glanced around the room and leaned into Grant. "I heard the Moffit boy was suspended for fighting in gym class."

Grant shook his head slightly. "Oh, I hadn't heard."

"Yessiree. I always knew that Moffit boy was no good; I always knew it. I was his Little League coach a few years back, and all he did was sass back and argue." The chairman sighed heavily. "But I'm not surprised with his parents. That John and Pam were always late for church, never brought snacks in for school parties, and do they fight!" The chairman winced. "The McConnells used to tell me that the Underwoods told them the Moffits had the police there more than a handful of times, breaking up those fights." The chairman laughed.

"I bet Missus Moffit is that crazed under the sheets, ya know?" The chairman and Grant shared a laugh.

"But seriously, Grant. That is why the Moffit boy is what he is because of that dysfunctional environment. I mean, really, when is the last time you saw them here?"

"It's been a while," Grant admitted.

"Indeed!"

CHAPTER 2
Cynicism

Digger / 1991 – Elkhart, Indiana

"A motorcycle? No way, nuh-uh."

"Oh, Grant, lighten up. He's eleven. It's just a minibike."

"That's not the point. It's just going to distract him from the things in life that matter."

"Such as what?"

"What does this teach him? What will he learn from this? How does this improve him?"

"Do you ever listen to yourself, Grant? If whatever Digger does can't result in some sort of an award for you to brag about, then you don't want him near it."

"And what's wrong with recognition in life?"

"What's wrong with him doing what he likes other than what you like? He's not you, Grant."

"How dare you! What's wrong with wanting my son to learn values? Is he going to learn them behind some handlebars, revving up and down the road?"

"You don't care what he learns. You just want him to learn it your way. That's your real goal."

"You just don't get it, do you?"

"No, you just don't get it, Grant. Those values you mention need to be learned organically, not from you spoon-feeding it down his throat like stale gruel."

January 2019

Thoreau once said, "Most men live lives of quiet desperation." I always thought it pretentious and downright showy to quote literature in everyday conversation, but so is using words like 'pretentious,' I suppose. Nevertheless, I must admit, I often think about that line from him. Maybe to sound smart, or maybe I am actually a contemplative thinker, I do not know. All I do know is that I would say in modern-day America, that quote isn't valid. Life has changed in the fact that the desperation is not so quiet anymore.

With the advent of social network sites, and such things as text messaging and reality television, the overabundance of people who openly complain and lay their life's troubles and idiosyncrasies out for all to see is ever increasing. People's five minutes of fame come at a cost, and because it's so commonplace to do so, most don't realize that cost, nor do they care.

Aside from pretentious types, I also hate the term 'old school.' Yet I am old school, I suppose, since I keep my problems to myself and don't announce to the uncaring and voyeuristic world what is happening in poor ol' Digger's life. These people who wear their heart on their sleeve make no sense. There's a reason why the Old Man upstairs put our hearts deep in a crevice surrounded by bone and muscle because, if left to the elements, then you are forced to count on people's goodness to keep it from being damaged.

If the cynicism is showing through, then I am getting my point across incredibly early.

I think these things. I think these things a lot when I'm out on the road. The mystique of the open road has been praised in poems, limericks, and inspirational blurbs, but the facts are, unless you are where I am right now, you will have a harder time understanding it. The passion that a winding, unexploited road with miles of ghosts before me brings to me is not explainable. Some attend church in a building. My church is here, behind my handlebars, with my soul free to think, feel, see, believe, and to solve. God created this beauty, and it's an insult to Him to forego it. Man's natural state is freedom. Those who willingly give that up are those who won't sing a song from the sound of the rubber on the road.

I know you've heard it all before, but the words are true. The ride of freedom is truly in one's soul, but only if you've been behind the chrome bars, looking at the dotted, yellow lines through the eyes of a warrior. It is only those who can genuinely appreciate the spirit of the road—roads that Internet maps barely know because nobody of substance rides these roads. But alone on these roads means something different. Whether it's special or not is debatable, but it is, for certain, a tranquil feeling. I mean, the hardest person to get to know is yourself, so the more time you spend getting to know the real you, the better the relationship you'll have.

I wake up to familiar faces, but also strangers, new sounds, smells, and sights. But regardless of those differences, I'm always there. I need to know what I think and why. The therapy of the two-lane highway can open old wounds but also help heal them, giving a sense of optimism over the horizon. As I ride and ride, the road continues; it doesn't end. The asphalt never disappoints me. It can be smooth, straight, and unencumbered, but I'm guaranteed a patch of curves, potholes, and then every biker's nightmare—gravel. But the dotted lines keep zooming past me, and the pavement goes on and on. The sense of knowing the road will, once again, be smooth and open keeps my spirit alive and my sense of adventure from reverting to the cynicism of the world that sucks me in once I put the kickstand down.

I am my own best friend, and I am my own worst enemy. I am every man.

But we are all hungry for human contact, company, a validation of our existence, and a sense of purpose that only the two clenching hands can provide. When I cruise in parade style with my brothers, bound by our patch, through these same streets, I find purpose, love, commitment, and pride, which keep me sane.

The fact is, when loyal people get lost in a world where they feel it doesn't exist, they create their own world. We people find one another, and we share that value with each other. Just because ninety-nine percent of the masses don't understand it doesn't limit its importance. Lost, lonely people in search of purpose have been creating their own world since time began.

We scare the citizens, and I'd be a liar if I said that didn't sometimes inflate my ego. But to take a citizen from fear, to one step back, to 'on guard' is what I like. They see the scruffy beard, or the long hair, or the endless ink, but when they see that iconic patch—and that we all have them—they faintly smile as they move aside and let us by. If you respect me because you fear me or because you like me, I don't really care, because the end results are the same. They leave us be, they pull their children closer, they instinctually gulp and look away when I try to meet their eyes, but their fear is working for us. Step aside and just leave us be. We are who we are, and we will not stop because a mother might glare at us disapprovingly.

Nothing enrages authoritative types more than people who don't conform and who have a strong distrust of government and the establishment, the two real areas that seem to believe laws don't apply to them. The mindset permeating American culture is not only pernicious by stripping away personal identity and freedom, it is intellectually lazy. The desire to be left alone, seek privacy, and not be under scrutiny is now considered 'suspicious' in our dumbed-down, paranoid culture. When you perceive motorcycle clubs as the enemy, don't be too surprised when they then view you as an enemy as well.

All of us in the club are the same, but we all have our differing reasons, our 'causes' if you will, of why we seek this family life. And let us be clear here: we are a family. Those who think blood is thicker than water apparently never thought one second beyond the words of how profound that statement is *supposed* to be, or they'd know how empty of logic it truly is. Your family life molds you in childhood. No matter how long you live or the changes you go through, it's your childhood you remember the most, and it just seems unjust that it not be remembered with fondness.

However, I'm getting ahead of myself. For any of you to understand, fully, you need to have an open mind, a free spirit, and a rationale that what they taught you in kindergarten is not true. Life *isn't* fair.

It is social Darwinism at its best.

CHAPTER 3
The Prospect

Solomon / 1968 – Limestone, Florida

"Are you out of your fucking mind, Tommy? The Marines? Why? Why now?"

"I thought of all people, you'd understand."

"Why? Why on earth would you think I, of all people, would understand why you'd want to fly off to an early grave, trying to prove something to nobody?"

"I don't know what I am supposed to say here, Mom."

"It's not what you're supposed to say; it's what you're supposed to do. You're supposed to not end up like your dad. You're supposed to do something with your life other than lose your fucking mind in a foreign country and come home drooling on yourself until one day you eat your gun!"

"I see, Mom! The lunatic doesn't fall far from the tree, is that it? I'll end up like Dad, right?"

"I'll tell you what, Tommy! You just do whatever the fuck you wanna do! You're a selfish asshole! You're already like your dad! Go follow in his *footsteps! You're a loser like him, anyway! I won't even let you back here in a pine box with a flag draped over your coffin! Now get the hell out of my fucking sight!"*

January 2019

Kickstand down. I am the first to arrive. As the sergeant-at-arms, I make sure to be the first. I was just elected sergeant-at-arms. I ran against Crispy—a good brother in his own right, but too short-fused to be in a position where it's the job to keep the peace. When he lost, he beat feet for Las Vegas. When he rolled out of here, he said he would be back in a week. One week turned into two and two turned into three. We lost contact with him for a while. But he finally threw Tophat a text yesterday saying he was leaving that day and should be back by the weekend. Ah, Vegas! It hijacks your soul, I guess.

And speaking of those who are not here, the prospect is supposed to be here, but he's late. The refrigerator needs to be stocked, ashtrays dumped, and these floors look like hell in need of remodeling. I pop off the padlock and open the creaking door. The dank smell hits me. The dark, cold room is void of life. I try to reinvigorate the life back into our home as I take the padlocks off the windows and air this stench out. That fucking, lazy prospect! I shouldn't be opening windows.

The sunlight peers in. It can get cold here in January, so I shovel some coal in the stove and salute Old Joe. Old Joe's patch hangs on the wall next to that old picture of him in that stupid welder's cap. I laugh. Old Joe wouldn't know a plasma cutter from a pizza cutter. He and Solomon founded the club back in 1972 when they returned from Vietnam. That was an era where many clubs had their inception. Joe was a Sailor and Solomon a Marine. The only action Joe saw was a South Vietnamese concubine at a Saigon port. Solomon, on the other hand, saw the fighting up close and personal. At least I think he did. I wasn't there to verify it.

The buzzer sounds, alerting me to a person on the grounds. Normally I hear the rumble of the V-Twins. Prospect swings open the door and greets me with a halfhearted hello.

"Place looks like shit, Prospect," I exclaim. "I am not supposed to be here prior to you."

"If I get here early, then I have to wait outside," he replies.

"Seriously?" My indignity shows overtly. "That's an actual response?"

"I . . ." He pauses.

"Yes?" I say, pushing for an answer.

"No, I get it. Sorry," Prospect replies faintly.

"See, Prospect, that's what you do not get. You don't get it! You get here and sit in the wet, fucking grass in your britches if that is what it takes," I say, wrangling my finger across his pale countenance. "If I tell a prospect to go dig a hole until he spots his first Chinaman, that's what he does!"

Prospect stares at me with a combined look of contempt and fear, a combination I never believe existed until I saw it.

"You earn this shit!" I bellow as I tug at the club patch. "We don't sell this shit on the fucking Internet. This is earned by lots of things, all boiling down to loyalty."

Prospect looks down, unsure what to say.

"We are *the* premier motorcycle club of Florida, Prospect. We are Demons Rising Motorcycle Club . . . we are the shit here, pal. You want in? Then you fucking fly right and know we decide what the definition of 'right' is!"

"I'll get the coal, Digger," he says meekly.

"No, you'll do what I say, Prospect." I wait for a response. I expect none and get none. "Go get some fucking coal and warm this joint up before Solomon gets in and sees his breath in the air. God help you then, and God doesn't have access to the front door, either."

"Okay, Digger," he says with a tinge of what I perceive as passive aggressiveness.

I continue the onslaught. "This isn't some *F.J. Club*, Prospect. We wear this diamond because we earned it. So I guarantee that nobody—*nobody*—will wear this patch until I feel he earns it, and I'm easy. Solomon is the king of what is what here. Learn it and learn it soon."

"Is all okay with you, Digger?"

"Are you a therapist, Prospect?" I shout. "I don't need or want your kindness. I only want your loyalty, and that starts with doing what I say, when I say it, and with a bit of pizzazz. So get this place clean and warm . . . and I mean now!"

"Yes, sir," he says submissively.

The prospect abandons his idea of trying to bond with me and create some disingenuous family unit for now and subjects himself to just the obedience. When push comes to shove, Prospect is on the losing end of both.

Now that I temporarily emasculated the prospect, I don't know what to do. I often question my motivations—in silence to myself—on why I berate the prospects. The core of me says it's to preserve the history and dignity of this club, but the caveman side of me thinks maybe it's just a cathartic release of aggression or old-fashioned machismo. When I want to respect myself, I convince myself the former is true.

The thunder of a few bikes roars down the roadway. The prospect still wades through the coal.

"Uh . . . Prospect? Do you hear that?"

"Hear what?"

"The bikes? There are bikes rolling into the clubhouse, so who are they?"

"I dunno, Dig. Oh, I get it. Sorry," the prospect says as he peers out the window. "All good, Digger. It's Zonk, Pancake Dave, and Walt and Willie."

"Then you better have . . . what waiting?"

"Yeah, yeah," the prospect says excitedly. "One Budweiser, two Pabst, one Coors, and one shot of Yeager and three shots of Jack."

"And they better go to the right people."

"I will do it, Digger. I will."

Walt and Willie Henshaw are two blood brothers. Walt is the oldest, and Willie not the oldest. They prospected at the same time approximately ten years ago, but Walt was patched in three months before Willie. Walt looks out for Willie. They are brothers, and I don't mean just in the MC tradition. I mean if a kidney is needed for Willie, Walt is a match.

Pancake Dave got his patch in the mid-nineties. He is a good and loyal brother with noble core instincts. You know the next word is 'but'; but he doesn't catch on to life's nuances well. He graduated high school but did so in special education classes. In fact, as the story goes, he obtained his moniker one day when the guys were making pancakes and one of the brothers said, "Pancake, Dave?" and he responded with, "Why are you calling me *Pancake Dave*?" The name sort of stuck, as do so many monikers in this biker subculture. Solomon told me that they met him one year in Daytona where a bunch of cretinous yahoos were calling him *Shortbus* and terrorizing him on the beach during bike week. Solomon has this thing he calls *Brothers Without Bikes* for guys he likes, but who don't ride. Solomon said the club adopted him, in a way, and helped him rebuild an old blockhead and taught him to ride. Originally, Pancake Dave was just going to be a hang-around of sorts, but Solomon said he proved himself worthy of our patch over time. And in Solomon fashion, he never did elaborate.

Prospect scrambles behind the bar, clanging bottles together and grabbing a fistful of shot glasses. The rumble of more engines grows louder down the driveway. I point to Prospect to cue him to finish the drink orders as I check the cameras of who is rolling down on us. Solomon leads approximately twelve more riders through the dust.

"Solomon!" I say to Prospect. "That means what?"

"Uhh . . . double Jack and a Bud?"

"Are you asking me?" I say forcefully, pointing at myself.

"No," Prospect retorts.

"And his drinks better be in front of him when he sits, and you know which stool is his. He brought it from the old clubhouse. He loves that stool."

"I will," is all Prospect says this time.

The crowd ambles in, slowly pulling off their gloves and stripping off their cut to remove jackets underneath.

"It's fucking cold in here!" Solomon bellows. "I mean, it's Florida. I have a prospect, a stove, and more coal than my ex has—minus the Christmas ribbons—so why the fuck is it cold?" Solomon looks about in rhetorical fashion. "Walt? Any idea why it's cold in here?"

"Not a clue, Solomon," Walt says.

"Digger? Answers?"

"Yes, yes, I do, Boss. Prospect here," I say, pointing at Prospect, "did not want to wait outside until a patch holder got here, so he didn't scoop up the coal and prime the furnace or any of that."

"Aw . . . poor little prima donna," Solomon says, patting Prospect on his back. "Get yourself some hot cocoa and then see us in the meeting room in five minutes."

"Okay, Solomon," Prospect says sheepishly.

"Better yet, come in now," Solomon says, grabbing him by the collar.

Solomon guides Prospect into the meeting room behind the other sixteen members. After we all get in, Solomon shuts the door gingerly with his foot. I turn on the monitor, exposing twenty different views of the perimeter of the clubhouse. Not a lens inside, though. Solomon and I remain standing on each side of Prospect.

"We are demons!" Solomon shouts.

"And we are rising!" we all bellow in unison.

"Digger? Do you have something you want to say to Prospect?" Solomon asks calmly.

"Yeah, I do."

I quickly drive my fist into his rib cage, sending Prospect down on one knee. Solomon takes a half step and pommels Prospect's chin, driving him to the floor where he instinctively covers his body and head with his hands. Prospect's curled-up body is met with a plethora of boots along his midsection and head.

"Enough! That's enough!" Solomon shouts. "Had enough, Prospect?" Solomon asks, as he tears Prospect's bottom rocker patch off his worn, denim cut. "I guess we won't call you that anymore, will we? I guess we will go with your God-given name of 'Myron.' Man, oh man, God hated you by giving you that name."

"Wanna watch a movie, Myron?" I ask, grabbing his cheeks with my thumb. "Do ya?" Myron lies still as he shakes in fear. "Answer me, you piece of shit!"

Myron says nothing. His face is beaded with sweat and his breathing is shallow. He tries to make eye contact with me occasionally, and with every look away from me, he skips a breath. Myron, unsure how to respond, moves his head in a circle in perfunctory fashion.

"Sure you do," I say, squeezing his face harder. I snap my fingers, and Walt hands me his phone. I pull Prospect's face around and have him look at the screen. "Hit the play button, Myron." Myron says and does nothing. "I said hit the fucking play button *now*!" I scream.

Myron awkwardly pushes the start button as his finger slips off the screen. He dabs the sweat off his finger on to his shirt and looks up at me. Myron shakes nervously as he reaches slowly to tap the phone's screen.

"You see, Myron, we thought we had a thief in the place. We track our bar shit pretty good. So we did the unthinkable. We placed a couple of cameras *inside*, and what do we see?" I ask, squeezing his cheeks harder. "That's you, isn't it?" I ask, pointing at the screen as I slap him. "Isn't it?"

The video plays, showing a smirking Myron grabbing a quart of whiskey and putting it in his duffle bag as he looks furtively at a seemingly empty room.

"But wait, Myron, wait . . . watch what you do after you steal from us."

Myron grows panicked as he looks away from the screen, looks away from all of us. As the video continues, we see a sharp image of a grinning Myron removing small items from his pocket and fastening them in three different areas of the bar.

"What did you put there, Myron?" I ask cryptically. "What did you put behind the molding in the back cupboard? Was it the same thing you tucked on the ridge of the door leading into this here meeting room?" I squat down and place my nose nearly on top of his. "Was it this?" I ask, pulling a small recorder out of my pocket. "Answer me, you fucking scumbag!" Myron says nothing. His body goes limp in a reflexive moment of submission.

"Ya know the irony, Myron? The irony is you are a fucking thief, which caused us to place cameras to catch a thief. And what do we catch?"

Myron grows pale but had an almost look of surrender on his face. I have seen that look before, including in the mirror. Whether it was the mild jolt of reality he just forced me to contend with, or whether it was just my disgust with him, I grab him by the back of the neck and slam his face into the table leg, causing a stream of blood to slowly drip from his head and then into his eye.

"That's a question you should answer, Myron. We thought we caught a thief, but what did we really catch, Myron? Or is it 'Agent' Myron?"

I stand up and step back from him. "Get up," I say tersely. "You are so fucking stupid. You steal about a hundred bucks of whiskey as you are planting bugs? That's so fucking careless. What academy, Myron? Huh? Which one? A.T.F.? F.B.I.? Which pile of shit fed agency are you with?"

"Digger, I swear—"

"Shut up! You shut the fuck up!" I say, as I jab my finger at him with every syllable. "I don't want to hear it! We don't want to hear it!" I swing my fist wildly in a fit of rage, origin unknown, and completely miss him, causing me to fall to the ground. Willie quickly grabs Myron by the neck from behind. "What now, Walt?" Walt motions to Solomon, and Willie redirects the question to him. "Solomon? What now?" Willie asks.

"What now? Hmmm . . . good question, Willie. What do you think, Myron? What now?" Solomon leans down some and gets face-to-face with his newfound enemy. "So what do we do with our sticky-fingered record producer now?"

"Okay, guys," Myron says curtly between gasps of air. "So what would you do if I was a fed and you kill me? You want that kind of grief? You want to see SWAT come through here and just fucking wreck this place, leaving it as something you'd never recognize again looking for me? That is, after they find kilos of coke, cash, guns, and whatever else they bring with them. You want to take on that big fight and bring on that nightmare?"

Solomon appears taken aback some. He stands back up, brushing the muck off his pants a bit. Solomon smirks at us and rubs his thumb into his achy palm. The rest of us have the same look on our faces—confused, scared, unsure, and angry.

"Ya see, Myron," Solomon says in his trademark, phlegmatic way, "you're overthinking this." Solomon clacks his tongue off the roof of his mouth. "You're not an actor in some cut-rate 'B' movie. We're pragmatists, aren't we fellas?" Solomon says to us in unison. We all reflexively nod our heads unenthusiastically. Solomon kicks a chair, draws it underneath himself, and perches down. He leans into Myron somewhat and says, "It's January, it's cold, and none of us are going to take the time it would take to dig a hole big enough to bury you."

CHAPTER 4
The 'In' Crowd

Venus / 1996 – Moorefield, Nebraska

"You look like a whore, Mary Ellen, a common, street-trash whore."

"Thanks, Mom. I can always count on you to be supportive."

"Supportive of what? You being a whore? You making me look like a white-trash mom raising some white-trash kids? Do you want the neighbors thinking that? Is that what you think I am?"

"Is that what you think I am, Mom? Do you think that little of me?"

"Aw . . . poor Mary Ellen. The guys don't think she's pretty enough, and the girls just think she's plain weird. Blame us, child, go ahead. Blame your dad and I for trying to get you to think and stop trying to be something you're not. The girls are pretty, and you're not, so you're going to be a whore instead? Will that make up for no slumber party invites, no date for the prom? Being a whore?"

May 2019

"Where's Venus?"

"It's the planet east of Mercury and west of Earth," I say comically.

Solomon shakes his head slightly. "Okay, Digger, now that you showed the smart-ass that you are, again, go find her so she can tell Prospect to get at least six big bags of that charcoal. We are expecting the whole western hub of the coalition."

"She's inside. She said she wanted to grab some flag banners and some red, white, and blue napkins," I say.

"Then definitely go find her and tell her we don't need a decorator. This is a coalition meeting, not a. . . ." Solomon, unable to find a clever metaphor, blurts out, "Just go fucking get her. She's your ol' lady, not mine."

Solomon is a bulky man, nearly six feet tall, with a surprisingly trimmed beard, but a chaotic mustache that seems to have no beginning or end—just a mesh of solid, white hair follicles. He gowns himself in traditional, old-school, biker garb containing ratty blue jeans, a cut-off T-shirt from some concert he went to in the late 1970s, and a pair of boots that resemble western wear more than customary riding boots. His eyes are a piercing blue that strangely darken to a pale green when he is angry. His hands and arms tell tales of woe in each faded tattoo and aging scar—each with a story, each with its own brand of style, but inscrutable, nonetheless.

As Solomon and I walk into the store, we see our shiny, new prospect with Venus, talking to an old man in a wheelchair accompanied by a younger man behind him. Prospect is one step at the back of Venus, watching over her.

Venus complements me with her fiery, red hair that she normally wears in a modest wave. She is a few inches shorter than me and wears these *geek chic* glasses over a pair of soft, brown eyes. She dresses tamely when judged through the lens of our biker subculture. She has a natural beauty about her that I can't really explain, but it starts with an infectious smile and a flair for speaking to others through facial expressions.

"Hi, Digger!" Venus says energetically. "This is Milo Breamish," she says, pointing at the man in the wheelchair. "He's a World War II veteran cutting the ribbon in the parade in Tampa today. I was telling him about our Memorial Day picnic today."

"A pleasure, sir," I say, grasping his hand firmly. "I'm Digger Garcia, U.S.M.C., two tours Fallujah."

Solomon reluctantly reaches his hand down to Milo. "Solomon, Marine Corps, Vietnam, 1969 to 1972."

The younger man with Milo looks at Solomon and me and turns pale. He is a taller man, but thin with neatly trimmed, sandy-brown hair, and he is gowned in a dressier, pullover shirt and khaki slacks. His counterpart looks to be in his late eighties and sits in a wheelchair covered from his waist down by a blanket that he uses to continually clean the lenses on his glasses.

Venus touches the younger man's shoulder and says, "This is Mister Breamish's grandson, Roger." Young Roger slowly raises his hand, unsure to whom he offers the extension. Solomon, without looking at him, says, "Charmed." Roger slowly lowers his arm.

"Some kind of bike club, huh? What's that patch mean?" Milo asks, pointing at Solomon's diamond-shaped patch with the iconic *1%* trademark.

"It just means they're a serious club, Mister Breamish. It symbolizes they're not a F.J.C. type club, but truly authentic," Venus says excitedly.

"F.J.C.?" young Roger says inquisitively.

Venus smiles and waves her hand in mock feminine fashion. "It stands for *Family-Job- Club,* meaning most motorcycle clubs, like ninety-nine percent of them"—Venus grows a self-satisfaction grin on her face—"have a protocol where their families come first, then their job, and then club responsibilities. A one-percent club means the club comes first in front of everything. The club is your family and your job. We are so all about motorcycles, most of us don't even own a cage."

"Cage?" young Roger inquires.

Venus laughs. "Oh, it's just a slang term for a car. Real bikers feel that a car is a cage."

Solomon sighs heavily and glares at me. Venus, oblivious to Solomon's gesture, continues. "You and your grandson should stop by today for our Memorial Day picnic. We just built a new clubhouse in Balm; it's this little nowhere town near Sun City."

"And on that note, Miss Venus, we all got to scoot on out of here. Long day ahead," Solomon says, looking at Milo. "Thank you for your service, Mister Beamish—"

"It's *Breamish*," Venus interjects.

Solomon pauses, and his hands remain in a holding pattern. "Anyway, you have a good day, sir. Enjoy the parade in Tampa. I'm sure you've earned the accolades. But we are out of here," Solomon says, pushing Venus gingerly down the aisle. "Prospect!" Solomon shouts. "Get charcoal, and get your ass out to the parking lot." Solomon places his fingertip on Venus's back and walks her toward the door, quickly. "Digger?"

"Behind you," I say.

"I know you are," Solomon replies.

We egress out, and Solomon guides us behind a dumpster and a large propane tank. He stops and takes one giant step around and faces Venus. "I love this man right here," Solomon says, pointing at me. "This is why I am not knocking you on your dimwitted ass right now." Solomon wags his finger inches from Venus's face. Her eyes grow wide, and her skin seems to pucker and get clammy. "Where the fuck do I start?" Solomon asks. "Who were those guys, Venus? Who? Huh? Who?" Solomon's interrogation leaves no pauses for Venus to reply outside of a stammer here and there. "Don't just look at me with that stupid, blank, fucking stare. Answer me!" Solomon pauses this time, awaiting an answer. Venus, still visibly shocked at the verbal onslaught, peers at me with mouth open, searching for an answer—not just to the question, but to the blitzkrieg she is currently facing.

"I . . . uh . . . they're going to the parade. He's just a harmless, old man," Venus says awkwardly and with a modicum of panic. "I mean, they're just going to a parade, that's all."

"Really?" Solomon says, as the vibrant blue of his eyes turns a pale aura of green. "Because they say so?" Solomon says rhetorically. "Because your street-smart nature that you discovered since you've been with Digger for six whole months just blossomed? You have no fucking clue who they are, Venus. None! And here you are, giving your own version of Wikipedia biker section on what a one-percent means and all that crap! Telling him where the fuck we are? Just give them a Google map of our locale, Venus. Why didn't you just spit some saliva in a napkin and give him Digger's D.N.A. that you collected a few times at 'our' clubhouse? *Our* clubhouse! That's what you said, Venus! You actually said that! 'Our' clubhouse! Let me educate you, little girl," Solomon continues mercilessly, "it's *my* fucking clubhouse!" Solomon says, swinging his hand toward himself. "It's *his* fucking clubhouse!" Solomon says, shoving his finger in my chest with a tad of anger aimed at me. "It isn't yours and it never will be! So you don't get to invite anyone there unless a patch holder tells you to do it!" Solomon continues the bombardment. "And it's not a picnic. It is a coalition meeting/Memorial Day run. We have thirty sanctioned coalition clubs coming today. Clubs like *Rebellious Youth MC*. Clubs like that don't go to 'picnics.' Little, old, blue-haired ladies and farmers with bad haircuts wearing shabby overalls go to fucking picnics!" Solomon sighs heavily and catches his breath. He grits his teeth, clenches his fist, and then kicks the dumpster. Solomon then begins to calm. He puts his hands down and gently, but firmly, grabs Venus's cheeks with his forefinger and thumb. "And one more thing: don't you ever, ever, *ever* 'correct' me when I am speaking to someone again. You got that?" Solomon asks through gritted teeth.

Venus gulps and nods her head affirmatively.

Solomon rubs his face and sighs heavily. He leans back some and places all ten fingers together. He closes his eyes and tilts his head back a bit. "Digger, I'm jumping on the bike, getting a little wind therapy. Take Prospect," Solomon says amidst an expressive sigh, "and her," he says, pointing demonstrably at Venus but remaining focused elsewhere, "and go back to *our* clubhouse. Tell the boys I will be there when I get there."

"I got it, Solomon," I reply.

Solomon sighs calmly. "I know, Digger. I know you do. See you soon," he says, giving me a halfhearted hug.

Venus, still seemingly in shock from the verbal ambush, wipes tears from her eyes. "You just stood there," Venus says to me bitterly, continuing to ward off tears. "You just stood and did nothing. Is this what I can expect? If some guy goes off on me, you do nothing?"

"If some guy ever does something like that, you can expect he'll end up in the ground after we make him dig his own damn grave to China. If you don't know that by now, then you and I have nothing to talk about anymore."

Venus glares at me and places a cocksure smirk on her face. "Is this the part where you try to tell me this was *different*?"

I pull on Venus's shirt and move her to the side of the building. I place her against the wall and place my palms on each side of her, resting them on the brick and mortar, and lean in toward her. "I'll now explain it to you with a bit more composure, but with no less passion." I tug at her chin and make her look directly at me. "This is not, repeat *not* a reality TV show, Venus. This isn't one of your books, or some of those bullshit *mock*-umentaries you watch. This is real life." I release her chin and step back some. Venus continues to look at me, expressionless. "Losing its luster, is it?" I ask her. "Losing the romantic intrigue of all this?" I ask again, waving my hands, looking about. "You're seeing the other side, the real side. That, my dear, is how you know you're no longer in a fantasy or hanging out with the cool kids at the lunch table. It isn't just getting stoned in the clubhouse, getting fucked on the pool table, and raising hell with the forbidden crowd. No, no, no, it's much more. So if you thought hanging out with a motorcycle 'gang,'" I say, using finger quotes, "would make you feel important and help you escape from life, then you just now realized today, there's no escape—at least not in the way you think." Venus gulps and her eyes grow bigger. Her breathing is shallow, and she scratches her nose because she feels as though she needs to do something.

"I get it," she says.

"No, no you don't," I say, wiping the tears away from her face. "You thought hanging out with the *bad boys* would rev you all up and you'd be in with the 'in' crowd, right?" I say.

"Wrong," she retorts.

"My question was rhetorical," I say forcefully. "You are intrigued by the bad boys, but in all reality, we are just plain bad, okay? You're not in the *'in'* crowd, Venus, you're just along for the ride, and as you learned, that ride has many bumps and curves, and that just made reality push saga out the door. Sorry, but this is how it is." I give her an affectionate kiss on her forehead. "You're important to me, Venus, very important," I say, waiting for some type of response. "But something tells me that now means a bit less to you," I say. Venus starts to speak, but I just put my finger to her lips and shake my head. "You get all excited when you talk about how a one-percent club puts the club first over everything, until you just now realized that part of that 'everything,' as you called it, includes you." I stare at Venus, trying to magnify my point to her. I know it is important for her to fully understand, but it feels like telling a child that Santa doesn't exist.

"Know your place, Venus, and stay in your own lane." I turn and walk away. I hear Venus sigh. She suspends any movement briefly. I listen to my own heel clack against the pavement, waiting for Venus to act. I speed up my gait and wave at Prospect to meet me by the truck. Venus sighs again, but I continue walking. I hear her rifling through her purse, and then nothing. Seconds later, I hear her footsteps behind me.

CHAPTER 5
A Moment

Walt and Willie / 1985 – Reseda, California

"*Just paint it green like Dad wants.*"
"*I can't find any green, Walt.*"
"*Shhh . . . quiet! You wanna wake him? Just do it like he said. The paint is on the bottom shelf.*"
"*Walt?*"
"*What?*"
"*Stay here, please?*"
"*I can't, Willie. It'll be okay; he's sleeping now.*"
"*But he always wakes up. Please stay?*"
"*If he finds me here with you, it'll start again. Is that what you want?*"
"*No . . .*"

May 2019

The fiery, red embers cool to a pale orange. Approximately a dozen charred burgers and a few scraggly hot dogs lay motionless on the blackened grate. Walt and Willie lie in the grass next to one another near the grill with their coveted patch clutched in their arms. Walt, the older of the two brothers, is over six feet tall, with long, shaggy, unkempt, flaxen hair. Occasionally, he braids the misdirected follicle train, but mostly just pulls it back into a rubber band. He sports a five-o'clock shadow that appears to be in perpetuity. One pierced ear in his left lobe is home to a makeshift earring made from a wadded-up, RC Cola bottle cap, the origin he never shares with anyone. Willie, on the other hand, is a good four inches shorter than his older brother. His hair is a mixture of an orange and dark-red pelt that he cuts to his scalp to hide the odd color. His nascent mustache is in search of respect as it looks to connect in a natural way with his sporadic whiskers along his cheeks. His right ear appears to suffer from some cauliflowering, and his nose is also bulbous and ruddy in appearance.

We all love Willie, and he is our brother, too. But he has this childlike quality about him that can be unsettling at times. When we were building our firepit, we had a truckload of dirt delivered. I saw him once in the dirt, running his fingers through it, mimicking 'motor' sounds. Walt noticed and snapped his fingers a few times, and Willie grabbed his shovel and started working once more.

Walt is in his mid-forties, and Willie turns forty this year. They keep to themselves a lot and talk little about the chaotic and brutal life they endured at the hands of their sadistic father and apathetic mother. From the few times Walt has discussed it with me, it sounds as though Willie received the crux of the abuse. But Walt is so furtive about discussing their childhood, I can only surmise the extent and the targets of the abuse.

Willie tends to stay with Walt overall. When we ride, Willie rides alongside of Walt. When we eat, each sit with each other. When questions are posed to Willie, he looks at Walt. And as I stated earlier, both came to us at the same time, but Walt was patched in three months before Willie. Walt managed to get himself in trouble a few times once he was patched in because he took umbrage with anyone who still treated Willie as a prospect, even though he still was. It's clear that Walt has watched out for Willie their whole lives, but there are times Walt needed to curb his sense of loyalty to Willie and realize that his loyalty now belongs to all of us, not just Willie.

Solomon is hugging the last club's president before they leave. They exchange graciousness and pleasantries to one another. Pancake Dave is helping Prospect find the stuff he needs to clean up the kitchen. He points here and there, and the look on his face shows some confidence as he quietly directs Prospect. The day appears to be a successful one. It is the first time we hosted a coalition meeting in approximately five years. Demons Rising lost their standing, in a sense, around that time due to some stupidity, and the coalition recently said they want to reestablish relations.

Demons Rising has been a one-percent club since its start in 1972. We earned it and deserve recognition as the premiere club here.

Prospect is getting the bonfire started for all to unwind. The time of night comes where we get to just sit, drink, get high, and earn our reprobate credentials. Most of the time, we let the ol' ladies out here, but this is not one of those nights. Willie is walking with Venus and Prospect toward Solomon and me. Venus sheepishly looks at Solomon and tries a faint smile. "I just wanted to say good night to you boys. Babs and a few of the girls invited me out with them." Venus looks at me and mouths softly, "I guess I'm one of the girls." Venus smiles, then pauses a bit. I reach up and pull her hand toward me. She leans down, gives me a kiss, and stands again, saying nothing.

"I'll walk you girls out, Venus, but can you show me how to whistle some more next time?" Willie asks, pursing his lips and merely exhaling wet air. Venus pinches Willie's cheek in kittenish fashion. "Of course I will." Venus continues the awkwardness by remaining still. She clears her throat and looks at the ground. "Solomon," she says self-consciously, "I just want to apologize about . . . uh . . . all that stuff today. I . . . uh . . . understand now."

Solomon looks at me, then rolls his eyes and grunts mildly as he stands. "Come here, you ditzy bitch," he says to Venus with a smile. Solomon hugs her and sits back down. "Venus, grab Digger and me a bag of ice and that bourbon bottle that is behind the cash register before y'all go."

"Absolutely," she replies.

"I'll get it, Solomon," Prospect chimes in quickly.

"I told Venus to do it, Prospect."

"Yes, you did, Solomon," Prospect says as he places his hands behind his back.

The fire starts to crackle more as the flames flirtatiously kiss the tree branches. I can hear the occasional popping noise, bits of flame escaping the roar of the fire only to die out in the night air alone, and the commotion of the party ending yards away diminishes.

"You never told me. Where did you meet this chick, anyway?" Solomon inquires.

"Where you meet all good Catholic girls—at the Tip Top Tavern in Bradenton."

Solomon laughs slightly. "Yep. Been there a handful of times over the years."

Solomon leans back some and twists his foot in the air a few times. I can hear the grinding and the crackle of years gone by in his ankle. "Is her name actually 'Venus'?"

"No, it's Mary Ellen."

"Mary Ellen?" Solomon says amidst a laugh. "Are you sure you didn't meet her on Walton's Mountain?" Solomon laughs again.

"Nope, never been there," I say with a smile.

"And she thought renaming herself 'Venus' would help her lose her good little Catholic girl/country bumpkin image?"

"Actually, I gave her that name," I reply.

Solomon pauses, then just stares at me and tosses his arms outward. "And?" he queries.

"And what?" I say, knowing full well what his question is.

"How did you come up with that name? Are you a closet Frankie Avalon fan?"

"No," I say, smirking some.

"Yeeees . . ." Solomon pushes on.

"Well, she's a goddess, and when I think of a goddess, I think of the Roman goddess, Venus. My Venus is a goddess, too."

Solomon shakes his head at me disapprovingly. "You're such a fucking girl! A 'goddess'?" Solomon says sarcastically, using air quotes. "Where'd ya pick that up? On Oprah?" Solomon shakes his head and looks away. "Geez, Digger, what the fuck? You watching *Lifetime* now? Swapping meatloaf recipes with the other suburban whores?"

"What's so bad about that?" I ask with a halfhearted smile.

"I could see it if it was 'Venus because she's red hot' or because of her fake-ass, red hair, or even 'Venus swallows my penis'—"

"She does do that," I chime in quickly with a laugh.

"Too late, Digger." Solomon laughs. "Don't try to be a man now. Now I know who you are. You sound like a lovesick high schooler banging the head cheerleader."

"You're a cynical old man," I say, stripping off my cut so I can lie flat on the ground, placing my patch gently on my stomach. "Cynical old coot."

Solomon also strips off his cut and lies back on a mound of dirt. "If by 'cynical' you mean a 'realist,' then that's me, Brother."

"Nooo," I say with an elongated 'o' sound. "I mean cynical. And old." I snicker. "And a coot!"

We lie there looking at the fire and just relax a bit. I take out my flask and start to grab a swig.

Solomon, breaking the silence, begins singing the Osmond song "Young Love" aloud and starts laughing uncontrollably.

I retort back with, "Hey, you whippersnappers!" I yell aloud, fighting back a laugh. "Get the hell off my lawn before I tan your hide! I just planted them thar azaleas."

"See? You even know names of flowers." Solomon laughs. "You're such a girl. Go rub some Monistat on your cooch!"

I pause, chuckling some. "When I was a boy, we walked to school five miles in the snow! Uphill! Both ways!"

"I love chocolate," Solomon says amidst fake tears. "It helps with the bloating."

Venus and Willie hear the sound of laughter as they approach us.

"Here, Solomon," Venus says, handing him the freshly poured bourbon and an ice bucket filled with ice cubes.

"Thanks, Venus. Your ol' man and I will take it from here." Solomon twists his neck a bit to make eye contact with Willie. "Walk her all the way out, Brother, and come back and join us if you want. We're going to burn a few and abuse our livers."

"Thanks, Solomon, but I am going to go back inside and see what Walt is doing."

Solomon sprinkles a little green in a rolling paper and lights it up. He inhales deeply a few times, almost exposing his cheekbones. Solomon hands the joint to me to share.

"How do you believe it went today, Solomon? I saw you and ChuckForce from Rebellious Youth talking."

"It went great, I think. I sense we're square with them. Demons Rising has a solid rep. We are the kings. We flew the diamond the nearly fifty years we've been flying colors. I've known ol' ChuckForce since he started Rebellious Youth in Fort Myers in '68."

I shake my head and laugh. "The name kills me," I say. "Their youngest member is that fucking asshole *Elf*, and he's at least forty."

Solomon looks at me perplexingly. "You got something against elves?" he asks with a laugh.

"Just that asshole. Where did he get such a stupid nickname anyway?"

"His name is John Elfman," Solomon retorts.

"That's why? Nothing significant?"

"Not everything is deep and philosophical, Digger. You are always trying to complicate simplicity."

I sigh. "Fine. I simply hate him because he's young and stupid."

Solomon smirks and shakes his head. "He's older than you, so does that make you younger and more stupid?"

"No," I say curtly. "I'm smart."

"You're a *smart-ass*, Digger. You're young as well. The young need to have more smarts and less anger."

"Oh," I say with an incredulous laugh. "Of you and I, I'm the hotheaded one?"

"No, you're the smart-ass one."

"At least I am not in a club full of old codgers like you, paradoxically named *Rebellious Youth*."

"Paradoxically?" Solomon says sarcastically. "What did you do, Digger? Masturbate to a thesaurus last night?"

I laugh as I take another hit off the joint.

"And remember, Digger, ChuckForce was nineteen when he started that club. At that age, you never think you'll be old." Solomon snickers some. "He talked to me about patching in, but I was already on my way to Vietnam via Paris Island."

"Had to teach those Vietcong a thing or two, did you?" I ask with a laugh.

Solomon perches a bit of a blank stare on his face. "You know war, Digger. It's always the same. The enemy just looks a little different with every war. We always find enemies. We always find different ways to kill them. But in the blink of an eye, that same enemy comes back with the same goal, wearing different garb."

I look perplexingly at the lit joint in my hand. "What the fuck did you put in this thing? The deepest shit you ever talk about is why Wile E. Coyote just didn't go to the supermarket instead." I look over at Solomon, only to see him swallowing bourbon from the bottle with one hand and giving me the finger with the other.

"It's the fire, Digger. The heat and the power make my mind go deep," Solomon says with a smirk.

"Yeah, well, don't discount this Hawaiian bud you're smoking, either." I take two or three quick hits off our joint and hand it back to him. "Ever regret anything in Vietnam, Solomon? I mean, you know, anything?"

"Oh, for fuck's sake, here we go," Solomon clamors.

"Now what?"

"This is the part where you get me to 'open up' and cry about all the horrible things I saw and did in Vietnam. Well, save your breath, Digger. I have no regrets, no ghosts, no nothing."

I sigh. My frustration grows some, but I try to keep from projecting it. "I went to war, too. I am just trying to see if what I experienced is similar, that's all. We're just talking here, Brother."

"No," Solomon says tersely. "You're talking. I'm smoking weed and guzzling whiskey."

"I know," I say with a surrender in my tone. "I was just curious, ya know?"

The glow of the fire intensifies the aging eyes and withered skin of my brother. He focuses in on the flames as they peak higher and higher. The crackle of the burn echoes some against the silence. Solomon nods. He smirks a bit and emits a compulsory laugh. "In the winter of 1970, we were all chowing down on some morsels—me and six guys from my platoon. We were about a half mile from base center, but we got cut off and were tracking our way back east." Solomon swigs another gulp of bourbon and wipes a bead of sweat from his brow. "It was quiet and all, just the usual chatter from a bunch of grunts. I mean, nothing was stirring, not even a mouse. But through some thicket about sixty feet away, we heard a few twigs snapping and some low gibberish. We grabbed our rifles and started to bunch together a bit. Then the silence grew. You know, Digger, that deafening silence you hear just when primal fear meets reality?" Solomon says. "Anyway, out peeks these three 'Cong guerillas. They charged from the bushes and shot blindly. I heard screams, saw fire, and with one hand, I fired off all thirty rounds. That split second seemed to last for hours. I wasn't sure what happened and if it was over." Solomon takes a deep breath and spits something out of his mouth. "One tried limping off with his gun in his hand. I managed to get up, jump over the meal wagon, and shoot him again in the leg. He turned and looked at me. He was only twelve years old."

My interests begin to peak further. I run all the possible scenarios in my head in a matter of seconds. My thoughts are lost when Solomon continues his tale. Solomon repositions his body and faces me straight on.

"Now, Digger," Solomon says, pointing at me, "this is the part where I say I shot him anyway and never forgave myself for killing that boy."

I sit stunned, in silence, as a veteran of the brutality of war. I clench my fist, and my breath becomes rapid and terse. The laughter from the clubhouse morphs into white noise. I can feel my brother's pain, this man whom I heartfeltly taunted moments ago, this man whom I love unconditionally, this man, my friend, my brother. I don't think I ever felt closer to him. I have known him for nearly a decade, and I harken back to the night he struck up a conversation at some local watering hole near Sarasota, inviting me for a ride with his brothers. I know his pain right now. I know the tears he has inside for an innocent boy whose life was snuffed out by the futility of war, and by a man who sings the songs of regret decades later, here and now, at our house, at the bonfire where Solomon and I have had many talks about the MC life, family, brotherhood, loyalty, and now inner pain.

"But let me stop you there, Digger. Part one of what I said was true: I shot that boy in the head as he gripped his rifle, pointing it at us. That is true." Solomon resituates himself; his frustration shows through his fist, gripping in the dirt. "But part two, Digger," Solomon says, holding up his index and middle finger, "part two . . . no! No, my Brother. That is not true. I never had to forgive myself because I didn't care and," Solomon says forcefully, amidst a pause, "I still don't. I'm glad I shot that boy dead then, and I am glad today. He tried to hurt my family, and that is all that mattered. I don't think about his face, his name, his cry, his eyes—none of it. I don't care. He deserved what he got." Solomon calms himself some and sits back down in the dirt. "This is real life, my friend and Brother, and only in the movies do they feel remorse or regret for killing a child when that child, only seconds before my bullet pierced his head, was trying to kill me. I was proud that I did it then, and I am today, and I could give a fuck about what he might have become because what he was, Digger, was a killer. I have not shed a tear for him since and I never will."

"I don't believe that, Solomon," I say in a perplexing fashion.

Solomon repositions his body and sits upward. He shakes his finger at me demonstrably. "Well, believe it, Digger! Because it's true. You're looking for some 'moment' here with me and it ain't there. I feel nothing. Notice I said 'nothing' and not 'numb.'"

"I . . . just don't. . . ." I stop my words because I don't know what to say. What's my line? Where's the script?

"You just don't what?" Solomon asks, tossing his arms out. "What? What are you looking for here?"

"I just . . . he's . . . he was a twelve-year-old boy. I don't think . . . I just don't see how. . . ."

"I'm sorry, Digger. If you were looking for me to cry like some bitch, it ain't happening." Solomon stares at me a bit. I don't know whether he regrets the look of disappointment on my face or is taunting it, perhaps trying to teach me a lesson in a warped way only he can understand. He looks at me sideways a bit and says, "Sorry, Digger, I'm just plain evil, I guess. One-way trip to hell."

"I don't believe that."

"You must!" Solomon snaps back. "Or else why are you disappointed that my conscience is totally clear? After all, I am a demon and we are rising!" Solomon raises the flask to me, gulps the last drop, and screams "*yahoo*!"

I sit, stunned a bit. Maybe not so much for what he said, but in regret of a moment that I wanted to share with him. I nod respectfully at Solomon and stare for a few seconds more than is comfortable. For some reason, I hold up the peace sign to him and then tap my chest. I do so because perhaps I am still living in a movie drama and am looking for that portal back to reality. I slowly lie back down in the dirt. I reach over for one more hit of the joint and a slug of bourbon from his flask. I see the trickles of embers fly from the top of the fire, expire, and burn out as the cooler night air ends their brightness. It seems almost cinematic. The light begins to die, the energy of the conversation wanes, suddenly that white noise disappears, and I can hear the laughter of my brothers back in the clubhouse. My moment is gone. I can live with it, I suppose. Life can be bland at times when your expectations die.

"Damn kids today," I say with a quip. "No respect no more for their elders."

Solomon smiles and lays his head down as well. "Come over tonight, and we will have a topless pillow fight and do each other's nails!" Solomon snaps back with a laugh.

"Did you see that cold front coming from the north? Dagnab winters!"

"Do you sometimes not feel fresh . . . 'down there'?" Solomon asks in-between bursts of laughter.

"Let's hit the early bird special, Mable!" I retort quickly.

"Sally's husband still brings her flowers. Aren't I as pretty as her?"

"I think I have some leftover meatloaf in the icebox."

"Does this dress make me look fat?"

"I have some hard candy in my pocket . . . at least something is hard near my pocket!"

"Do any of these multiple vitamins have estrogen in them?"

"May I have prunes with my tomato juice?"

"If I watch *Titanic* during 'that time of the month,' I just cry all night!"

"Gumption, I say! Gumption! Back in my day, we had gumption!!"

The laughs continue as the fire burns bright. My tears come from laughter, love, comfort, and, most of all, confusion. But I let them flow down my cheeks. I smile at the night sky and allow the peace to settle in for the night. Morning will come soon enough.

CHAPTER 6
It's Earned

Pancake Dave / 1980 – Deland, Florida

"Oh, look! It's retard!"

"I just want to get on the bus, please."

"Why aren't you on the short bus, retard? That's where you should go, you fucking dribbler."

"I just want to get on the bus, please."

"Aw . . . baby wants the bus! Baby want a brain, too?"

"Please, I just want to get on the bus, please. I wanna get to school."

"So you can piss your pants and eat beans?"

—Pause—

"Fucking retard!"

June 2019

The weekend arrives. We fill it with curative wind. The unwilling turns and the tingles on our hands are home to the solitude that only our symbiotic existence can glean. The day belongs to the randomness that is us—no plan, no direction, no destination, no goal, other than to reestablish our oneness with each other and the road and the surprises it gives us. We drift east, inland, to the rural bastion where nothing is everything and individuality nestles in with the family orientation we feel.

Walt and Willie ride in unison, absorbing a semblance of peace. They occasionally glance over at one another to affirm the continuity of a safeness they feel. Solomon leads the way, his gray ponytail whipping to and fro in the crosswinds that the travel east often brings. Tophat, our vaunted V.P., smiles glibly at an alligator aside the two-lane stretch as he offers up the universal sign of peace. The cold-blooded reptile seems to extend its only hint of respect it can by remaining aside the highway, waiting for the last echo of the rumble to pass by before he scurries across the road to the dampness of the swamp. Venus lays her head on my back occasionally as she lightly rubs the sides of my legs. I see her smile intermittently as I peer into the rearview mirror. Her countenance shows gratitude outwardly, and with each peek into her face I get in my rearview mirror, she grips my legs tighter and flicks her eyebrows upward at me.

We ride parade style, twenty-four inches head to toe, and in unison. We ride east, away from the coastline and away from the fast-paced, confusing aspects of Florida. This is my favorite part of being in this club. We look tight to the citizens; it fosters trust between us. And the adrenaline from the thunder from our exhausts perpetually feeds my need to stay positive and upbeat with the wind singing in my face, the smiles from my brothers, and the warmth of Venus's body pressed against mine as I lean in and then accelerate out of the corners. All of what I describe may not define life, but it accentuates it for certain.

The lonely highway of State Route 70 has been encroached upon some by urban sprawl, but there is still at least thirty miles of it that runs straight through some swampland and farm country with only an occasional cage continuing past us, heading toward the city. The curves are few and the bumps are infrequent, allowing us to roll east, unencumbered by man or nature's invasions.

Pancake Dave has a cagey and silent smile on his face. His head slowly bops back and forth to a song in his head. That face! That's the face every biker wants: peaceful, serene, and self-owned. Like all of us, Pancake Dave has had it rough, but he is in his realm with a Demons Rising patch proudly earned on his back while rolling down the road with all those who love him. We don't pity him. No . . . pity is the conman's form of abuse masked in a smile and a handshake. But we know he's limited, so we focus on where he can—and does—shine for us. He is no less than a Demons Rising brother, but no more, either. In our world, we do have equality amongst those we allow inside our domain.

The road widens some as smaller edifices begin to come into play. I can see the tattered American flag whipping in the wind from a watering hole replete with motorcycles, barbecue smoke, and leather-clad chatterers milling about the parking lot. Solomon raises his hand up, snaps his fingers, and points. I ask him all the time why he bothers snapping his fingers when he knows damn well nobody can hear it. Solomon always says, "The friction from the fingers creates magic." I never bother following up on what the hell that means; I just usually give him a quick fist bump, a respectful nod, and move on. Solomon circles about the parking lot, looking for a spot large enough to hold all our bikes. We all wheel into the lot in harmony and watch as the citizens nudge one another and furtively point in our direction. As we climb off the steel horses, Prospect grabs an old canteen, douses his mouth with water, and then lights a cigarette. Solomon nods at Prospect slightly, conversing to him with an old-fashioned edict of eyeball communication.

"Got your back, fellas. Have a good time," Prospect says as we all walk toward the entrance. Prospect then stands erect in front of all our bikes as we all saunter in the door of the old bar, suitably named *The Open Road*, just outside the city limits of Arcadia. Tophat and Solomon never drive by this place. They affectionaly call it a great spot on a long, lonely road. Tophat says he met his ol' lady, Babs, here in the 1980s. Solomon grew up less than five miles from this bar. He recalls his cousin and he would ride their bicycles here to see all the motorcycles in the parking lot when they were about nine or ten years old. The owner at that time would give them bottles of soda and hot dogs if they picked up trash on Sunday mornings. That tale is one of the few Solomon revealed to me over the years of his childhood.

As we walk inside, instinctively, the citizens part the crowd and greet us with a nervous smile, allowing us room at the bar. "Eight pitchers of Bud, eleven shots of bottom-shelf bourbon, and four of any kind of some fruity sissy drink for Babs and her chick crew," Solomon commands.

"Fuck that!" Babs clamors with a boastful smile as she latches on to Tophat. "Give me the sour mash, too!" Babs laughs with the support of all of us. Venus, clearly looking uncomfortable, chimes in and says, "I . . . uh . . . will take whatever. Thanks." She smiles as coquettishly as she can.

Solomon smirks at Venus and rolls his eyes, then looks back at the bartender. "A fruity drink for the fruity chick, and a shot of bourbon for the psycho chick." The bartender laughs and goes about preparing the order. Babs jams both her thumbs at herself proudly to show she wears such an appellation with pride. Venus mounts a crooked smile but stays in form.

I like Babs, I really do, but she is, shall we say, without restraint. I don't think Babs is her real name, but Tophat said she introduced herself as *Babs* when they met. She is always first on the dance floor or on top of the bar. Babs does not have subtlety of tongue, but she's not cruel to others. She is just *loud and proud*. I would describe her as a kind person overall, but do not cross her. She's a scrapper. I have seen Babs fight, and she does so like a man—knuckles up. She will dance topless at local taverns and wrestle other women in coleslaw. In fact, Babs often brags about being crowned champion during bike week in 1981 and 1990. I don't get the sense she's being intentionally provocative to garner attention, it's just part of her boisterous personality. I find her quite beautiful in her own style. She's got swarthy features born of a Greek heritage. She still wears her jet-black hair curly and combed to the side, as she most likely did in the 1980s, and she has a small hoop nose ring. Normally, I'm not a fan of the hoops, but it looks sexy on her. And Babs is rarely without her old, leather cap atop her wavy hair.

As the sergeant-at-arms, it is my job, in particular, to size up the room, examine who is here, how many, where they're standing, and if any other patches are present. I see the men's room door fly open, and I count six younger men walking out—two are wiping their noses, and only one spots us, pokes his contemporaries, and points our way. They slow their gait a bit and motion for one another to amble out the side door to the patio. Through the dense crowd, I manage to spot a glimpse or two of a back patch. The club name and center patch allude me, but the *Florida* bottom rocker patch is inescapable. I whisper to Solomon and Tophat and let them know. It's their ultimate decision, but I already know what that decision is. Solomon and Tophat hunker together quickly and point and look elsewhere. The others' instincts draw them to the controversy and conversation. Although the chatter doesn't weaken, and the volume of the juke doesn't dissipate, it seems as though the attention in the bar focuses on our serene and reticent huddle.

The men scurry outside. The threat is low, or. . . .

I whisper to Solomon, "They seem young, like neophyte punks who watch too much TV."

"I wish that was conclusive," Solomon replies back to me as he slaps me on my back. I think Solomon appreciates my input but filters it through his own understanding and wherewithal.

"Tag 'em outside. Get 'em near the wall and take two on each end," Tophat says. As the sergeant, it's actually my job to size that up, but I bow to experience and allow ego to take the down escalator.

Fingers point, tongues silence, and movement begins. We slide to the side door; the crowd looks on. Their curiosity and fear mute their thoughts. The cluster spreads wide, kicking stools behind them, eyes to the floor, drinks tucked in to their chest, heads nodding, and perfunctory eyeballs support us for reasons born of fear only.

"Hit the door with force," I say. "Wake them up, and let them know where they are and what they are doing."

I think it was Pancake Dave or Crispy who hit the side door loud enough to cause a reaction. All I am sure of is that we follow tight and close, solidarity unmistakable. I now count five. Apparently, Sesame Street failed me as a child.

It's my role, and I take it. I look for the oldest, the strongest—the president. I grab him by the shoulder. I know he expects it, but I cannot be certain of his reaction. I use enough force to spin him back around. I work my index finger to tuck inside his cut and draw him an inch or two to me. I remind myself that I owe no explanation. I am the inquisitor; he is merely the answer-bot.

"Florida?" I say with force. "And," I say, spinning him back around to read the top rocker, "Black Shadow?" I say this with curiosity and accusation, a mix of passion I have worked on for quite some time now.

I let the silence work in my favor. I stare at him, eye-to-eye. I know I got him. But I also know control doesn't negate crazy, so I remain alert.

"I made a statement disguised as a question, genius," I say to him, massaging his cut patch leather vest. "Explain! Now!"

The stillness is on my side. Solomon and Tophat stand silently but boldly, one on each side of their small pack. Prospect's instincts tell him trouble is afoot, and he meanders inside with us.

"Guys, please," a voice from the bartender chimes in from behind the bar. I snap my hand toward the voice. I make a cutting motion on my neck. He waves his hands and cuts the volume on the jukebox.

"Waiting!" I say to the interloper.

The small but weighty five-foot, six-inch frame, with tattooed, sleeved-out arms accentuating his repeated Nazi symbols tattooed on his knuckles, sporting a blond crew cut, tries to mix survival with grace. "Yeah," he says, clearing his throat, "Black Shadow, established club from West Virginia."

"Yeah?" I say in mock praise. "That's six states away, and . . . I never fucking heard of you."

"I have," Solomon chimes in, as he shoves one Black Shadow out of his way and into the arms of Pancake Dave. "But they folded in

'62, probably a quarter of a century before you were born," Solomon continues.

"My granddaddy was a charter member in 1950," the man says as he nervously clears his throat.

"Jesus-fucking-Christ!" I say. "Nineteen fifty?" I continue with incredulity. "Who cares? You think it matters that grandpappy was a charter member of some club that closed down before J.F.K. was killed?"

"Hey . . . uh . . .," the man says with a pause, searching for his next word in a newly discovered world of pride meeting abject fear. He starts to speak when I cut him off mid-sentence.

"Take 'em off! All of them! Off! Now!"

I can see by the look in his blank stare he fails to grasp the obvious.

"The cuts! Your patch! Off! Now! Give them all to me and slink away from here, and we will allow you to do so vertically," I say sternly.

The crowd stays back, but a saturnine-type curiosity keeps them focused on the two motorcycle clubs standing off on one another. They form an informal arc around us and struggle on where to focus their eyes in fear that someone's eyeballs will connect with theirs.

"And what . . . uh . . .," the man whispers with little confidence. "And you do what with them?"

"Are you interviewing me?" I ask. "Us?" I say again in an attempt to correct myself. "You are not leaving here with them. The only way this scenario ends is that you leave them, drenched in sweat and estrogen, with us, or you leave them drenched with blood." I step in closer to the man. My peripheral view belongs to my brothers and I trust their sight.

The man looks back at his cadre in search of answers, confidence, reasoning, or logic, but finds none.

"We just thought that. . . ."

His pause shows his weakness. I pounce. I exploit. "I'm thinking you don't know how to think. You want colors? You want legitimacy? You come to a coalition meeting, with hat in hand, and you present! And by 'you,' I mean someone entirely different because your opportunity to be legit died today, in our hands."

—Pause—

"It's over, Frank," I say. "Take them off, now."

"Who is 'Frank'?" he asks with a quizzical look on his face.

"You are. I just named you. I don't know who you are, so I named you. Now, hand them over . . . last time before we just take them."

The man I named Frank looks behind him as he strips off his cut slowly. I see the weakness in his eyes, I see the weakness in his speed of undress, I see the weakness in all of them. The remaining Franks follow suit and remove their cut, handing them to various brothers of mine.

"You made the right choice, Frank," I say, patting him on the shoulder condescendingly. "Although your choices were pretty limited, right?" I say, as I tap his back harder. "You all may now slink away. And if I ever see you with a Florida rocker again. . . ."

—Pause—

"Yes?" Frank says with confusion.

"It's not a situation that will ever happen again, so I need not finish."

"No," Frank says sheepishly.

I squeeze his shoulder a bit tighter. "I am waiting to say 'you're welcome,' Frank."

"Oh . . . k . . . so I need to say. . . ."

We both say "thank you" simultaneously.

"*Jinx*!" Solomon yells.

Frank looks at Solomon confusedly, unsure what to say.

"Never mind, Frank. You need to be older, wiser, smarter, and more experienced to get that reference. And clearly, you are none of those."

Frank looks up, then to his left and right. He sighs. He fidgets with his hands. "Thanks," he says awkwardly.

"You're welcome, Frank," I reply, patting him on the shoulder again. "But it is us," I pause and look back at my brothers and the full crowd of onlookers, "who want to thank you," I say, tapping him on the nose, "because we are a thirsty bunch." I follow up with a smile. "Drinks are on Frank!" I shout with a hand pump. The crowd pauses, but soon follows suit and cheers.

I reach into Frank's pocket and yank out his wallet. I grab a fistful of credit cards and toss them on the bar. "Find one and run it," I say. "Frank is picking up today's tab."

The bartender rummages through Frank's future debts and picks a credit card. "Got it!" he shouts.

I hand Frank back his wallet and shove him and his contemporaries toward the back door. The bartender smiles as he pours countless shots of liquor to awaiting glasses. Solomon muscles through the crowd a bit, smiles, and hugs me. "That's the guy I saw in Sarasota! That's the future leadership of this club!" Solomon then points to Prospect to follow the defunct Black Shadow out the door.

After many drinks on Frank, some cheers, some heads throwing back, we, Demons Rising MC, kings of this state, gather outside and get ready to saddle up.

CHAPTER 7

I hear a pop. Then another. Then three in a row. I see Pancake Dave, looking confused. I watch him clutch his chest and look perplexingly at the blood on his hands. He glances back up at me and he falls. He doesn't scream, he just falls.

CHAPTER 8
Balance

Tophat / 1970 – Portsmouth, New Hampshire

"Oh, Travis, you're such a handsome man."

"Thanks, Mom. Do I look okay? Dawn Seaburn is supposed to be there tonight."

"Dawn? She's just a little girl, Son. She's got a long way to go to be a woman."

"She's only a few weeks younger than me, Mom."

"Travis, stop calling me 'Mom.' I told you that you're old enough to call me 'Lu-Lu.'"

"I . . . I know."

"When are you coming home tonight, Travis?"

"Uh . . . by eleven?"

"Okay, sweetness. I'll make some snacks, and we can watch some TV in my room again, okay?"

"Okay. I . . . uh . . . will be there."

"Travis, honey?"

"*Yeah?*"
"*Shhh . . .*"
"*I know, Mom. I mean . . . uh . . . Lu-Lu.*"

June 2019

That fucking song. I hate it. But we play it at the clubhouse whenever we bury a brother. I purposely parked my bike away from our clubhouse but still within our fence. I shoo Venus inside with a slight nod and a perfunctory smile. I signal to her to go without me because I want to be alone with my thoughts.

I can't get the sight out of my mind of Tophat ripping off his shirt, trying to get the blood to stop flowing. I can't stop hearing him scream Dave's name over and over again, telling him to '*wake up!*' I can't forget the way he shrieked at the EMT people after they looked up at him despondently and lightly shook their heads.

I don't understand why there was no sound of a motorcycle roaring away, no sign of a cage rolling by, no figure scampering through the woods. Gone! A ghost. Nothing happened like I thought it would. I wasn't prepared for any of this. I don't know how I am supposed to act or feel.

As I slow my gait to a near halt, I ponder the day of mourning for Dave that we held at his favorite hamburger joint in nearby Ellenton. Every club in the coalition was there, as well as a plethora of independent clubs—even the ones not seeking entrance into the coalition. Although they are not part of the coalition, they still must come to a meeting and, essentially, seek permission to wear a patch with an *MC* tag if it is three-piece. They are vetted to see if they are legit and such, e.g., no past or present law enforcement members, actually own and ride a motorcycle, etc. You may scoff at the latter, but there are some who buy patches and fancy leather doodads, and then try to obtain a motorcycle. We call them Internet clubs or *pop-up* clubs—suburban dentists, IT geeks, etc., playing make-believe by sewing patches on their back and buying leather outfits. They're not serious people by any means. But as we just discovered, non-legitimate is not akin to harmless. Sanctioned clubs, even those not in the coalition, are allowed to come to our events, *required* if you are looking to be in the coalition someday.

I digress, which I do a lot when my brain is being peppered with thoughts I don't want and ones I am trying to dissect. I watch Venus walk and give sideways hugs to my brothers and their respective ol' ladies. With each hug she then pulls back, says something I can't hear, and then hugs again. I can't tell whether she is feeling comfort in her sadness or just cinematic emotion.

She's so beautiful, more so at times and less so at other times. The occasion, the moment, the heat, and the disparate way the neurons are firing sways the mood. My brain creates a firestorm where my thought patterns flow in all directions. I think the chaotic nature of it is designed to keep it from being overloaded with a flush of realism.

I am trying to discern if the massive turnout for Pancake Dave's funeral run was a telltale sign of respect for us, or just a chance to get inside a one-percenter's clubhouse to say, "Yeah, I was there!" But either way, it was a turnout of epic proportions. I will say clubs like Rebellious Youth have nothing to prove, and they were there in full force. They will be watching us to see how we react to one of our own being murdered in cold blood.

I don't know what happens to my short-term memory. Maybe it's still the shock, but I only recall bits and pieces of the ride from Dave's memorial, where we all met and spoke of Dave, to the ride back here. We picked our remembrances of Dave carefully.

Solomon said we have to keep the recollections upbeat and lighthearted because so many clubs were there, including neutral clubs, and although part of the coalition, they are ready to prey on their *incorrect* interpretation that our temporary troubles with the coalition make us weak. They may want to be the dominate club in Florida; we don't know. We had to discuss . . . *discuss*! . . . our stories we told. That angers me! I want to talk about the time Dave and I had breakfast at this Amish place in Sarasota where he helped some little kid in a wheelchair get a whole plate load of bacon. Dave knelt slightly and peeked up at this kid's mom to assuage her fear and then said to the boy, "When people ask if you did crunches this morning, you can say, 'If you mean the crunch of bacon, then yes'!" The boy's mom laughed, as did I, and Pancake Dave went on to load up on—you guessed it—pancakes. Pancake Dave knew what it was like to be minimized, marginalized. I often wonder whether he really liked pancakes that much, or whether he just tried to live up to his name. That nickname made him feel important, like one of us. And he was.

But Solomon voiced his dissent, and that anecdote showing kindness to a crippled child was voted down. We *voted* on that. We took a vote on whether I could tell that story. Never mind that it was voted down. Where do I follow up on that comment and how? But the pragmatic side of me understood. I hate my pragmatic side. It's not 'me,' but it is who I am. The vote was needed. I lost. But we did tell stories of Pancake Dave in a good, lighthearted manner that preserved our sincerity and our survival.

I was in a goddamn war! *War!* Strangers in a strange land wanting to kill me, and I don't remember having to have that balance.

I am almost at our clubhouse, our home where Pancake Dave leaned and rocked in the corner to some imaginary song near our slot machine. He would tip his glass at us if we directed our attention at him.

I'm an officer in this club. The coalition is here. I chased out the nobodies who permeated the so-called 'Black Shadow' MC. The coalition needs to know what I did and what they face. They need to see me at the podium. They need to know what I did without me telling them. They need to see Pancake Dave in the corner. They need to see we loved him so. They need to see us as strong.

I know when I slowly walk up to the podium, I will have at least one hundred eyeballs looking my way. I think of Pancake Dave. I think of today. I think of the roar of all the motors. I think of the sporadic memories. I think of Pancake Dave falling. I see that look he gave me. I see him fall again. I think of him being called 'Shortbus.' I think of that kid in the wheelchair. I think of Dave's sense of purpose Demons Rising gave him. I think of the club's future. I think of the way my horses used to run to the barn back in Indiana. I think of the first time I heard a motorcycle engine roar. I think of Dave trying in vain to get his bandana on his head when he was drunk. I think of the sand beneath my boots in Fallujah. I think of my Eagle Scout induction. I think of Pancake Dave posing for a snapshot, holding a bottle of syrup in that masterful, self-deprecating picture. I think of my mom. I think of my first girlfriend, Wendy, and her weirdly shaped bicycle. I think of me. I think, 'why am I thinking of me'? I think of Venus. And I think of why. I think of what is important. I think of why it is important. I think of love.

I am ready! I can create this balance. I see my biggest fan—hopefully—in the crowd. I see Venus, fake-ass red hair and a charm, in question, that builds me and completes me. Or depletes me.

I miss you, Dave. I really do.

I hear the music as I walk into our home. That fucking song!

CHAPTER 9
Delilah

Venus / 1994 – Mooreland, Nebraska

"Oh, Mary Ellen, when we said anyone could sit here, we didn't mean 'just anyone.'"

"Look! Now you made her cry."

"Oh, geez, don't just stand there looking like an idiot, Mary Ellen."

"Yeah, go sit with the smokers and special ed kids."

"Yeah, take that shitty lunch meal with you and walk away in your three-dollar Walmart shoes."

"Gonna wear them, alone, to the dance next week again?"

"Aw . . . she's gonna cry."

"What a fucking weirdo!"

June 2019

"That was a great speech, Digger," Venus says as she drapes her arm over my chest, nuzzling as close to me as she can. "Well . . . I wouldn't call it a speech, really."

"I know. I just meant everyone's ears were tuned and they were looking intently."

"I tend to ramble and gab all at once," I say, stroking her bare back and drawing her in closer to me.

"I was listening. You were definitely 'on.'"

"I loved Dave. I just spoke from within."

"But the other stuff, too. The stuff about the coalition, and the clubs, and what these pretenders from ol' West Virginia did at the bar, and the future, you know?" Venus says with enthusiasm.

"Yeah," I say with some skepticism, "like I said, Venus, I just spoke. My short-term memory isn't what it used to be . . . Neptune."

"Asshole!" she says as she tickles me.

"Hey, Venus, let me rub Uranus!" I say as Venus laughs again and hits me with the pillow.

"How about 'Venus sucks your penis'? Is that a better quip?" she asks as she slides her lips along my chest.

I laugh. "That's what Solomon said once."

Venus stops and looks at me peculiarly. "He doesn't like me, does he?" she asks as she lies back down slowly, pulling the blanket over her naked body. She looks up at the ceiling and lies there quietly.

"Solomon?" I say inquiringly. "Yes, of course he does."

"No, no, I am sure he doesn't. He hasn't treated me the same since the day at the store."

"Oh Christ, Venus, don't read anything into that. He is not a warm and fuzzy guy, believe me."

"No," Venus replies emphatically. "I'm sure of it. He just wants me to disappear. He just thinks I'm another club whore. I can tell."

"Venus!" I say briskly. "You're talking about a man who literally punched out a mall Santa Claus last year near the *Nacho Pit* as twenty kids watched on in horror. The man is a joyless, fucking freak!" I say. I perch a look of disgust on my face as I regret not thinking of that barb during our last verbal spar at the bonfire.

"He-did-not?" Venus retorts animatedly as she leaps up from the bed.

"Yep," I say, nodding my head. "He even screamed, *'Ho-Ho-Ho this, you glorified, fucking, rodeo clown'* as he pummeled him."

"Now I know you're kidding."

"I'm 'fraid not," I say with a smirk.

Venus laughs. "Why?"

"Who the fuck knows," I say as I throw my hands up. "His ex giving him shit, all coked up, and Christmastime bring out the worst in him, any or all of the above."

"What happened after that?"

"Oh, he spent the night in the warm, clenched fists of the Hillsborough County Sheriff's Department. No charges were filed, and they kicked him loose the next day."

"They didn't press charges?" Venus says.

"The mall—and 'Santa'—didn't want to pursue the hassle."

"So cool!" Venus says with a smile. "They're that afraid of you guys?"

I emit a small chuckle. "I think they just wanted to be rid of us. Mall security said something about 'Demons Rising being well above their paygrade.'"

"You guys can just do whatever the fuck you want, can't you?" Venus asks, still beaming.

"I like to think that beating random Santas down is not on that list, but. . . ." I reply with a cocksure smirk, knowing Venus is pleased.

"That's freakin' hilarious!" Venus continues laughing. "Does he really hate Christmas?"

I sigh and smile. "Does the man hate Christmas?" I ask rhetorically. "Venus! He roots for the sun when Frosty comes on TV. He once said the Island of Misfit Toys were just a bunch of weak-ass, whiney pussies."

Venus explodes in laughter. Whether it's rooted in the humor or the euphoria of connecting to our world alludes me, but its origin I care not. I just enjoy the smile she gives.

"Now I know you're lying," she says, still laughing.

"Okay," I say in surrender. "I made the Rudolph part up, but he did go off last Christmas during Frosty. Called him a 'thief and a pedophile.' I'm telling you, the man is Scrooge on steroids at Christmas."

"Oh my God, I can't wait for Christmas so I can pick on him."

"Uhh . . . no, you won't be doing that."

"Can I please say something to him?" Venus pleads.

"Umm . . . that's a big negatory, sweet thing."

"Why?"

"Venus, he would be pissed. Don't."

Venus's smile disappears. She sits, silent, and then lies back down. "I told you he didn't like me."

"Why?" I ask, "because he doesn't want you teasing him about stuff like that? I probably shouldn't even be telling you that."

"Oh, I won't say a word, Digger. Not-a-word! Not about anything! I swear it," Venus replies eagerly.

"I know you wouldn't," I say gently.

"I mean, at the bar, he rolled his eyes and called me a 'fruity chick' right in front of Babs and the other girls." Venus pauses. A distance grows in her eyes a bit and she sighs. She lies silently momentarily and then says, "I've never seen that, you know. Have you?"

"Seen what?" I ask confusedly.

"I mean, I know you were in the war and you saw stuff like that, but right in front of you? Out of nowhere?" She continues as she gently rubs her nails across my chest. I see the chipped paint and faint hint of the glitter that coated them hours ago. She uses her index finger to gently twirl into my skin.

"If you're talking about Pancake Dave, I—"

"Yes," Venus says, interrupting me.

"Look, Venus, I. . . ."

Venus props her head up slightly and looks at me. She smiles and kisses me as she runs her hand down my body.

"Dave is gone, and we have to move on from here to the next phase," I say.

"I know," she whispers softly as she continues to caress and kiss me. "Next comes the revenge, right?"

Demons Rising

"Revenge?" I say, sliding her away.

"You know what I mean, Digger," she says with a genteel smile. "You guys hit 'em back, right? Take one of theirs out?"

"What the hell?" I say bewilderedly. "What do you think this is, *the Sharks and the Jets*?"

"Who? Never heard of them. What part of the coalition are they from? Or are they one of the West Virginia clubs?" Venus asks as she returns to circling her finger along my chest.

"No," I say, looking perplexed, and now too embarrassed to admit I am familiar with *West Side Story*.

"But you guys are going to get payback, right? I mean, I would assume the coalition of clubs is expecting you all to step up, right?" Venus presses on.

I stare at Venus, unsure what to say. I pause momentarily. "What happened to 'Venus sucks my penis'?" I ask, not realizing why I was unsure of what to say. I mean, that seems like the most logical response.

"Come on, Digger," Venus says tersely, slapping my arm. "You just said you know I won't say anything."

I say nothing as I stare at Venus with a blank look on my face. "Soooo," I say curiously, "for the record, the . . . uh . . . 'Venus, penis' thing is done for now?"

"Stop trying to be funny, Digger," Venus says as she lies flat and covers herself more.

I lie with her and hold her. "Venus, the women don't know stuff like this, okay?"

"Babs—"

"No, Venus. Tophat does not tell Babs shit, and she doesn't know anything more than you, got it?" I say, anger showing.

"Yes, she does. She—"

"No!" I snap. "No, she-does-not! And I don't think she tells you that she does."

"I didn't say she does," Venus says. She rolls over slightly, facing away from me.

"Why is this shit so important to you?" I ask. "You and I exist with or without this club."

55

Venus rolls back over with more alacrity this time. "You're not thinking of quitting, are you?"

"Would it matter?" I ask defensively.

Venus, again, rolls over slightly, facing away from me. "No, Digger, of course not. That's not what I meant."

"Again, Venus, why is knowing this stuff so important to you?"

"It's not," Venus retorts, muffled by her pillow. "It just makes me close to you, that's all."

I give way to a smile. I lie and rub up close to her. "Hey," I whisper. "I love you," I say, kissing the back of her head.

Venus reaches back and pats my hip a few times.

Fortunately, the ring of my phone rescues me from the awkwardness. I roll back over and grab my phone.

"Mallet! Hey, Bro, how's it going?" A few *uh-huhs* and *that's cool* are exchanged. "Okay, get here in one piece. See you tomorrow." I hang up my phone and lie back down. I look over at Venus and stare at her, listening to her breathe. I rub her hair slightly and yawn. "That was Mallet, sweetie. He's one of our nomads. He's leaving now and will be here by tomorrow."

Venus remains facing away but says, "I've heard you mention him. You two are tight, right?"

"Oh, hell yeah. I love that guy. He's true blue. He's a cut above the rest."

"Do I even need to ask why y'all call him 'Mallet'?" Venus says.

I laugh slightly. "No, you guessed it. He's one hell of a scrapper."

"Why, *if* I may ask," Venus says with noted sarcasm, "didn't he come to the funeral?"

"Yes, you may, *wise-ass*, and the answer is he has stuff going on in Virginia and he couldn't get away."

"Virginia?" Venus says, as she rolls back around hastily once more. "So he—" Venus silences herself. I look at her as comforting as I can.

"Venus..." I pause. Venus lies back down and rolls away once more. I sigh. "Do you know why I gave you the name 'Venus'?"

She reaches back and attempts to rub my chest. She sighs. "Yes, yes I do," she says amidst another sigh. "I'm sorry."

56

I lie back down and place my hands under my head. I stare at the ceiling, making shapes out of the swirled and mismatched paint and random water stains. I like moments like this at times. I play a song in my head and almost lightly self-hypnotize myself. I look over at Venus again and whisper softly, "You're gonna be the death of me." I smile, although she cannot see it.

Venus breathes deeply but rolls back over and drapes her arm over me. I think she feigns sleep some and she says softly, "I'm sorry."

I stare at that beautiful face, covering an irksome and enigmatic creature at times. I think to myself: *I should have given her a different moniker from ancient times. Yeah . . . like Delilah.*

CHAPTER 10

The Rat

Digger / 1990 – Elkhart, Indiana

"Change our last name? Are you insane, Grant?"
"Productive response, Kate."
"And what do you want me to say? 'Great idea, Grant'!"
"Did you even ask why I want to change it?"
"I already know why. Because 'Garcia' isn't elite enough for you."
"You're being overly simplistic."
"Then elaborate, Grant. And then explain how you will tell Digger."
"It's a Latino name, and I am blond and blue, Kate. My stepdad adopted me; you know that."
"And you say he was a good man, so why dishonor him?"
"Thanks, Kate. Make me the bad guy. I just want to be taken seriously in my life. I have goals."
"What you have is a warped sense of values."
"Because I want a name that matches me? Really?"
"Then how about 'Asshole,' Grant."

"Real productive again, Kate."
"Then change it to Bunker if you want! I don't give a shit."
"Yeah, real funny, Kate."
"I'm not changing it, and I will not allow you to change Digger's name just so you can impress some stuffed-shirt blue bloods."

June 2019

Willie is the first to hear it. Our entry buzzer alerts him to an interloper. Willie looks up at the monitor and sees a man stopped at our front gate. The man departs from his bike and strips off his shirt, pants, boots, and socks. The man, thin build with a grain or two of muscle sporting no tattoos, begins walking down our driveway toward the clubhouse. I'd say he is in his mid-thirties and looks like some factory-made action figure come to life. He is tall and lanky, at least six-feet, six-inches tall. He sports a weak ponytail hairstyle, deep black in color, that is trying to morph into a mullet, and his pasty skin puts him out of place for Florida. He gives the impression of a wayward *surfer dude*, only pale.

The only thing that would give him any semblance of ruggedness is a zigzag-style scar just above his left eyebrow. But even though it is a zigzag, it seems to spread out at the end, looking like a carrot, and almost appears to be burnt orange in nature. It's just plain weird looking. I can't seem to take my eyes off it. Maybe it's a burn. Maybe it's a birthmark. I just know it's weird looking. A zigzagging carrot.

"Walt!!" Willie shouts. "Something's going on here!" Willie reaches for his waistband and pulls out his snub nose .38. Walt runs to the bar area and sees Willie. Willie then whistles for the rest of us, who are outside making some small repairs to our fence.

"Hey! We got company!" Walt shouts. Tophat, Mallet, Solomon, Crispy, Jack, Zonk, and I run to the clubhouse with guns drawn. We huddle around the monitor as the man approaches slowly up the walk, waving his one open hand.

"Holy fuck, he's holding up a Black Shadow vest!" I say fervently.

"His other hand?" Jack asks.

"Empty. In fact, he's holding it up and wiggling his fingers," I reply. "Not only that, the damn fool is down to his gym shorts and bare feet!"

"What the fuck is going on? Any more of them?" Zonk inquires.

"I don't see any," I reply. "Let's get out there. I'm taking point," I say as I run to the door. "Walt and Willie, go around back."

The man sees us, guns drawn, and stops. "Please!" he shrieks with passion in his voice. "I don't want this," he says, shaking the vest. He tosses it on the ground and then keeps both hands up slightly. "Please, guys, I'm down to my shorts, dudes. I got no weapon, no mic, no camera. I swear it," the man bellows. He drops his shorts to his knees and pirouettes. "Nothing!" he says as he reaches back down and pulls up his shorts. "I know I'm taking a chance here, but I don't know what else to do." The man stands there, awaiting a response, as he stares at seven men, angry and unsure, with guns aimed at him.

"We look scared," I whisper to my brothers. "Put the iron down." We all lower our guns but keep them in our hands.

"I just wanna talk, dudes. That's it, I swear."

"Take 'em!" I say forcefully.

Willie and Walt grab him by his arms, and Mallet tears at his hair. The three drag him into the clubhouse and hurl him to the floor. He quickly props himself in a crab position. "Please," he says as he gulps. "I am requesting to speak, and then I'll take what comes my way."

"Are you setting the agenda here?" I scream.

"Damn, man, come on! I'm a fucking accountant!" he shrieks tearfully.

"You going to do my taxes or something?" Solomon asks with false confusion.

"No, no, no," the man says, holding up his hands. "I'm trying to point out I'm not a real biker."

"Wow!" Walt says with a quip. "We are forever grateful you pointed that out to us."

"Exactly!" Crispy says, looking at Walt. "We would have never known otherwise."

"Please," he says once more.

"If you think we are going to see your actions here today as some sort of courage and believe this is the part of the story where we say, *Gee, he has guts, don't he, fellas,* you're out of your motherfucking mind," I say calmly.

"No, no, not at all," the man says. "My name is Brett—"

"Good!" Mallet chimes in quickly. "Now we know what to write on your headstone." Mallet's small, five-foot, eight-inch wiry frame stands over the man named Brett. Mallet gowns himself in his traditional long-sleeved, pullover shirt with a ratty, old, faded-blue bandana. His beard has become more salt than pepper over the past two years, and in that beard is where he tucks in his trademark yellow sunglasses.

"I am not trying to show machismo," Brett says. "I actually studied risk management in college."

"And . . .," I say with a pause, motioning my finger around the room, "this was your best risk? Coming here?"

"Believe it or not, yes," Brett says. "I know your guys' rep, and eventually you would have found me and every Black Shadow, and I cannot live my life looking over my shoulder every second. I am ready to squeal like the pig that knows he's dinner. Do you think me ratting out everyone else would impress you? No, I am acting out of pure fear, self-preservation, and I don't care. I'd rather be breathing than have people say nice things at my funeral. I owe those clowns nothing! I wasn't even there when your friend got shot."

"Friend?" I shriek as I drive my foot into his face. Brett emits a quick mumble and falls flat on the floor. "That man was our brother! You fucking scumbags don't know the difference, do you?" I say, punching him twice in his head as he tries to cover himself.

"I'm sorry! I'm sorry!" he says in a panic. "I know who killed him, and I can tell you where he is, please. . . ."

I cease the beating and grab Brett by his neck. I motion for everyone else to stay back. I throw him into a chair forcefully, but still gently enough so he ends up sitting upright. "You have one chance to please us here, Brett, and then we might just let you walk on out of here with no more bloodshed."

"Okay, okay, I will, I swear," Brett says, still shaking and turning his head away from me. "The dude you named 'Frank'... it was him," Brett says as he sighs. He slowly lowers his hands and looks at the half circle of angry bikers.

"I knew it was that little turd," I say.

"Yeah, it was him," Brett says. "My understanding is that nobody else wanted anything to do with it."

"Yeah?" I say mockingly, "well nobody stopped it or gave us a heads-up, did they? So they are just as guilty."

Brett nods his head slightly. "Well, 'Frank's' real name is Donald Heidlberg. He calls himself *Torch*."

"I like *Frank* better."

"Yeah," Brett says with a halfhearted smile, trying to find some way to bond with me. "He also fancies himself some sort of right-wing militant who wants to eliminate minorities, etcetera. I mean, he's just some millennial crybaby nut who thinks the world revolves around him. He's a spoiled, rich kid whom mommy and daddy doted on, and he was never challenged a day in his life."

"Was his *grandpappy*," I say mockingly, "actually a charter member in 1950?"

"Yeah, yeah," Brett says while panting. "He showed Torch some old snapshots of them back in the day and regaled him with all these war stories. But even his granddad told him that he can't just buy some patches and start running the roads. Even his granddad said the stuff about finding the dominant club in the area and asking permission to start a legit MC."

I emit a soft chuckle, born of disgust. "And you put on a patch with this guy? Why?" I ask more out of curiosity, not necessity.

"Oh, man, just to," he sighs, "you know... to get girls," he answers uneasily.

"So," I say, grabbing him by the neck, "our brother is dead so you fucking geekwads could pick up girls? Is that what I am hearing?" I ask, shaking him.

"I know. I got... I got nothing, man. Torch took it too far. He was so embarrassed that you took his shit and made a fool out of him that he just stewed and stewed about it. He had the prospect take his bike back to our clubhouse near Nocatee, and then Torch went to a store in Arcadia, bought a rifle, and hid in the woods." Brett stops talking, looks up at me, and swallows some dry spit. "He was aiming at you, dude."

Brett's words stun me and fill me with emotions I have not immediately processed. This is the part of the show where I grow enraged at hearing those words and waste this guy here and now. I see that look on Dave's face, and now I wonder if it was him saying to me, "This was meant for you. I took it for you," as he collapsed.

"Okay," I say calmly. "Enough of Frank's fucking bio. Where is this piece of shit now?"

"He's back in West Virginia. He's from some Podunk town named Duckwall."

Brett stares at all of us, trying to read the unreadable. His eyes slowly move across ours, one by one. Each of us receive a different look, but they all equate to fear.

"Where's your keys, Brett?"

"Keys . . . keys to what?" he asks bewilderedly.

"To your ride you left out by our gate. I need the keys so it will be easier to bring it into our clubhouse."

Brett pauses momentarily and says nothing. He just stands motionless with a blank stare.

"Well, Brett," Mallet says as he pats him on the back. "You don't expect us to push it in here, do you?"

"You mean . . . my bike? Pu-pushing it?"

"Yeah, I mean, Mallet is correct, isn't he?" I ask, looking over at Mallet as he gives me an affirmative nod. "Making us push it in here would make you a poor guest to your hosts."

Brett looks around at all of us and finally understands what we are saying. For some reason, he appears to stare at me for an extra moment or two in some vain effort to sway my position. I merely return the stare and say nothing. Brett finally exhales a deep and surrendering sigh. "They're hanging on the rear foot peg," he says sedately.

"Thank you, Brett," I say, patting him on the back condescendingly. "In all fairness, my friend, I did say we'd let you *walk* out of here." I continue with a spurious smirk on my face. "But nobody said a thing about riding."

CHAPTER 11
It's Just Two Brothers Riding

Mallet / 1999 – St. Paul, Minnesota

"We are happy to have you stay with us for Christmas, Richard. It's our honor."

"The honor is mine, Missus Velez."

"Well, we certainly weren't going to allow you to spend Christmas at Fort Benning eating rubber ham and watching reruns of 'It's a Wonderful Life'."

"I am very grateful, ma'am."

"When my son said a friend in his platoon had no family to go home to for Christmas, it just . . . just broke my heart."

"That's nice of you, ma'am."

"Where are your parents going for Christmas?"

"Nowhere, ma'am. They're back home at the farm in Pennsylvania."

"And you didn't want to go be with them?"

"I think it was more their idea, Missus Velez. They haven't spoken to me in years."

"My stars! That upsets me so."

"It's okay, ma'am. I had given up on having a fatted calf waiting for me since I was twelve."

"No, no, no, that won't do, Richard. Why would you give up at such a youthful age?"

"It's okay, ma'am. I don't care much for veal anyway."

"Oh, Richard, you're too funny."

June 2019

I meet Mallet back at the clubhouse at first cock-a-doodle. Mallet, being one of the club's nomads, has no actual home base chapter. He runs across all of Florida and up the Eastern Seaboard, staying in touch with our chapters in North and South Carolina, Georgia, Virginia, and Delaware, and he is getting another chapter started in Maryland. We have additional nomads who cover the chapters in the mid-Atlantic, and others covering out west. Mallet's bottom rocker denotes no particular state, only the word "nomad." He helps start new chapters, rolls in and assists charters in trouble, and essentially goes where he pleases. No one chapter directs a nomad's movement. Mallet knows we have a pressing issue to address: one Donald 'Torch' Hessenberg and any remaining Black Shadow members who were involved in taking our brother.

Mallet makes an excellent nomad in the practical sense and in the philosophical sense. Mallet's own life outside our life is, well, *nomadic* in nature. He is estranged from his family, and has no legit ol' lady, no real past that explains the ingredients that define him.

He and I are tight, tighter than any of my other brothers here perhaps—except for Solomon. But although Solomon and I are equals because we are club brothers, our relationship definitely has the mentor/mentee component to it that makes it unbalanced.

Mallet is more my age, former war vet as an Army Ranger, and our outlook on life is just on an even keel with one another. There's a mutual respect for each other, and there's never a moment that we feel, as us men too often do, the innate need to outdo the other. We're not afraid to be who we are. He likes Jim while I like Jack. It's that last part where I believe it is the only time we denigrate one another: he calls my whiskey a pussy whiskey and I do the same to his. We always laugh and swig from the same flask anyway.

Once Prospect cooks us breakfast, Mallet and I are heading out on the road. While on higher alert than normal, there's an unwritten rule that while flying colors in times like this, nobody rides alone.

Venus is in the real world today, and I told her Mallet and I are hitting the road for a few days to kill the cobwebs in our brain. If this were a movie, I would take my cell phone and toss it in the fire or smash it against the wall, but reality is also saddling up with us, requiring us to be tethered to the world of which we are trying to flee. Only in the movies do you break *all* contact from the real world.

We holster our irons, give the kickstands a jolt, and meld our hands into the throttle. As the engines roar, I instinctively sigh deeply as a smile forms, and I close my eyes. Music starts playing in my head, and the sensation in my body begins to slowly caress my brain. Sometimes I think this is the best part of the ride. People say it about sex, food, and such, and it's the same here—the anticipation of the uncertainty. My father always said I thrive on it. Yes, I agree. However, my father did not phrase that comment as a virtue to be upheld, but rather a flaw in need of repair. I never understood how people rise to challenges, or even discover challenges, if they do not embrace uncertainty. There are varying degrees—I get that, I do—but uncertainty is the genesis of the passion of life itself. If that is not the goal, then I am unaware of what is. In a land where certainty is king, you will find uniformity, conformity, malaise, and a sickness of the heart and mind. Dignity dies, and life abandons you. And the vessel by which it travels is of your own making. Birds fly, children cry, and dreams die. There are your certainties that you can't control, but anything else is fair game. I have forever believed that all men should always be the sole architect of their lives.

What's pineapple on pizza taste like? What happens when you add this to that? Where does this road go? And this one? And that one? Ya know . . . pineapple on pizza is pretty fucking good.

The cobwebs in my mind trap the ghosts that exist there. On days like this, on the road, I swear the wind whips through me and breaks those spider-like shackles, releasing those ghosts. I know eventually they are replaced, but for these few hours, there's an emancipation in my mind. It's an atypical feeling that is indescribable for most, and that is why I don't share thoughts like this with anyone. Well, anyone other than the man riding next to me right now. Mallet's approach to life is like mine. I feel both sympathy for and give thanks for that fact. Not even Solomon would understand what I am talking about, even though he probably feels the same way.

A cager rolls upon us and then tempers their speed. I glance in my mirror to make certain all is satisfactory. I spot Mister and Missus Front Porch, pulling a fifth wheeler with their two point three children and dog named Spot behind us. The wife pokes at her husband as she sees who is in front of them. What a sight she must see, the two of us rolling along, free as birds, without a care in the world. Lights! Camera! Action! She pulls out her phone as the traffic slows, heading into a lone stoplight. I don't know whether being a curiosity to citizens is a compliment, or if it is supposed to be degrading. As Mallet and I sit at the red light, I raise my left hand for a fist bump to my brother. I seize his hand and shake it high in the sky. I see the wife go crazy with her snapshots now, one after the other. I contemplate whether I am truly showing my brother heartfelt admiration and respect or posing for the camera, perhaps being theatrical for a couple of drone-like, passerby types who feel energized at the sighting of us. Mallet smiles and says, "Love ya, Bro!" I smile back and nod.

The Iowa suburbanites turn right as Mallet and I go straight. "You're welcome," I mutter to myself softly as they pass by.

The moment ends. What the moment was, I am not certain. I will replay it in my head and question my motives.

Eighty miles across flat terrain, eyeballing an occasional bobcat, one gator, and maybe five cages passing west as we fly eastward, is when it hit us. It was at a red light near the town of Avon Park. Both Mallet and I look at each other, but he is the first to say it. "Where the fuck we going, Bro?" Mallet asks as he demonstrably tosses his hands out. If I give him any other answer than the one that he is expecting—the answer I know to be true, right, and powerful—his disappointment in me will be forever.

I smile at him as beads of sweat drop from my forehead. The engines continue to roar, and I throw my hands out, too. "I have no fucking clue," I reply, with all the grace I can muster. "I do know there's a joint on Route 27 called the Wild Turkey that has cold beer, good, fried tomatoes, and they don't give a fuck if you burn a few on the back deck."

"Yeah," Mallet says inquisitively. "Do they serve that pussy-ass whiskey you like, or do they have a real man's bourbon?"

I laugh. "They have what you like. They serve it to you with a straw or a sippy cup."

We swing the bikes around the parking lot and back up right on their walkway. The citizens take a step back and look, point, and whisper. We drop our kickstands and walk to the door. A couple of weekend warrior types gowned up in leather vests and newly pleated bandanas hold the door open for us. I give the one a gracious nod of acknowledgement. I hear him whisper to his friend, "Biker royalty right there, Kevin."

Mallet and I walk in and see about three or four members of Grizzlymen MC. They are a non-one-percent club and haven't joined, or asked to join, the coalition, but we sanctioned them about three years back. They sent two representatives to Pancake Dave's funeral. They're legit, but they don't want the hassle, or the perks, of being in the coalition. They spot Mallet and I as we walk in. They immediately pop up from their bar stools and greet us. "Hi," one guy says. "Louie, Grizzlymen MC, Avon Park," he says, extending his hand to me.

I accept his offer. "Digger, Demons Rising, Florida." After the mutual politeness and condolences on Pancake Dave, I run out of artificial pleasantries.

"Hey, look," Louie says, "you both don't need an invite to sit with us, but at least let us set you up with your first round."

"Obliged," Mallet says with an amiable nod. "A cold pitcher, a shot of Jack, and a shot of Jim."

"Sure thing," Louie says. "I'll have one of the girls send it your way. Enjoy." Louie offers a sideways salute and goes back to his table.

Mallet and I sit out on the back deck, talking about life—his life, my life, the club's life, Pancake Dave's life, Venus's life, my dog's life, and how life operates in our world and how and why we will protect it, while cherishing it, at all costs.

The idea of us leaving this town becomes less and less likely as the earth's rotation steals sunlight minute by minute. One pitcher of beer replaces another, and the whiskey shots seem to never end. Not once do we reach for our wallets. The crowd shows respect for our patch with their fascination in paying our tabs. We nod occasionally as they amuse us with tales of how they met one of our brothers in North Carolina, or how someone's nephew was close with a chapter in Arizona, or how they saw a documentary on Demons Rising last week—any inroad they can find to live, even for a fleeting moment, vicariously through us. We drink our whiskey, we smoke our weed, and we nod. Every now and then we spot Avon Park cops driving by slowly, probably concerned our visit to this small town on the north/south strip to nowhere is something more than what it is. But it is two brothers with their commitment for each other, their passion for the open road, their motorcycles, and the self-defined freedom we garner from all of it, seeking an escape for today from the other world. That's all it is.

The Grizzlymen begin rounding up their members and start making an exit. Louie comes over to say goodbye and asks us if we need anything.

"Got a couple of bumps before y'all go?" Mallet asks.

Louie looks up at his own club brother, nods slightly, and looks back at us. "Yeah, man, sure. If it's just a bump or two, it's on us."

"Can y'all clear the back deck for a minute? We want to talk with these boys," I say to the crowd of patrons. They disperse almost immediately as they walk back into the bar's main room.

Louie unwraps a piece of cellophane and dumps out a few small drops of cocaine. He takes a small spoon and places a scoop on Mallet's hand, then on mine. We both rub our hand to our nose and take it in. Both Mallet and I nod our heads in keeping with the universal sign for *thank you*.

"Uh . . . Digger? Mallet? Our clubhouse is off North Dressell Road. Y'all don't need an invite."

"Thanks," I say. "Appreciated. We are heading to Fort Pierce next month for the next coalition meeting. If we got time, we'll swing by." The Grizzlymen smile as they egress to the parking lot. The crowd makes their way back to the deck, resuming their hedonism.

Mallet spots two girls, probably in their late twenties, one with bushy, red hair and the other with black hair sporting some sort of 1980s-style, 'big hair' look. We wave them over to join us. They look at each other with glee and sashay over to our table.

Tomorrow we will ride somewhere else. The next day, we will go back to the real world. But tonight, that world stays there. I tug at the redheads' ears to get a closer look at her earrings. "Badass!" I say to her. She smiles beamingly.

"Thanks!" she retorts.

"And is this fake-ass, red hair?" I ask, gently tugging at her locks.

"Ha-ha," she laughs. "Nope! I'm the real deal! I am authentic."

Even though parts of that world I left this morning I love very much, tonight I am here. Tomorrow I won't be.

Tomorrow our colors are back in the wind, cruising down, up, or wherever, as civilians drive behind us, seeing the bold, red patch outlined in demonic green with our center patch showing who we are, the top putting a name to us, and the bottom rocker telling them where we are from. Their minds range from wonder, to disgust, to envy, to fear, but rarely, if ever, to self-assurance.

Simple respect.

CHAPTER 12
Church

Solomon / 1972 – Wauchula, Florida

"Are you crazy, Tommy?"

"Don't fucking say that, Sheila!"

"You spent four years in a jungle, in a war with no purpose, to come back to this?"

"Maybe it'll give me purpose."

"Really? I don't give you purpose? Your son doesn't give you purpose?"

"This is a different kind of purpose, Sheila."

"Ten-year-olds put on costumes and ride beat-up, old Harleys, Tommy."

"We're going to do this, Sheila, with you or without you."

"I can see that! You're a selfish asshole, Tommy!"

"You always see the shitty side of things, don't you?"

"There's a good side to starting a motorcycle gang?"

"It's a club, Sheila! A club! We promote brotherhood! We promote unity!"

"You have us, Tommy. You have your buddies from the Corps."

"They might be coming with Joe and I."
"You just have a fucking death wish, don't you?"
"With you or without you, Sheila."
"Since you are persisting . . . without!"

June 2019

It's church night at our house. Church is once a week and mandatory for all of us to attend. Every second Friday night and fourth Saturday afternoon, we have an open house where, essentially, we *open our house* to the public. Most people who attend are members of other clubs, stopping in to have a drink or two, and then there is the regular citizen population that attends. Although it is an open house, familiar faces are the only ones we let in with us on any given occasion. Sometimes a strange face or two will drop by and say they are a friend of so and so. Those folks get a quick pat-down and agree to relinquish their cell phones for the duration of their stay. We don't sell beer or liquor; it's free to anyone. But donations are highly encouraged to keep our bar bill down to a minimum.

As Venus pointed out to complete strangers back in May, our clubhouse is a blip on the map in a town called Balm, just outside Sun City. When we roll on out for the night and exit the town limit, the population goes down fifty percent. But for many years prior, Demons Rising's clubhouse was in the aptly dubbed rough neighborhood of *Sulphur Springs* in Tampa. Old Joe and Solomon bought the dilapidated edifice in 1973 for two thousand dollars, and Demons Rising's home was born. Solomon tells me there was no working plumbing, electric, or any power source of any kind. He used to say that the rats were irritated because they lived there for years unencumbered. It wasn't until the early 1980s that the house was fully functioning with central air and other modern amenities. Most motorcycle clubs start out in poorer neighborhoods of the city for the simple reason that property is so cheap, and our former home was no different. I was a patch holder there for the first few years, and I had reservations about relocating.

It was the first happy home that I had to move from, so it was an emotional struggle for me. And if I felt that level of a connection, I am certain the old timers like Hal, Tophat, Zonk, and, although he denies it, Solomon did as well.

But that damn, old pragmatism wins the day. Although the neighborhood thugs know better than to target our clubhouse during the havoc, the very essence of being in the city brings with it traffic, peering eyeballs, and an excuse for Tampa's city cops to routinely drive by our home, snapping pictures. And we are even on the underground tourists' circuit, it seems. It was not out of the norm to have someone in a cage with plates from other states attempt to take a *selfie* in front of our clubhouse, regardless of the fact the neighborhood is extremely high crime.

Which explains why I am presently on a dead-end road leading to another dead-end road in a part of the world filled with orange groves, alligators, and solitude. We bought a parcel of land about two years ago off the main road that is only a tenth of a mile long and at the end is all swamp. But Solomon learned that after about a hundred yards of swamp, there was a large parcel of dry land, which is where our home now sits. We built a road eight feet up off the swamp leading back to the clubhouse and fenced it all off. The swamp provides a natural barrier from vehicles coming onto our land. The entrance to that road is only about ten feet wide and is secured by an old, wrought iron gate. The feds, Solomon's ex-wife, or Solomon's ex-wife with the feds, will need helicopters to blitzkrieg us.

When you are permitted up the driveway, the first sight you see is the north end of the clubhouse emblazoned with a full-covering mural of our patch. We have two huge pig smokers out front, along with our ever-growing bonfire pit. There are horseshoes out to the side, but they go unused primarily. Attached to the clubhouse is a large garage for our bikes and supplies. We have four flags flying high atop the pole: the American flag, the Gadsden flag, the Rebel/Confederate flag, and then the state flag of Florida. Each chapter has a state flag, and each chapter that is in a state that was once part of the Confederacy has the rebel flag.

The inside is parceled off in four sections. The main room is a wide, open-spaced area with an old, coal stove for those few days of the year when even the Bay Area gets cold. It's fully furnished with two pool tables, a slot machine, a foosball table, and a seventy-two-inch TV for our vaunted Superbowl events. The bar area stretches along the back and is made of an exceptionally fine, finished cherrywood engraved with our name along the top. There is a community bathroom for when we have other bikers or citizens here.

Behind a steel door located at the end of the bar is our meeting room, off limits to anyone not personally invited inside. We have a full bathroom there with a shower. One of our former brother's ol' lady donated a bathtub. You should have seen the look on Solomon's face at the thought of some debutant tub in our home. There are two bedrooms off the meeting room for brothers who want to stay a night or two, or those who bring in late-night company. Hanging on the wall nearest the bathrooms is a host of bras. Each prospect needs to add one on the night he is patched into the club. Venus often asks which one I brought in. I tell her it's the one with my fingerprints on it. The walls are painted red with white trim in keeping with our colors. We all hang up our own stuff here and there, whether it be a picture we took while out with brothers, in local strip clubs, or perhaps just an innocuous shot of us in the city.

It's our home, decorated for us and in conjunction with our tastes. Pictures of every former member who has passed on, regardless of the chapter, hang on the wall by the pool tables. Frankly, the pool tables see more screwing than the actual playing of the game. Just about everyone's ol' lady has experienced the sensation of that green felt on their back. There's always that house joke about balls bouncing and sticks being stroked on the pool table during a game, and often afterward. It's part of the machismo we all must have to save face. That and an occasional cigar. I feel at home here.

"Prospect!" Solomon bellows. Prospect dutifully walks over to Solomon near the bar.

"What do you need, Solomon?" Prospect asks.

Solomon hands Prospect an empty cardboard box. "Make sure everyone drops their fucking embryo in here that so many can't seem to be without before we go in for church."

Prospect smiles and pulls his own phone out from its holder and drops it in the box. "Will do, Boss!" he says enthusiastically.

"Take your last swig, dump the phones, and let's go. Church has been called!" I shout.

Walt and Willie, Crispy, Zonk, Tophat, Jack, Blitz, J.J., Hal, Preacher, and Big T all enter the meeting room. Solomon is already in the room in his chair that has more duct tape than original material. Mallet is not required, but I have never heard of any nomad from any club not taking part when they are in town. Prospect is still uncertain on his role regarding meetings, causing him to pause before entering.

"You, too, Prospect. You're in until you're out," Hal says with a smile. Hal always has a smile. He joined Demons Rising in the late 1970s when he was nearly forty years old. Hal is a great guy, always upbeat and very shrewd. He never wanted officer roles, but he's been the unofficial ambassador for Demons Rising. He rides a 1950 Indian. He's the only brother without a Harley-Davidson, but our club charter only says American made, and in 1950, Indian fit that bill. Hal is also one of a few handfuls of men left in the world who can work on the old Indians made in the '20s and '30s. People often tap him all over the country to rebuild their old Indian.

I love when Hal orders a drink when we are out on the town. He orders a glass of Black Velvet and ginger ale with only one ice cube. Why some bar rags challenge it or don't pay attention at times, I do not know, but it's the only time he can be unfriendly to citizens. "I said one ice cube! One!" he will say with a bit of punch in his voice.

The smoke fills the meeting room, and the chatter begins to wind down as Solomon stands to begin the meeting.

"We are demons!" Solomon shouts.

"And we are rising!" we all bellow in unison.

"Quorum?" I ask.

"I count fourteen members," says Zonk.

"Our club secretary says fourteen. We have a quorum, agreed?" Tophat asks.

In unison, we all yell, "Agreed."

"Treasurer report," Solomon says.

Preacher stands and clears his throat. You would think a guy named Preacher would make an honest treasurer, but he's a die-hard atheist who has a tattoo on his arm that reads, "God's last name is Krenwinkle." Significant for him in some way, I am certain.

"We have $14,854.92 in the house account, $1,397.76 in the bar account, and $419,569.44 in the trucking business ledgers. We took in $4,932.88 at the Memorial Day run and spent $1,334.09 on it. We spent $4,998.54 on bar supplies and took in $11,008.55 since June first."

"Agree to accept?" I shout.

In unison, we all yell, "Agreed."

"Okay," Solomon says, "let's take care of the candy-ass shit first. Our sister chapter in Miami is going to the Frenzied Few's brotherhood run in Hollywood next weekend, meaning I need one more volunteer because I already know Digger is going," Solomon says with a smirk.

"Fucking-A-Right! I love Hollywood and I always will. Great memories there that I'll never forget . . . and mammaries," I say with a smirk.

"Yeah, okay," Solomon says while rolling his eyes. "We get it, Digger. You got laid there once, *bon voyage*! Now, who's going with Digger to make sure he comes back, even though you know damn well Venus will want to go."

Mallet says, "I wish I was still going to be in town, or I'd go with Digger. I miss Hollywood."

"I'll fucking go," Preacher says with a heavy sigh.

Why don't you pick a town to truly be in love with, like Vegas?" Solomon asks, pointing at his iconic, snake eyes, dice tattoo.

"Lost Wages?" I say mockingly. "I don't like the desert."

Solomon shakes his head and continues. "Smart-ass!" is all he says. "Okay, back to real business," Solomon says. "I took this next part on myself because I knew it wouldn't be an issue. An old buddy from the Corps has a son with a cement business, and we need at least two truckloads for that back deck. He's giving us a rate," Solomon says placidly.

"Agree to yawn?" I shout.

In unison, we all yell 'yawn' demonstrably.

"Assholes," Solomon mutters.

I look over at Prospect and point at the door. "Go tend the bar," I say to him. Prospect's attention is refocused at my edict, and he nods and exits the meeting room.

"Black Shadow MC," Tophat says with a follow-up pause. "Rumor has it they disbanded, and nobody is flying colors now. But in case some lone wolf type who thinks he is a tough guy still wears it, do we agree to take him?"

We all nod in unison.

"I make no excuses for these guys at all, but these guys are nobodies," I say with authority. "That having been said," I say, following up, "if they fly, they die. Simple as that." I look around the room measuring feedback to my words, both for clarity and for their reactions to how I said it.

"What about Torch?" Willie asks.

"What about him?" I say.

"What Willie is asking . . .," Walt begins to say as I motion for him to stop.

"What about him, Willie?" I press on.

"We are taking him out, right?" Willie asks.

"You tell me, Willie," I say.

Willie looks at Walt as Walt tacitly nods his head. Willie looks back at me with a stern look on his countenance. "Fuck yeah!"

I smile back at Willie and wink at him. "Fuck yeah, yes." The club doesn't show much reaction other than some anger refomenting as they think of Dave. "This may not count as some sort of club-to-club hit, but we buried our brother, nonetheless, and if some citizen dressed in a clown suit takes a page from some badly produced TV show, then we shan't disappoint the lad on making his acting dreams come true."

"But since this is not some TV show," Tophat chimes in, "this is going to take time. There is a reason why after nearly fifty years of this club's existence, the feds have never been able to make a case."

"Tophat is right," Mallet says. "We are not tough *and* smart, because to be tough, you have to be smart already."

"This from the guy who tossed an off-duty Polk County deputy through a plate glass window in 2010, but whatever!" I say as the club roars in laughter. Mallet smirks some and takes a fictitious bow. "But Mallet is right," I say. "We have had feds attempt to infiltrate and make cases against us, regardless of the fact we aren't doing anything wrong, but they always fail."

"Torch is going to meet *hell's fire*, but give it time, brothers," Tophat says. "Fuck the coalition, fuck their peering eyes. We will do this when it's smart to do it. Mallet is heading back up to our Virginia chapter, and he will be doing some intel on our friend in the neighboring state to the west."

"Okay," Solomon says, "let's table this. There's no point in planning who, how, when, where, and all that crap until we have some semblance of a roadmap on where to start. And that means nobody talks about it unless it's new information. Got it?"

"Yeah, Boss," Zonk says. The rest of us nod our heads.

"We got one last thing. Another old Marine I know is coming here with hat in hand and will end up leaving with an empty hat. Now, for the sake of perception, only myself, Digger, and Tophat are speaking with him. He is due here any minute."

"Why?" Crispy asks as he stands up. "Our charter specifically forbids secret or separate meetings."

"Yes, it does, Crispy, but this is neither of those," Solomon says with his irritation growing.

"Oh?" Crispy says with sarcasm. "So y'all are in a separate room, but it's not a separate meeting? Is this *separate but equal* redefined?" A few brothers can't help but laugh.

Solomon has little room for patience, and less so for Crispy. He leans in and points his finger at Crispy. "Because—"

"Because," I say, interrupting Solomon's certain paroxysm. I continue to stare at Solomon. "Solomon's friend asked to speak with him as his old friend, not as president and founder of Demons Rising MC." I pause and look away from Solomon. "The details of what this guy wants are not clear. We just know it could mean some money flowing in, that's all. He will share it with all of us afterward."

"Yeah, we get it," Crispy says, "the meeting is for jarheads only."

Crispy stands motionless, and his expression is nearly impossible to read. The pause is only a few seconds, but it seems as though the discomfort of that moment lingers. I stare at Solomon in an effort to communicate to him the need for calm.

"Motion to end the meeting," Hal says.

"Second!" I shout quickly.

"All in favor?" Solomon says, staring at me.

In unison, we all yell, "Aye."

Mallet and I lock eyeballs. He smirks, shakes his head, and walks toward me. "What the fuck, Bro?" he asks probingly.

"Bah," I say, swishing my hand like some Frenchman's wave, "that's just Crispy. Gets irked easily."

"Yeah, he's a good brother, but clearly, the club's choice for sergeant went to the right guy," Mallet says.

"Thanks," I say sincerely. "I really do try to keep the peace. But when two of the loosest cannons butt heads, it takes all I have."

"I may take him to Virginia with me when I go, you know, have a talk with him," Mallet says.

"It couldn't hurt. We don't have a disruptive force here, but he is the closest thing to having one," I reply.

Mallet slaps me on the shoulder. "Y'all are in good shape here, seriously. This is the toughest state in the union to be in a high-profile MC—tougher than Cali and tougher than New York."

I smile. "I thrive on that shit, though."

"And it shows," Mallet says. "Y'all know too well the feds are trying to get through our door nationally, and what better place to start than the original chapter here."

"Yeah, we do understand, given what happened last January with our former prospect, Myron."

Mallet laughs. "Yeah, him . . . fucking turd." Mallet grabs me by the back of the neck, perches a sinister smirk once more, and whispers, "Whatever did become of that poor lad?"

"Oh, Myron?" I say with false surprise. "The last I knew, he was looking hard for some Chinaman with shovel in hand."

CHAPTER 13
Offer, Consideration, Acceptance

Tophat / 1995 – Portsmouth, New Hampshire

"Travis, I am so sorry. Your aunt and I loved your mom, we truly did."
"Thanks."
"Where's your sister?"
"I . . . uh . . . not sure. With my aunt Marilyn, I think."
"There she is. Lisa! I'm sorry about your mom, sweetie."
"Thanks, Uncle Ray."
"We are meeting at the Elks Club afterward for a luncheon, when you two are done paying your respects to your mom, that is."
"Thanks, Uncle Ray."
"Well, I'll leave you two alone."
"Nice guy, our uncle. He leaves us alone like we like each other."
"At least you'll get a free meal, Travis."

"At least . . . oh, forget it. Just go away, Lisa."

"And leave my baby brother alone in his time of grief? Aw . . . never."

"Then go see if you can blow the undertaker, Lisa. Maybe he will trade you some meth."

"Aw . . . poor little brother, still a bitter boy? Don't know why. You were always Mom's favorite."

"Yeah, I see you are still America's sweetheart."

"Yeah, I see you are still a real motherfucker, Travis . . . or . . . is 'was' more appropriate now?"

"You're such a piece of shit, Lisa. Get the fuck out of my sight before I knock your teeth in."

"Okay, sweetie, I'll go. I am sorry. I'll just . . . um . . . leave you two alone. You know, like I always did."

June 2019

The laughter seems scripted and the hearty handshakes appear staged. But here he is, Benjamin Austin, Marine, quasi-local resort owner of a nice spread along the coast of Naples and contemporary of our president, whom he met in the jungles of Vietnam some half century ago. Here's a man who seems to personify success as described in the traditional sense of the word. His silver hair is thick and full. He sports a mustache, neatly trimmed, but still fuller than most. His pale-blue shirt seems to be silk, and he tugs at his Rolex occasionally, either because it annoys him at times, or he wants us to notice it.

"Okay," Solomon says, "the amenities are out of the way. We know you're married to your college sweetheart, Beth Ann, have two sons, Michael and Benjamin Junior, and built up a very successful resort in Naples. And we know I divorced the queen of the harpies, have one son, own a successful trucking business, founded the most famous motorcycle club in the world, and that I am still devilishly handsome. So let's move on," Solomon says, motioning with his hands.

"I didn't catch your son's name," Benjamin says.

Solomon pauses a bit and says, "We call him *Iggy*."

"Iggy?" Benjamin says with incredulity. "That can't be his real name."

"Well, it could be, but it isn't," Solomon says while manufacturing a smile. "His name is Xavier Ignacious, hence the moniker Iggy."

"Where'd you come up with that, Tommy? Family name?"

"No, or I would have named him Thomas after me or 'Chief Crazy Fuck' after my dad."

Benjamin, sensing his old friend's angst, eases off. "I'm sorry, Tommy," he says, amidst the clearing of his throat. "I was just making small talk and wonder why you chose such an unusual name."

Solomon smiles and leans into Benjamin. "Because *Kris Kringle* was already taken," Solomon says quietly. "Now let's get on with it, Ben. You didn't look me up after twenty some odd years to learn my bio."

"Okay," Ben says, shuffling some papers in front of him. "I am assuming I can count on discretion?"

Solomon pauses and then quips, "I hope you're not actually asking that."

"No," Benjamin says, growing more uncomfortable. Any hope he had of controlling the conversation through appealing to Solomon's sense of '*we go way back*' is lost. "Anyway, I'll lay it out, Tommy. My business is worth forty-two million dollars. It's an extremely successful resort that gates about sixteen million dollars a year in the front door. I have been working on this since we got back from Vietnam."

"Since *you* got back, Ben," Solomon interrupts. "Remember, I did three tours. I got out in 1972."

"Okay, Tommy," Benjamin says, "understood." Benjamin clears his throat again and starts his tale once more. "Anyway, I borrowed twenty grand from my dad to get the place going. My sister was busy being a flower child and protesting what we were doing as an excuse to smoke dope, fuck random guys, and be a dilettante. She got real lost in the sixties and just never really came back, ya know?"

Solomon nods.

"As I was saying, Dad gave me the seed money, and I grew it to where it is today. I haven't seen or heard from my sister, Molly, in decades."

"I'm following, Ben," Solomon says.

"Okay, well, out of fucking nowhere, a few months ago, her husband calls. Thirty years her junior and a total pile of shit. Never did an honest day's work in his life. Molly is seventy-three now and completely out of it. I mean, fried totally. Her new husband was a maintenance man in an assisted living home where Molly was at. Gossip was passed here and there, and they discovered she comes from a family with money. So he swoops in, somehow convinces some douchebag notary to marry them, and gets power-of-attorney over her finances. Now those finances are limited because she stuck most of her inheritance in her arm. But . . . he finds out her brother is rich, hires some shitbag P.I.—probably related to the scumbag notary who married them—and discovers Dad's money seeded my business. He is now trying to make the argument that my business was, and still is, part of Dad's estate." Benjamin pauses and stares at his old friend, but with a whole new outlook and a realization that Solomon has a new sense of loyalty that does not include old war buddies. "They want half, Tommy." Benjamin sighs heavily and catches his breath. "And my high-priced, Jew lawyer says they have a case."

"Hmmm . . .," Solomon says, looking at Tophat and myself. "So if my third-grade math is correct, then you're talking about twenty-one million dollars of your assets go to her."

"I'm guessing you don't want this lad as a partner, right?" Tophat asks.

Benjamin looks at Tophat and then back at Solomon. "Tommy, please, I need your help. I'll pay you whatever you want."

"You're in a pickle, Ben," Solomon says. "What do you want me to do?"

"Can't you and your guys, like, scare him off?" Benjamin inquires.

"For how long, Ben?" Solomon asks. "I mean, time is meaningless to guys like this. They live in the moment. Two weeks after we talk with him, he'll be back. You know that."

"I do know that," Benjamin says. "I do."

Solomon leans into Benjamin. "Then why talk out of the side of your mouth? You could hire a couple of meth heads for a few hundred dollars to rough him up, and you know that, so why come to me?"

"I don't want to lose my livelihood, Tommy."

"So you want him or her as the focus?" Solomon asks.

"Oh, him, just him. My sister doesn't even know what this guy is doing. She lives on benzos and vodka and watches infomercials all day. Remember what we used to say back in the day? Cut the snake's head off, and the rest of it dies."

Solomon grows a manufactured look of confusion on his face. "Did y'all say that in the kitchen?" Solomon asks.

Benjamin leans back a bit and gets indignant. "You going to minimize my contribution to the war because I was a cook? Is that what you're saying?"

"No," Solomon says, jamming his finger at Benjamin. "I'm pointing out the concept that *semper fi* grows and changes and adapts to your life and is not supposed to be used in a veiled attempt to grease an old Marine into a favor!" Solomon yells.

"Did I say 'favor,' Tommy? I said I will pay you. Let's just put it out there—fifty thousand dollars."

Solomon's eyes grow some, and he looks at me and then Tophat. Solomon smiles some and says, "Yeah, that's pretty good, Ben. But we were thinking more of a percentage, like one half of one percent of your gate."

"Half a percent?" Benjamin says with a confused smile. "What the fuck, Tommy? That will cash out to about one hundred shares of stock at the most and about six thousand dollars a year, and that's if profits stay up. You could lose money some years. Take my offer, old friend, it's better."

"You didn't hear what I said, 'old friend,'" Solomon says mockingly. "I said one half of one percent of your gate. That's one half of one percent of sixteen million dollars a year. That's eighty thousand dollars a year, free and clear."

Benjamin fixates his sights on Solomon. He wets his lips a few times and seems to be searching for words. Not just words, but the right words—words that will somehow make Solomon's proposition palatable and pragmatic. He looks at me, then Tophat, hoping we will say something that helps him make sense of his life as it is right here and now.

"Tommy," Benjamin says dumbfoundedly. "You're crazy and you know it."

Solomon leaps up, slams his hand on the table, and closes in on his old jungle comrade. Solomon stays silent and pauses momentarily before he sits once more.

"You're talking an average of eighty thousand a year, Ben. That's one maître d' or a bump in price of the rooms of one percent." Solomon smiles gloatingly. "Then you can appreciate the irony of that percentage and save your business at the same time."

"So . . . half a percent every year? Half a percent for the big, bad one-percenters? For how long?"

"For how long?" Solomon says histrionically. "In perpetuity. What did you think? There's an expiration date?"

"How do I explain that to the shareholders? 'Hey, ignore that entry in the ledger. It's going to a bunch of one-percenter thugs in Tampa'?"

"Watch your fucking mouth!" I scream. "You show some goddamn respect!"

"Respect?" Benjamin says incredulously. "Respect? Why don't you just ask me to fuck my mother?"

Tophat suddenly leaps over the table and grabs an angry but frightened Benjamin by his silk shirt, tearing the buttons. "You think you're funny?" Tophat screams as he shakes Benjamin like a ragdoll. "Do you? You find shit like that funny?"

"Whoa!" Benjamin says as he pulls away. "Tone it down, fellas. Come on. In the end, we are businessmen negotiating a contract here. Offer, consideration, and acceptance; let us stay on this, please?" he says nervously.

Tophat regains his composure and looks at me and Solomon sheepishly. He rubs his face and sits back down calmly.

"Okay, this is going sideways, Tommy. Let's recap: you want half a percent of the gate in perpetuity, right?"

"Cor-ect!" Solomon says, folding his arms.

"And how do I do this?" Benjamin asks inquisitively.

"Cash," Solomon says placidly.

"Cash?" Benjamin says disbelievingly. "Like, do I give it to you every month in some dark attaché case under the viaduct at three a.m.?"

"I don't care if you give it to us in a canvas sack with a giant, black dollar sign on it at McDonald Land," Solomon says sternly.

"How do I syphon off eighty G's a year to avoid the I.R.S., and my partners, and the board?"

"You're asking me?" Solomon says. "That's your problem, Ben. Do it the same way you do now to keep a whore or two I know you must have hidden from Beth Ann. I don't care."

"And how will you explain the influx of cash to the feds? The I.R.S.?"

"That's not your concern, Ben."

Benjamin looks around the room and sighs heavily.

"And your deal is with the club, Ben, not me," Solomon says. "Chances are you will outlive this old biker, so don't be thinking that cash flow ends, because it doesn't. And—"

"There's an 'and,' Tommy?" Benjamin says indignantly.

"Yes," Solomon says quickly. "You update your will to give the C.E.O. of Bay Trucking the value of your shares equivalent to eighty grand a year upon your death. Obviously, I understand once you die, payment in the form of cash must end, but we will still get paid."

"Bay Trucking?" Benjamin says in wonderment.

"It's our trucking company, Ben. We are an L.L.C. and everything."

"Oh," Benjamin says with a smirk, "so that's how you laun. . . ." Benjamin stops mid-sentence. "I have to think about this, Tommy."

"You do that, Ben," Solomon says, as he stands up and grips Benjamin's hand, shaking it fervently. "You think about whether it is too high of a price to pay. But when you do, consider what dear old brother-in-law will do when he wins half your business. What do you think he will do, Ben?"

"I don't know, Tommy," Benjamin says blankly. "Buy a fucking bowling alley and a meth lab?"

"Be like me, Ben. Be a pragmatist," Solomon says as he pats Benjamin on the back with a tad bit more force than needed. "If dear old brother-in-law wins, do you think he's going to want to be a partner? No, he'll want to liquidate and liquidate quickly, and he will sell his shares for about fifty percent of what they're worth. And you know that will make your stock do a nosedive, pissing off your shareholders and making your business worth . . . less . . . than you hoped."

Benjamin stares and sighs once more. He shakes his head in frustration and sighs again. "Okay, Tommy, you win. But I'm disappointed in you, I really, truly am. I thought you were a man of honor. I walk away from here no longer your comrade, only a business associate."

"We'll be in touch, Ben," Solomon says.

"K . . .," Benjamin says as he begins to walk out.

"Oh, Ben?" Solomon says. Ben turns and looks at Solomon.

"Yeah, Tommy?"

"*Semper Fi*, Ben."

"Yeah," Benjamin says, turning and walking away. "Whatever you say, Tommy."

CHAPTER 14
Maturing

Willie / 1989 – Grants Pass, Oregon

"Dad! Please! He's had enough; he can't breathe! He's bleeding!"
"You back talking me, boy? You want it next?"
"Mom? Please?"
"You two know better, Walt. Why do you two provoke your father?"
"Dad, please stop! He won't do it again, I swear."
"Damn right he won't, boy! I'm making sure of it. Goddamn ungrateful fucking kids have no respect!!"
"You're going to kill him! Please!"
"You wanna take his place, boy? You want what he's getting?"
"Yes, Dad, I'll take it. Leave him be!"
"Get outta here, Walt!"
"Dad!! I-said-no-goddamn-fucking-more!!!! Leave him alone!! NO MORE!!!!"

July 2019

Dusk is coming earlier on this hot July night in Florida's Bay Area. But still, a handful of us meander out from the coolness of modern technology invented by Mister Wills Carrier, in all places, Buffalo, New York, the heart of some of the worst winters known to mankind. Oh, some say the ancient Egyptians first discovered the theory, and some say it was Benjamin Franklin and John Hadley who first conducted experiments exploring the principle of evaporation to rapidly cool an object. But in July, in Florida, we salute the two greatest inventors in history: Mister Wills Carrier and Mister Jack Daniels, the inventors of the air conditioner and of ambrosia, respectively.

But with all due respect to Mister Carrier, a few of us opt to sit by the bonfire tonight and decompress from the day. Solomon has Prospect start the fire like he always has all prospects do. Solomon made hundreds of copies of his marriage license and has the prospects use it as kindling. Then, it's Prospect's job to get the fire up to par, grab a cooler of ice, some whiskey, and some rolling papers.

"I'll be right back with the bonfire kit, fellas," Prospect says. "Do you need anything else?"

"No," Solomon replies. "You can go home if you want after that, though."

"Why don't we let Prospect sit for a few minutes with us?" I ask.

"No," Solomon says, staring at me and shaking his head demonstrably. "Nobody with only a bottom rocker ever does. When he earns his top and center, he can sit with us."

"I get that, Solomon, but he's a damn good prospect, and I didn't think it would hurt."

"But it would," Solomon retorts. Tophat then nods his head in the affirmative. "When he earns this"—Solomon tugs at his old, ratty, denim lapel—"he can sit with us because he will be 'us.' Don't rob him of that honor, Digger."

I nod my head as well. "Understood."

I see a shadowy figure walking from the clubhouse toward us. As he approaches, I see that the man is Willie.

"Hidey ho, Willie," I say enthusiastically. "You two going to join us tonight?"

"It's just me," Willie responds.

"Where's Walt?" Tophat inquires curiously.

"He's watching TV with a few of the girls along with Zonk and Crispy."

Solomon and I and Tophat impulsively look at one another. Solomon gives a 'thumbs-up' and says, "Well, pull up a rock, Brother, and sit. We are going to—"

"Burn a few and abuse our livers?" Willie asks rhetorically with a smirk.

Solomon laughs. "I guess that is one of my proverbs, ain't it?"

I pass the flask to Willie, and he throws back a hearty gulp and wipes his mouth. I hear the cackling from some of the girls moseying toward us. Their words are inaudible, but their giggling overrides any hope of hearing them anyway. It's Babs, Jackie, Cricket, and Kathy.

"Howdy, boys!" Babs bellows as she and the girls saunter out. "We're done watching *Lifetime* and syncing our menses, so we are going to the city and celebrate!"

"Women really celebrate that?" I say with a quip.

"Fucking right we do, and we are celebrating the fact there are strippers in Tampa tonight. We are gonna show 'em the chicks from Demons Rising know how to party," Babs continues.

Venus looks down at me with a visibly awkward expression. "I really want to go with the girls," she says softly and apologetically.

"Then go!" I say. "You don't need my permission, for fuck's sake."

"Are you sure?" Venus replies.

"Venus," I say as I swing my seated position toward her. "The *'Property of Digger'* patch you wear is on you to protect you. It doesn't mean I have to give you permission to wipe your nose."

"Oh, she will be doing that tonight!" Babs says amidst a loud, boisterous laugh.

My attention is drawn away from Venus temporarily as I look at Babs. I focus back on Venus and say, "My point is, I don't need, nor do I want, to give you permission to do anything."

"This isn't like when I asked you if I could run to the grocery store the other day. This is . . . well . . . a strip show."

I emit a manufactured chuckle. "You've never seen a guy's dick before?" I ask. "Sweetie, that thing you were slobbering on last night? That's a dick."

Venus puts on a fake smile and says, "Thanks."

"My point is, *go*. Leave us be for the night. We need a break from the estrogen anyway."

"That's right, girl," Babs says to Venus. "We wear these property patches because we are part of this family, only in a different way."

"I don't have a 'property of' patch," says Jackie.

"That's because we don't have any 'property of everyone in the fucking club' patches yet. But when we do . . .," Solomon says with a sarcastic grin. Jackie sticks her tongue out at Solomon in coquettish fashion.

"Nobody has given me one, either," Cricket says.

"Sweet thing," Solomon says with an immense, ear-to-ear grin, "I'd give you a kidney if you needed it."

"I'm honored!" Cricket says buoyantly. "That's the second different organ you have offered me this week."

"Well, we know it wasn't his heart because he don't have one, and it damn sure wasn't his liver since it's shot," I say with a laugh. I then peer up at Venus. "Go," I say to her with a halfhearted smile. "Enjoy." I then peer at a jaunty and fidgety Babs. "Keep an eye on her, Babs," I say pleadingly.

"Great fucking strategy, Digger," Tophat says. "You want my ol' lady to keep yours in check while they're going to see strippers."

Babs points at herself boldly with both thumbs. "He has known this hot bitch for over thirty years; he knows the deal." Babs laughs. "Let's go, girls!" Babs shouts. "The girls are gonna rock the house tonight!"

Tophat looks back at me, Solomon, and Willie and then sighs. "Yeah . . . this will end well. My ol' lady is going to do a couple of lines, chase it with Vodka, and then once she eats a chili dog, her hormones are going to take over, and she will be chasing down every swinging dick off the stage and through the parking lot."

"And didn't you tell me last week she's calmed down a bit over the years?" I query.

Tophat nods his head slightly. "Yep, she was worse," he says as he shakes his head. "You should have seen her in the '80s."

"I bet she's like that *in her* eighties," Willie says with a quip.

We sat quietly for a moment, perhaps stunned a bit. Then the laughter roared. "Damn, Willie," Solomon says, "you're on fire!"

"No worries. Most of those guys are gay anyway," Tophat says.

"So are you happy with how the meeting went with your old, rich pal?" I ask Solomon.

Solomon nods his head slightly and purses his lips. "Yeah," he says sedately but with confidence, "and that money will cover every single house expense we have, including the truck business. It's a good deal: taxes, upkeep, utilities, etcetera. All that shit."

"Not enough for our bar bill, though," Willie says.

"No," Tophat says with a smile, "that will not be covered." Tophat laughs, not so much as the joke was funny, but as he is gleeful at Willie's interaction with us.

"That Ben was a bit of a tool, though," I say to Solomon.

"He was back then, too," Solomon replies. "Fact is, he was scared to death he'd be drafted so he enlisted, and daddy helped get him a nice, safe M.O.S. in the kitchen. He hasn't changed a damn bit."

"And what was up with riding you about Iggy's name?" Tophat asks.

"Bah!" Solomon says, as he swings his hand in disgust.

"Why did you name him Xavier Ignacious, anyway?" I ask with a smirk.

"Fuck you, Digger," Solomon says.

"That's not an answer," Tophat says with a laugh.

"Sheila wanted to name him that, all right? I didn't have a say."

"You're passing this off on your ex? You? You want us to believe you took orders—any order—from her? Ever?" I say.

"Meaning?" Solomon says derisively.

"Is it or is it not true that Sheila once told you to put the toilet seat down and you responded by removing not one, but both toilets, and then smashed them in the backyard?"

"You listened to Old Joe too much when he was alive, Digger," Solomon says with a false look of anger on his face. "That son of a bitch is lucky he's dead, or I'd walk in there and kill him now."

Through our laughter, we hear a set of footsteps walking toward us. As the light from the fire spreads, I see that it is Crispy.

"Hey, Brother," I say.

Crispy looks at me and nods. "Uh . . . the nomad wants me to go with him to Virginia tomorrow," he says bitterly.

"That 'nomad' has a fucking name," Solomon retorts brashly.

"Ohhhh-kayyyy," Crispy says. "*Mallet* wants me to saddle up and go to Virginia tomorrow."

"Then you're going," Tophat says.

"Any idea why?" Crispy asks.

"Does he need a reason?" I snap.

Crispy sighs. "I guess not. I just don't like surprises, and I have a feeling a surprise is waiting for me."

Solomon looks at Crispy perplexingly. "Why would you think there's a surprise? For real here, why?"

Crispy pauses and sighs again. "I don't," he says. "I guess I better go get some z's. I have a long ride." Crispy offers a backward salute to us all as he walks back to the clubhouse.

"Okay, that was a buzzkill. Now, where were we?" I ask as I look up and massage my chin in false contemplation.

"We were asking Solomon here why he named his kid Xavier Ignacious," Tophat says with a smirk. Tophat looks at Solomon and fights off laughing. "Why did you name him Xavier Ignacious?"

"Because you touch yourself at night, asshole," Solomon says.

"All right, enough. Let's leave him be," I say. I poke at the fire a bit and turn some of the wood. "Solomon, why did you name him Xavier Ignacious?" Willie, Tophat, and I begin laughing uncontrollably.

"All right," Solomon says, standing up. "I'm going back in for a bit and get something to eat."

"Yeah, sounds good," I say as I stand. Tophat and Willie follow.

"Solomon?" Willie says, breaking the silence.

"Yeah, kid."

"Why did you name him Xavier Ignacious?" Both Tophat and I burst out in laughter. Solomon grabs Willie and playfully shoves him ahead of us. "Fuck you, Willie." Solomon looks at me and gently slaps my chest to get my attention. He points at Willie, smiles, gives me the thumbs-up, and nods.

I nod my head excitedly and then mouth softly, "I know."

Tophat saddles up to Willie as they walk and puts his arm around him. "I think there's ham left over, Willie," Tophat says.

"Yum," Willie responds. "And key lime pie, too?"

"Yep!" Tophat says. "Key lime pie, too!"

CHAPTER 15
Lessons Learned

Digger / 1997 – Elkhart, Indiana

"You did good, Digger. A 98.4 G.P.A. You get looks and brains from your Mama Bear."

"Thanks, Mom."

"Why are you congratulating him, Kate? He's salutatorian."

"Jesus Christ, Grant. What the hell is the matter with you?"

"Digger? Son? Who won the Heisman Trophy this year?"

"Uh . . . Charles Woodson?"

"Yep. And . . . um . . . who came in second?"

"Grant!!!"

"Digger? Who?"

"I don't know."

"You don't, huh? Well, guess why, Digger?"

"Grant!"

"Kate! What do you NOT understand about the humiliation of me having to tee off at nine a.m. with Bartholomew Vaughn's father and seeing that smug look on his face?"

"Really, Grant? The question should be 'why do you understand that'?"

September 2019

"Shit!"

"Don't fight with it, Zonk. Let's just go to the dealership and get a wiring harness," Tophat says.

"Oh, no," I say softly, knowing Solomon's next words.

"Dealership?" Solomon loudly proclaims. "Dealership? You mean *boutique*, don't you?"

"Oh, for the love of God, let it go," Tophat says as he fiddles with the wiring harness.

Venus, sitting patiently on the sidelines, just smiles.

"Yeah, let's roll down to the—*cough, cough*—dealership," Solomon says, using finger quotes. "I need my nails done and a good cry."

"Solomon, please!" I implore him. "Zonk needs a wire harness, and it's too much of a unique product to get anywhere else. We need to go to the dealership. Old man Chauncey won't have a wire harness this new."

"That's because Chauncey has parts for real bikes, Digger. He remembers what it was like before these dealerships started kissing the yuppie's asses and turning their fucking shops into places where you can get cappuccino and wash your fucking hands with perfumed soaps. And those are in the damn men's room! In my day, there was no need for a men's room, just a room with a steel door and a shitter because women didn't need to go inside."

"I know," I say satirically. "First it was the nineteenth amendment, and next, tampon holders in the condom dispenser."

"If that's the amendment that banned booze, then you're right," Solomon clamors.

"Nooooo," I say. "That's the one that gave women the right to vote."

"These Nurse Ratched battle-axes can vote now?" Solomon retorts.

"Very funny." I stand up as I wipe the grease on my pants. "Not everyone has an old Shovelhead that they bought new in 1966. Some of us like the modern shit."

"Modern shit gave us STDs, the A.T.F., the D.E.A., NOW, the E.R.A.—"

"That failed decades ago," I interject.

Solomon sighs. "I wasn't done griping."

"Continue," I say with an elongated sigh.

"Yuppies, and Fonzie jumping a shark on fucking water skis."

"Feel better?" Tophat asks.

"If you're a good boy, Solomon, we will stop and get you ice cream," Hal says amidst a laugh.

"If you weren't so old that you actually recall the good old days when women could not vote, then I'd bust your brittle bones, you old, fucking dinosaur," Solomon puffs.

"We should all go. It's good to make some face time there anyhow," I say. "We should try somewhere different than Manatee River Harley, too. Let's ride into Saint Pete and hit that dealership. We need to mingle a bit more." I look over at Solomon and give him a serious stare. "Solomon," I say pleadingly. "Just roll in, say 'hi' to the manager and the other staff, let them 'ooh' and 'aah' over your Shovelhead, and then when we get our harness, let's just roll out, okay?"

"Meaning?" Solomon asks.

"Meaning," I say with growing impatience, "don't go in and tell them that *Easy Rider* centerfolds used to hang above the urinals, or the coffee was six days old and was from a steel, dented pot and not in the form of a fancy Keurig in the lobby with fancy creamers, or how there were oil stains on the floor, and they were somehow synonymous with cum stains from a man's engine, or how if a woman came in, the first question the staff asked was, "Where's your ol' man, sweetie?"

Solomon laughs. "You kids today. You're all so cute and naïve."

"We roll into the parking lot just north of the rocky bay in St. Petersburg and see all sorts of hoopla going on in the form of a promotion: balloons, popcorn machines, young ladies in bikinis, and even a clown. I cringe at the thoughts that I know are currently roaming in the anger-filled hallways of Solomon's brain as he spots the circus atmosphere. As we ride in, the high energy ceases, and all eyeballs are affixed on us as we slide the kickstands down.

"Digger! They have a fucking clown!" Solomon says.

"I know, I know," I say in an attempt to mollify him.

The beer vendor walks gingerly out toward us, holding two draft beers. "Anyone else want beer?" he asks. Solomon waves his hand at him, but Zonk and I grab the free brew. Two staff members run to the door and open both ends of the door wide. One staff member is a younger man with red hair and partially clear skin, and he simply says, "Gentlemen, welcome."

"Thanks," I say politely. Zonk goes to the parts desk with his tattered, old harness in his hand. The parts clerk notices who is standing before him and gets nervous; his eyes hit the floor. I can't make out the words, but Zonk is talking as he waves his harness.

Hal gravitates toward a couple of women thumbing through the shirts. They respond with smiles, blushes, and laughs. Prospect stays with Hal. Normally, he will stay tight with an officer—usually the president—but I allow Prospect's instincts to take control.

"What the fuck, Stacy?" says a man garbed in a newer, leather vest and bright-orange bandana, sporting a neatly trimmed goatee. His anger is directed at one of the women giggling with Hal. "Stacy!" he shouts. "Let's go, unless you're into the geriatric crowd." Prospect flinches but stops in his tracks, not wanting to give the perception Hal needs help. I peer over as well but am not going to intercede on my nearly octogenarian brother, either.

Hal steps into the man's face and says, "May I help you?"

The man holds his ground but does appear to flinch a bit. Whether he is guided by the human's frailest instinct, *vanity*, which rarely guides in the correct path, or whether he is just devoid of a sense of common sense, he inexplicably continues his verbal onslaught. "No," he says. "I have my own link-to-life button if I slip in the tub."

Hal smiles and leans back a bit. "I'm betting you've slipped in the tub a few times."

"Yeah?" he says with a pause and no follow up.

"Brian!" the woman named Stacy yells. "Don't light this firecracker, for Christ's sake. Please . . . let's go! Please, Brian!"

"Your woman, who seems to like me, by the way, is definitely smarter than you," Hal says. "But then again, you set that bar pretty low for her."

"Oh, yeah?" Brian says in a cocksure way.

"That's your response?" Hal says.

"I'm thinking it is," Prospect says, intervening. Yes, Prospect is intervening, but I stand by my position to trust his instincts.

Prospect somehow pats Hal on the shoulder simultaneously as he grabs Brian by the scruff and pulls him to the back of the showroom. I whistle at my other brothers and point to the rear of the showroom.

"Back door?" I say as a demand disguised as a question to a staff member.

One of the girls in sales sheepishly points as she looks desperately at other staff. Prospect continues to pull Brian out the door and into the alley. The remaining Demons Rising brotherhood follows tightly.

"Please!" Stacy yells as she enters the alley. Venus follows close and looks at me. I snap my fingers twice and point at Stacy. Venus gently grabs Stacy and pulls her slowly inside the dealership, mumbling "It's all right, it's all right" along the way.

Brian fidgets a bit and walks in a circular motion. "Hey," he says, wiping his brow, "this is between me and the old geezer."

"Ya see, it's not," I interject. "He," I say, pointing at Hal, "is a 'we,' and you took on that nightmare."

Solomon stands in front of the door leading into the dealership, rubs his fingers into his palm, but says nothing. Solomon, the founder and leader of Demons Rising, hasn't earned and kept that role by not trusting the club's ability.

"So it's me against all of you?" Brian asks. "That's fair?"

"Did you go to kindergarten, Brian?" I ask rhetorically. "Life isn't fair. You should have learned that back when you were voted down as the milk monitor. Besides, it's you against him," I say, pointing at Prospect. "We are here for the entertainment of you learning about life."

Prospect reaches in his waistband and pulls out a long, steel, ratchet wrench. He immediately steps toward Brian, and Brian tries a desperate, wild swing at Prospect. Prospect takes a half step backward, then drives the wrench into Brian's rib cage once, twice, thrice, and then stops as Brian collapses, writhing in pain. He lies in the alley, clutching his chest, searching for a steady breath. Prospect then grips the wrench with both hands and vigorously hits Brian three more times sharply in his rib cage and once across his knee. Prospect then tucks the wrench into his waistband. Tophat, Zonk, and Solomon gather at the door and peer back inside.

"That was quick," I say sarcastically. I step over to Brian, lying in the alley. "Fair?" I ask. Brian looks up at me with a fearful look on his face. "Kindergarten" is all he can eke out as he huddles in pain.

I grab Brian, roll him over, give him a quick pat-down, and take his small, .25 caliber pistol from him. "Let's go," I say. We walk into the dealership, met by several peering eyes. Those eyes meet ours and then they drop to the floor. Venus still stands with Stacy. "I think Brian is looking for you, dear," I say to Stacy as I point at the alleyway. Stacy hesitates, but then hurries out the door.

"I didn't see any cameras out there," Solomon says with a smile.

"Just one," a staff member says awkwardly, "but it's aimed only at the door."

"Well then," Tophat says, "life is good here."

"Almost," Solomon says. He reaches in his wallet and pulls out two one hundred-dollar bills. He hands them to the manager by stuffing them in his top pocket. "We will take the thingy with us, Pal," Solomon says.

The manager looks visibly confused. He instinctively swallows some dry spit and says softly, "Thingy?"

"Your memory card, SanDisk, whatever it is you have that captures video on your security system. We will take that now."

"Oh," the manager says uneasily. "Give me a few minutes. It's a bit more complicated than that, but we will get it."

Solomon snaps his fingers at Prospect and points to the manager. Prospect nods and follows him. Solomon then picks up a few T-shirts and pretends to model them as we all give him a thumbs-up or thumbs-down.

"Here you go," the manager says, handing Solomon three memory cards.

"Two hundred cover it?" Solomon asks.

"Certainly," he replies. "And here's your wire harness y'all came in for. It was forty-nine dollars and five cents, but your two hundred covers it."

"Thanks!" Solomon says. "Your crapper smells lovely, by the way," Solomon follows up satirically as he smirks. The manager just nods.

We saddle up amidst a deafened crowd; the scuttlebutt apparently ran rampant. Even the clown looks scared as he holds two, poorly made balloon animals. We fire the motors, roll out, and head home.

We find our way home and back the bikes in toward the clubhouse. I tell Prospect to go inside and set up the bar and then help Zonk fix his bike. Tomorrow is just a ride to nowhere day. We are heading out east again to complete what we were robbed of when Pancake Dave was murdered.

I pull my phone from its holder and see three missed calls from Crispy but no voicemail.

"Uh-oh, no voicemail," I say to myself. I return Crispy's call and he answers immediately.

"Digger?" he says loudly.

"Yeah, what's wrong?"

Crispy sighs heavily. "It's Mallet; he's in jail."

"What? Why?" I shout, drawing the attention of my brothers.

"What's going on?" Tophat asks.

I slide the phone away from my ear. "Mallet is in jail," I say as I hold my finger up to the awaiting ears. "Where is he and what happened?" I ask Crispy.

"He's in Highland County. They busted him with a 9mm."

"Highland County? So what?" I say incredulously. "He has a concealed carry good from here to there."

"Digger, you know they are not going to share info with the likes of me," Crispy says. "All I know is they walked up to him outside a minimart, and the next thing I know, they're cuffing him and throwing him in the car."

"Where were you?" I ask with anger.

"What the fuck, Digger. They see two Demons Rising, and what do you think their reaction was? I had some twenty-something rook in a small-town sheriff's department shaking as he points his cannon at me, screaming 'stay back'!"

Solomon motions for me to cut off the call.

"All right," I say to Crispy. "Go back to the Richmond chapter for now. I'll call you back." I hang up and just repeat to the rest of my brothers what they already heard.

"Highland County, huh?" Solomon says.

"I was thinking the same thing," Walt says.

I just nod my head in agreement, as do the others.

"Throw a rock over the Alleghany Hills from there and it lands in . . .," Hal says with a pause for effect.

"West Virginia," I say.

"Okay," Solomon says as he nods in contemplation. He looks and points at me. "The sergeant has to go."

"Absolutely," I respond.

"Grab some cash from inside, some clean undies, and go and send Crispy back after you bail Mallet."

I just nod my head. Solomon stares at me, then steps into me, grabs my hand, and embraces it tightly. We just look at each other sternly, and a meeting of the minds occurs. I look at my other brothers and they look at me. I feel Solomon's hand tighten on mine. "Digger?" he says.

"Yeah?"

"Leave the bike and take the van."

"Yeah," I say. "Unquestionably."

CHAPTER 16
The Plan

Venus / 2005 – Oneco, Florida

"Are you my friend or my fucking therapist, Jessica?"

"Whoa, settle down, Mary Ellen. I am your friend who happens to be a therapist."

"And in what capacity are you now?"

"I'm your friend."

"Then act like one and just be my ear."

"A real friend calls you out on your shit, Mary Ellen."

"Shit?"

"Yes, shit! You let this guy beat you, control you, and for what? Good sex?"

"How shallow do you think I am? You think I like getting pawed at by some guy who hits me?"

"Not as it is happening, but you like it when he's good to you, the honeymoon periods."

"I'm telling you, you are sounding like my therapist."

"Maybe you need one, Mary Ellen. You want to please only those who are bad to you."

"Blah, blah, blah. . . ."

"The chaos, the pain, the torment, but then you do a few lines, he's sorry, and all is well."

"Blah, blah, blah. . . ."

"Yeah, go ahead, Mary Ellen, hide from the truth. You gravitate toward a warped sense of power. You see abuse as power, and you respect that in some sick way. The Vodka and coke are just your way of keeping you from saying how much you hate yourself."

"I am only hating you about now, Jessica."

"Don't burn this bridge, Mary Ellen. I'm your only friend left."

September 2019

"When will you be back?" Venus asks.

"Day up, day there, day back; maybe by Thursday," I reply.

Venus smiles. "Where's 'there'?"

"It's the reciprocal and square root of here," I say with a quip.

Venus grabs me and kisses me hard, and she digs her nails into the back of my head and breathes heavily.

"Well then," I say with a smirk. "I will make there, *here*, very quickly."

"I'll call or text, so you can let me know you're living."

"I can't," I say, shaking my head. "My phone stays here."

"Oh?" she says curiously.

"Yes." I clear my throat. "Babs will have a phone that I can call you on, okay?"

"Babs?" Venus says inquisitively and with a disappointed look on her face.

"Yes," I reply. "Just stick with her and the other girls. Stay away from the clubhouse unless she goes."

"Babs?" Venus questions again.

"Babs is Tophat's ol' lady, and she has been a fixture here since the '80s."

"I get it," Venus says softly, trying to feign a smile. "I suppose she knows where you're going."

"Venus!" I say, growing frustrated.

"I know, I'm sorry," she interjects.

"If it makes you feel better, she knows nothing more than where the spare phone is and when you can use it. She does not know anything more than you do."

"Okay," Venus says. She beams. "I think she likes me anyway. I think she's accepting me."

"Good," I say, not knowing what else to say. I pause, look at her, and smile. "I love you."

Venus nods her head slightly and rubs my face gently. "You're so good to me," she says as she forms a nervous smile.

I pause. "Well, you crazy, fucking redhead, time to go in my white, windowless van. O.J. is waiting."

I jump up in the van and look through the bags Prospect packed. I see coffee, water, a few *uppers*, snacks, and a handful of sandwiches. "Prospect kept the crusts on! Fucker lost my vote," I say to myself. He even packed napkins. Prospect must have realized it's summer in Florida and I won't be wearing sleeves, so napkins are a must occasionally. I shift into drive and look at Venus in my rearview mirror. I try to read her face and see what she is thinking. But that damn enigmatic persona of hers. And that fake-ass, red hair. I then ask myself why I am even trying. "Focus, Digger." I grin as I look down the road and begin the long journey.

From oranges, to peaches, to tobacco, and finally, ham! The *Welcome to Virginia* sign is a welcoming sign—no pun intended—but it's a big state, and there's a long way to go. Prospect made up a variety of sandwiches from turkey, to roast beef, to some kind of kosher crap.

There's one peanut butter and jelly. Walt and Willie probably tossed that one in; it's all they eat.

This town leads to that town along these backroad, country, pothole fortresses, but I glide into the hamlet of Monterey, the city seat in Highland County. I park near the library, jump out, and stretch my legs. I look around the area, seeking an inviting face. I finally spot one sitting on a cement embankment outside the local library. He is a light-skinned, black man, about fifty years old, wearing a long-sleeved, flannel shirt, tattered jeans, and boots. He bounces a rubber ball and is humming what I recognize as an old church hymn.

"Hey, buddy," I say to him. He looks at me quizzically momentarily, but then drops his head back down to his bouncing ball.

"Any old diner in this burg where I can buy you lunch?" I ask.

"What do you want, out-of-towner?" he asks, not looking at me.

"Great," I say, sighing in relief, "a man who cuts to the chase." I invite myself to sit next to him. "I want to buy an old Marine, who is also from out of town, a hot meal and put a thousand dollars in his pocket for about an hour of work."

"Yeah?" the man says probingly. "I'm a Marine? And I'm not a local? Yeah? You know this how?" he asks, still focusing on his bouncing ball.

"I'll start with the fact I know those boots. My cousin Elron was a Marine from 1985 to 1989, and he owned a pair of those boots. Paris Island issued. And you are in a long-sleeved flannel, you're lucid and awake, so you're not hiding track marks, meaning you just got off the bus from the north. Judging from the dialect, I'm thinking Minnesota area, near the border."

The man focuses on me now and smiles. "Yeah, okay," he says. "Okay, you've been around. You know the score. So what do you want that is worth a grand that won't put me behind bars?"

"Don't forget the hot meal, my friend. I want to hear about your time in the Corps, you know, because of my cousin. Then I will explain, and I promise, it's not illegal in any way."

"K," he says. "The name's Mason Allegro. And yep, from Greenbush, Minnesota. Closer to Winnipeg than Saint Paul. We call our town *'Santa's first rest stop on Christmas Eve,'*" Mason says with a laugh.

"Wow," I say with a chuckle. "I know an old coot who would wait with an M-16 for Santa to touch down so he could riddle him with lead." I laugh again.

After a slight pause, the old man speaks. "Gus's."

"Sorry?" I say, confused.

"Gus's Diner. Just up the road. Had me some eggs Bennie and sourdough toast yesterday." Mason stretches. "Real good food, and I saw a truly pretty woman there with a beautiful smile."

I pull out a wad of cash and flash it to him. "On me, Mason."

I genuinely enjoy my conversation with Mason. We talk for over an hour about the Marines and his sacrifice of ten years. He served in the first Gulf War with honor and distinction. We didn't get into the circumstances of his current situation. I have a job to do. I must focus on my current loyalties. I explain that I need him to go to the jail, lay out his identification, and bail out Mallet. Then I'll put a grand in his pocket and send him on his way. His only risk is the bail money, which isn't his to risk anyway. He agrees. He goes to the jail, an hour or two go by, and I see Mallet, hair disheveled, without his cut, walk out of the jail and down the road. Mason gave him adequate directions and Mallet spots me. I wave my arm out the window. Mallet sees it, lightly waves at me, and walks to the van.

"What the fuck, huh?" he says as he pops open the door, shaking his head. "What a fucking mess."

I reach over and give him a quick hug. "That old man came through for me," I say.

"That old man was a trip," Mallet replies.

"Yeah," I say with a smile. "He's a good, old dude."

"He says to tell you '*Semper Fi*,'" Mallet says. "Do you guys have, like, a secret handshake or something that identifies y'all to each other?" He laughs.

I smirk. "It's just a guess on his part. I never told him I was a Marine. Besides, the ten Ben Franklins I laid on him will give him amnesia."

Mallet grabs some chips from the food bag. "I see you brought the van. I guess y'all put two and two together."

"Yep," I reply, staring straight ahead. "I'm assuming you got a line on our pal Torch?"

"Sure did," he says excitedly. "Crispy and I were actually on our way back from our little recon mission when I got clipped."

I look over at Mallet. "What did they do with your cut?"

"It's back at the clubhouse," Mallet replies.

"Yeah," I say perplexingly. "I guess I figured you wouldn't be wearing it doing recon." I reach down and grab another sandwich. "How'd the bust go down, anyway?"

Mallet rolls his eyes. "Geez, it wasn't twenty minutes after crossing over from West Virginia when we got lit up. These two Barney Fife types were shaking and screaming. Patted us down, found the 9mm on me, and took me."

"So, what, exactly, did they charge you with, and what made them stop you to begin with?"

"Carry and conceal," Mallet says. "I didn't have my permit or any I.D. on me, for that matter." Mallet thumbs through the food basket and grabs some ice water. "As for the second part, they said we ran across the center line, the usual lies cops tell when they just want to pull you over."

"Crispy said you guys were coming out of a minimart," I say inquisitively.

"Well, sort of, I guess," Mallet replies. "We just pulled into the parking lot when they jumped out of their little clown car and pulled their guns."

I sigh a bit. "We need to fill up, and I need to take a piss. Can you grab a few of those gas cans in the back, and I'll find a side road so we can take care of both problems at once." I turn down a dirt road that appears to have no destination. "When we are done here, we will get some details on what to do next with Torch."

"Do you want to get Crispy first?" Mallet asks.

"Nah," I say, emptying the ten-gallon gas can in our tank. "Solomon said to send him back to Florida, and you and I will deal with this ourselves."

"That's a smart idea."

"Like you said, we are tough, which means we are also smart," I say with a quip.

"I'm fucking starving," Mallet says. "What else did Prospect pack us?"

"The usual garbage: chips, cheese doodles, and there's a bunch of sandwiches, too."

Mallet digs deep in the bag and drops about three sandwiches on his lap. "Prospect kept the crusts on! Fucker lost my vote," Mallet says with a snort.

I couldn't help but laugh.

CHAPTER 17
Surreal

Mallet / 1989 – Shunk, Pennsylvania

"And what about Richard, John? What becomes of him?"

"Don't lay this on me, Audrey. Nobody planned on Sandra dying."

"Nobody planned? Is that your reasoning? His mother dies, and now his father wants to abandon him, and you think it's due to poor planning?"

"What am I supposed to do? Marcy doesn't want kids; she never has."

"Then don't marry her, John."

"You're making me the bad guy. I told your sister years ago that I don't want children, but she pushed and pushed and pushed. I didn't ask for Richard, and I am not going to force him upon Marcy. You think that is fair to either one of them?"

"You bastard! So your son is an inconvenience to your precious new bride, and you want to . . ., what? Put him in foster care? Just be a man, John, and admit it. You just don't want him and you never did."

"What do I say here, Audrey?"

"Nothing, John. Absolutely nothing. You said it all."

September 2019

Mallet and I spend much of this time just jabbering about nothingness. We rarely, if ever, delve into his family upbringing. Like most of us, we are all drawn to this life for the search of many things, but one component is the search for family as we define it. It's like life starts again when you get your patch. You start new, with new family, new obligations, and new goals.

We both are old soldiers having experienced war, death, pain, blood, and confusion. And as those two old soldiers, we know this is going to be different, in a way. We know how this is going to end and why it must end the way it will. We know what we are going to do and why we are going to do it. We know the mission, we know the purpose, but what we don't know is the experience.

Mallet's time in the Virginias is fruitful. He discovers Torch is on an abandoned farm about thirty miles across the border with three other guys. He has apparently discarded his love of being in a motorcycle club and is back supporting his love of the Aryan nation. But even in this quest, he's doing a poor job. Mallet easily learns Torch has a routine he follows daily, which includes a 'brisk constitutional'—Mallet's words, not mine—to a local store for a cup of coffee and a bag of bagels. The irony of bagels is most likely lost on someone like Torch. Mallet also notes that the other three guys are gone at dawn and don't get back until dusk.

Mallet and I continue to talk as we drive the backroads of West Virginia, commenting on the small, meandering creeks and the mountains that are in forever formation as the wind whips through the crevices. I take note that we only have eleven more cans of gas in the back, and of those, one is only a five-gallon can. Pragmatism keeps us from absorbing the view granted to us by Mother Nature and from making small talk. Damn that pragmatism. I cannot count how many times in my life it forces me to face reality.

The sun begins to rise down the road from Torch's squatted farm he and his minions have dubbed their new compound. Mallet drives up the road slowly, allowing me to hear every crunch and crackle of the tires as they dominate the dirt and gravel beneath them. We view the barn on the property and take note of the small edifice they call home. The home rests in the rear of the property under the natural camouflage of untended grass.

I exit the van with my gun and a small gas can and slowly amble toward the barn. *"No talking, this is business,"* I repeat to myself softly. *"No talking, this is business. No talking, this is business."* I palm the revolver and tuck it close to my hip as I scamper quicker among the tall grass, my breathing growing heavier with every step. My hands, soaked in sweat, make holding the .38 snub difficult. *"No talking, this is business."* The barn door is so dilapidated that there is no need to open it. I enter. I sit. I wait. Mallet is driving to the store to spot Torch in his daily sojourn to get coffee and to, most likely, contemplate his pathetic life. The irony of his contemplation makes me snicker. The ferocity makes me calm. The wait makes me think. The fear makes my thoughts meaningless.

Waiting magnifies the intense breathing. The quiet, the solitude, I know are artificial and temporary. *"No talking, this is business,"* I say with a heavy breath. *"Loyalty, justice, faith, honor, sacrifice, commitment, pride, brotherhood."*

Mallet roars by the barn and beeps twice. I stand and walk to the window. I wait more and look. *"No talking, this is business."* I see the figure of a man walking through the field, holding a cup and paper sack. I see his face now. He appears to be whistling and keeping a tune in the mild rhythm of his body movement.

It is now when I set the fire; timing is everything on this. I wad up some papers and dump a few ounces of gasoline I took from the van. The wind is on my side, for it carries the billowing cloud of smoke out the window. I grab a piece of a rotted beam, pound on the side of the barn three times, and then hover by the door. *"No talking, this is business."* My breathing is spotty and shallow. I've been to war. I've seen enemies. *"Loyalty, justice, faith, honor, sacrifice, commitment, pride, brotherhood. Loyalty, justice, faith, honor, sacrifice, commitment, pride, brotherhood."*

I hear Torch running. I hear the tall grass being crushed beneath his feet. I feel the sweat on my hand. I hear his breathing intensify, the grass being crushed, his breathing. . . . "Holy shit!" Torch screams as he runs into the barn and spots the fire. He feverishly begins throwing mounds of dirt on the blaze.

I take a step out from the shadow and call his name softly, "Frank." He turns and looks at me, and the color drains from his face. He stands straight up and backs up to the wall. "Wait! No . . . please, you got it all wrong!" he says pleadingly.

"No talking, this is business!" I shout. I see an enemy's face staring at mine. I see the fear, I see the confusion, I see the pleading. I squeeze the trigger. It pops, it explodes, I fire twice, he falls. I stand motionless, holding the gun, still pointing at him as I shake uncontrollably. The fire burns, the screams stop, the sweat still pours. I back out the door, gun in hand, and I turn and run to the road. "Loyalty, justice, faith, honor, sacrifice, commitment, pride, brotherhood! Loyalty-justice-faith-honor-sacrifice-commitment-pride-brotherhood!" I say louder and louder as I run. I run uncontrollably, attempting to discover if it's fear, confusion, uncertainty, or satisfaction that motivates me.

I see Mallet in the van. He stops. My running increases. My breathing is panicked, and I still have the gun in my hand. The van is getting closer and closer.

"Run, Bro, run. Let's get the fuck out of here!" Mallet shouts.

I leap into the moving van and drop onto the seat, still breathing heavily, both from the run and from the adrenaline.

"Holy fuck, I don't even know what happened," I say.

Mallet looks at me somewhat pensively and replies, "But it's done, right?"

"Yeah," I say as I take a deep breath, "short, sweet, and to the point."

"Okay, take that thing apart," Mallet says, pointing at the gun. "We have lots of time. That barn will burn to the ground, and even if one of the other guys returns, they will just split. We have, at the very least, twenty-four solid hours before they even discover there's a body in that barn. By that time, the gun will be disassembled, caked in cement, and in various parts of the Jackson River."

"Yeah," I sigh and start disassembling the barrel and ramming a file inside of it.

"Then we go back to the clubhouse, get wasted, and we will head back to Florida tomorrow."

"Yeah," I snap the cylinder off. "Venus is probably lost without me."

Mallet smiles. "You okay, Bro?"

"Yes, of course," I say as I rub my face with both palms. "It's just. . . ." I pause. "I thought I would go off on him first, tell him about Pancake Dave, or what he did to our club through his cowardice, or make him beg as I showed him a picture of Dave, or something."

Mallet nods his head supportively. "I know, Digger, but only in the movies does it go down like that. We are stuck in the real world." He adjusts himself in the seat a bit and faces me more directly. "Digger, don't discount the fact that we've killed enemies before. We just never saw them up close."

I sigh heavily and laugh slightly. "Yeah," I say, rolling my eyes in surrender a bit, slightly embarrassed that Mallet saw in me what I didn't want him to see. "You're right. That's exactly what it is." I shake my head in disgust at myself. "I never saw someone face-to-face. It sure is really different. You see a man, a son, a father, etcetera."

"Well," Mallet says with a slight pause for effect, "trust me on this, Digger. Miles away or eye-to-eye, they are no less of an enemy."

I look over at Mallet as I begin to calm myself a bit. I emit a perfunctory laugh. I hesitate slightly and then paw through the lunch bag. "Want a turkey sandwich with the goddamn crusts still on it?" I ask, handing it to him.

Mallet snatches it and rolls his eyes in feign disgust. He tears into the sandwich with a caveman-style bite and begins chomping. "Fucking Prospect! He lost my vote!"

CHAPTER 18
Triggered

Walt and Willie / 1990 – Yuba, California

"Are both boys present?"

"Yes, your honor."

"All right then, boys. I've talked to both your mom and your dad, the child welfare worker, and the ad litem, and it's my belief that you belong back with your parents. But I'm going to need for you two to behave this time. Listen to your parents and obey them, got it? I do not want to see you back here again. Case adjourned!"

"You heard the judge, boys?"

"Yes."

"Then let's go back home now."

October 2019

Solomon goes all out tonight. He hires a band that looks as though they have been making the circuit since the late '70s, and he garners a few strippers who look like they were also from around that era. What he does do right is corral us two pigs to spit and eight kegs of beer, although I think Solomon drank one by himself, and Walt seems as though he adopted a keg of his own as well.

It's a closed party, meaning it's by invite only. If any club from the coalition stops by, they will be welcome—maybe even clubs not in the coalition, depending on who they are. But other than that, this is a Demons Rising's family event. Such an event usually follows a celebration, e.g., a brother gets out of prison or the hospital, or gets married, birth of a child, a patch party for a new member. Also, when newer members are awarded their one-percent diamond, which is usually six or seven months after they get their patch. I am not certain what Solomon's motivation is tonight. Things have been quiet since Mallet and I came back from Virginia last month. We all measure life by events, good or bad, and there has been nothing measurable since summer ended and the fall eked its way in. Hurricane season is nearly over. Perhaps that's what Solomon is celebrating tonight.

The aroma wafting from the spittle reminds my olfactory senses that there is a power greater than man, and that power is the *pig*. Venus is making time with the other girls, mixed in with sending me provocative text messages routinely. I read them, then look around for her and smile when I see her. She raises her eyebrows at me a few times and then moves on through the crowd.

"Digger, Digger, Digger, Digger!" Solomon bellows through a slurred dialect. "Digger! You're . . . uh . . . gonna take a swigger from a jigger, I figger!" Solomon says, followed by an outburst of laughter. "In fact," Solomon says, as he looks around the room. "Prospect!"

Prospect meanders through the crowd quickly. "What can I do for you, Solomon?"

"You can get Digger a jigger!" he replies. "Posthaste, my good man!" Solomon then claps twice. "Chop! Chop!"

Prospect looks at me, and I give him the thumbs-up. "One jigger of Jack, coming up," Prospect says.

"This is actually fun. You remember fun, Solomon?" Solomon says aloud but addresses only himself. He spots Walt and Willie near the bar. "Walt!" he yells. Walt smiles and walks to Solomon. "Walt! Walt! He needs"—Solomon pauses—"salt!" Solomon looks about the room. "Prospect!" he bellows once again. Prospect returns with the jigger of Jack. I offer a perfunctory toast. "Brotherhood!" I say as I throw back the whiskey.

"What can I do for you, Solomon?" Prospect asks.

"Salt!" Solomon shouts. "Get Walt some salt."

Prospect looks at me, and I smile, shake my head, and wave him off.

"Well, who is next?" Solomon asks.

"We don't have a brother named 'Joe Rob,' do we?" I say to Preacher as we both laugh.

"Willie!" Solomon shouts. "Willie needs a . . . a . . . a . . .," Solomon continues, as he struggles through the alphabet. "A filly!" Solomon proclaims proudly, finding the seemingly perfect rhyme. "Prospect!"

Prospect returns quickly. "What can I do for you, Solomon?"

"Did you get the salt?" Solomon asks.

Prospect looks at me and I smile, shake my head, and wave him off again.

"Anyway, get Willie a filly. Find one of the club whores and have her come here, naked and braless!"

Prospect looks at me with a smirk, and I, again, shake my head and wave him off.

"And while you're at it, Prospect, save me some time and get Hal a *gal*, too," Solomon says. "Get that old dinosaur a young vixen, ya hear me, Prospect? Not a motherfucking day over sixty-five!" Solomon laughs and looks at me. "Who's next, Digger?"

"Prospect, get Solomon a shot of something, will ya?" I say.

"Tophat!" Solomon yells.

"Okay," I interject. "Enough of this before you give yourself an aneurysm trying to rhyme something with his name." I put my arms around Solomon and walk him outside.

"Digger, Digger, Digger, Digger!" Solomon bellows once more. "Ya know what I saw at the Dollar Store today?"

"I don't know," I say as I shrug my shoulders. "Two midgets fucking next to a lemonade stand?"

"Huh?" Solomon says with a genuine, perplexed look on his face. "Why the hell would you think I saw that?"

"I don't," I say, waving my hand. "It was just a guess, Solomon. So what is it that you really did see?"

"Oh, Digger," Solomon says with a long sigh. "It's not even Halloween yet, and they are selling fucking Christmas decorations."

"Already, huh?" I say with disinterest.

"Yep." Solomon pauses. "I mean, what the fuck, right? Fuck Christmas!"

"Yeah, a bruised Santa at the mall knows where you stand on that issue."

Solomon burps. "I have to piss, Bro."

"Well, you know the way," I say, motioning him back inside. "You built this place."

I make my way back in after grabbing a slab of pork off the rotating pig. I spot Venus with Wanda, Preacher's ol' lady, and a few of the other girls.

"There's my mega man meat now," Venus says as she grabs my belt buckle.

"Hi, Digger," Wanda says. Wanda peers up at Venus. "You coming?"

"I'll be out there in a sec, I promise," Venus retorts. Venus's smile wanes slowly and she looks at me. "No matter how hard I try, I can't seem to get her to warm up to me."

"Wanda?" I ask.

"Yes."

"So?"

"Well, she's been here a long time."

"True," I say. "And she's not warm and fuzzy. Never has been."

"No," Venus says, shaking her head. "It's more than that. I see the look on her face when I come around. And she's snapped at me a couple of times over nothing." Venus sighs and stares out back where the girls congregate. "I mean, Babs seems cool with me and she appears to be the leader of the girls." Venus turns to me and smiles. "Kinda like the Alpha *Gal* of the bunch."

"Oh, Miss Babs is definitely something else," I say.

"But Wanda is so different."

"Sweetie," I say calmly, "just go have fun and relax, okay? Don't overthink shit all the time."

Venus's attention focuses back to me. She smiles tacitly. "I know," she sighs. "I will just go and be one of the girls tonight."

I kiss her. "You're my girl."

Venus smiles again. "Thanks, Digger."

I watch as Venus goes to be with the girls. Her first contact is with Wanda, and then my attention is drawn elsewhere. I wander through the house a bit and observe. Mallet makes eye contact with me as he sits virtually motionless on the couch. He smirks and gives me a thumbs-up. I return the gesture. I see Crispy sitting at the bar, smoking a cigarette by himself. I slap him on the back as I walk by. He turns his head and says quietly, "Love ya, Bro." I smile, nod my head, and keep surveying the area. Solomon leans against the pool table, eyeballing one of the girls, and although I cannot make out what he is saying, the look on her face of partial embarrassment and partial acceptance tells me it's something suggestive. Probably his usual line of *let me use my stick to drive two balls into your pocket*. I can't fault him for that; we've all used that line.

Willie walks out of the back room with his hair mussed, just wearing his T-shirt and jeans. He goes to the fridge, grabs a jug of water, and gulps it down. I am guessing Prospect found him a filly after all.

Willie walks over to the storage closet and peeks his head in. Solomon's attention is drawn away from the girl, and he moves toward the closet door. Solomon smirks, shoves Willie in, slams the door, and stands in front of it, holding it shut. "I always knew you were in the closet, Glen!" Solomon yells.

Willie begins screaming loudly and banging against the door profusely with all his might. "Let me out! Let me out! Let me out!" I can actually see the door's outline bow outward from Willie's impact slamming at the door.

"You wanna come out of the closet finally, Glen?" Solomon says with a laugh.

Willie's bloodcurdling screams draw the attention of virtually everyone but the pig spinning on the skewer. Even the band stops playing and looks on at the commotion. "Let-me-out!! I can't fucking breathe!" Willie continues to shriek.

Walt charges across the room, slamming into the pool table so hard that his force moved it across the room. He charges into Solomon and throws him to the floor. Walt then swings open the door and Willie rushes out, hyperventilating and gasping for air. Walt grabs Willie and yells for everyone to step aside. By this time, Solomon is back on his feet and enraged. I run to intercede between the two.

"Give him room!" Walt cries. "Let him breathe!"

Solomon, as he marches toward Walt with anger and fury in his eyes, is met by my stiff arm toward him. Walt is not taking notice of an infuriated Solomon as he tends to Willie.

"Solomon, stop!" I shout. "No! This isn't happening."

Walt finally notices Solomon and says, "Are you fucking crazy, Solomon?"

This question multiplies Solomon's rage. "Say it again!" Solomon screams. "Go ahead, Walt, say that again!" Solomon says as he tries to charge forward. Mallet grabs Walt from behind but does so gently, despite Walt's ferocious resistance.

I have both fists bunched up on Solomon's shirt, holding him back. This is the sergeant-at-arms keeping peace, not mentee subduing mentor. "Solomon, no! This is not going to happen," I say.

"You can't lock him in the fucking closet! You can't! Nobody is ever going to do that to him again—and that includes you!" Walt screeches at Solomon.

"How dare you think I would do that to any brother!" Solomon shouts. "I thought he was Glen. He didn't have his cut on, and I didn't see his face." Solomon breathes deeply. "But none of that excuses you putting your hands on me. Nothing does!"

I look over and see Venus and the other girls in the back of the room. "Prospect!" I shout as I remain holding Solomon forcefully. "Get the women out of here, now!" My edict creates them all scampering without Prospect's escort.

"Do you know how many hours, days, and sometimes weeks he spent locked in a closet?" Walt screams. "Do you? Do you know how many beatings I risked, sneaking him peanut butter and jelly sandwiches so he wouldn't starve to death, alone, in that closet?"

"I don't care!" Solomon screams as he pushes harder against me. "Who the fuck do you think you are putting your hands on me?"

"Solomon!" I shout, looking eye-to-eye with him. "This is not some squid in Saigon, this is not some blowhard, rookie cop in Saint Pete, this is not some tweaker running his mouth in some dive bar. This is your brother! And you, and he, are so fucking drunk and angry, there's no way I am letting this take place!"

"You don't have a choice, Digger!" Solomon shouts as he pushes harder.

"No!" I say. "You taught me what is important. You taught me it's not about me or any one of us. You taught me about the club—what it means and why it's important. Was that all crap, or did you mean it?" I ask. Solomon stays silent but no less forceful in his aggression. "That's a question requiring an answer, Solomon," I say again. Solomon's hold begins to lighten some, but the look on his face is still wrathful. "Yes or no!" I push harder. "You told me once that *'it's not about you, it's about the guy next to you,'* I say as my breathing gets heavier. "And this is 'the guy next to you,'" I say, pointing at a still-angry Walt.

I feel Solomon's body go limp, and he looks up at the ceiling. His breathing calms but appears to be labored exaggeratedly. "We are not done here, though, Digger. This will be dealt with at a later date."

"I am implementing the one-week rule here, Solomon, and as the sergeant, you know I have that right."

"It's a stupid rule," Solomon says.

"Nonetheless, it is in our club's constitution, and it gives carte blanche to the sergeant to table these conflicts until cooler heads prevail."

"*Carte blanche!*" Solomon says sarcastically.

"Semantics," I say with a forced smile, trying to calm the situation even more. I turn and look at the crowd, still in stunned silence. Walt is free from Mallet's grip now and is talking with him casually. I look at the band. "Are we paying you to be here?" I ask quizzically.

"Uh . . . yeah," one member says.

"Then strike up the band!" I say. I then look at the crowd again. "Okay, everyone, grab a shot and it's on Demons Rising!" The crowd cheers, most likely to aid in breaking the tension, but they all do hustle to the bar, nonetheless. "Glen?" I say, looking through the crowd. I see him peek his head up and look at me curiously. "Grab your shot and come see me real quick, okay?" Glen nods.

Glen comes to see me as I stand in the corner near the coal stove. "What's up?" he asks.

"First off, you didn't do anything wrong, but you need to go," I say, patting him on the back.

"No, no, I get it, Digger. I do."

"Thanks," I say. "It's just a weird night, and I don't want that ugly mug of yours reigniting the convo, ya know?"

"I understand," Glen says. "I like supporting you guys anyway I can."

"You've been a great supporter, even before I got here, according to Solomon, and we all appreciate it immensely. We will probably have some sort of Halloween bash, so you come to that and the first drink is on me," I say as I give him a hug.

Glen thanks me, waves at a few people, and leaves unceremoniously. I turn and look about the room and see Willie walking toward Solomon. I hastily move to both of them, but it seems all is well.

"I apologize, Brother," Solomon says as he hugs Willie. "I would never humiliate a brother like that with citizens here. I really thought you were Glen, and I was just having fun with him. You weren't wearing your cut, and you have a brown T-shirt like Glen—"

"My cut was locked in the bedroom because, well . . .," Willie says embarrassingly.

Solomon laughs. "You horndog, you!" he says, giving him another hug. "All okay with you and me? I really am sorry, kid."

"I know that, Solomon. All is well," Willie says graciously.

"You've really impressed me lately, kid, and I don't want that to end," Solomon utters.

"Don't worry about it, Boss. This is my home," Willie says, motioning his hand outward, "and you are all my true family. It's all I ever wanted."

Solomon smiles at Willie and slaps him on both shoulders. "Our Willie is all grown up!" Solomon says with a hearty laugh. "I'm going to crash in one of the back rooms, so keep your horny ass out of that one, Willie," Solomon says.

"Will do. See you in the morning," Willie replies. Solomon slowly walks to the bedrooms, occasionally slapping someone on the back and giving one or two of the girls a kiss.

"Digger?" Prospect says as he walks toward me, trying to keep the whiskey from spilling. "Here's your shot, too."

I shake my head and put my palm up. "Nah," I say. "I'm dry for the rest of the night. You hit it."

"I can have a drink?" Prospect asks surprisingly.

"Just this once. Cheers!" I say. Prospect nods at me and throws back the whiskey.

I feel my phone vibrate and look down at the screen. It's a text from Venus. I open it and smirk, fully expecting another provocative message.

I Love You is all it says.

CHAPTER 19

Love

Venus / 1992 – Moorefield, Nebraska

"I know what you 'think' happened, Mary Ellen, but you are wrong."
"No, Mom, I'm not."
"Mary Ellen! Why do you want to cause trouble? Huh? Your uncle didn't mean anything by it."
"But Mom—"
"This is a small town, Mary Ellen. If you keep going on telling people, then the whole town will talk about how Missus Webb's daughter has a wild imagination. Try dressing more appropriately, Mary Ellen. Act more like a lady. And stop using your wild imagination."
"I know what Uncle Emmet did, Mom. It's not my fault. I didn't imagine it."
"Stop crying, Mary Ellen! Your dad and I talked, and we are doing what's best for the family. Now we'll try to keep Uncle Emmet away from you, but until then, dress right, watch your tone with others, and most of all, keep quiet!"

October 2019

The beaches. It's the first thought that comes to mind when people think of Florida. The Sunshine State has the most coastal border than any other state, and yes, that means more than California. A once desolate area in American population, beachfront property values exploded since the 1950s. If you look at old photos from the beaches around the turn of the century from the 1800s to the 1900s, take note of what isn't there: people and houses. Swimming in the ocean was not the norm back then; the ocean was smelly, rough, and its dangers were well known based on the unknown. It was a place of natural disasters, shipwrecks, Biblical cataclysms, home to supernatural Greek tyrants, and home to so many indigenous creatures thought to be deadly for humans and all within the water's edge.

Fast forward to today where I walk, hand in hand, with my beautiful girlfriend in the powdery fluff that wriggles between our toes. An occasional renegade wave rushes up high enough to shore that we scamper away in childlike fashion. The caw of the brash seagulls dominates at times, but the other dulcet audibles the beach offers usually gives us peace. Pelicans fly majestically, only to change course ninety degrees, divebomb into the sea, and rise back up with a fish naked to the human eye, but somehow spotted ninety feet in the air by the predatory bird.

Venus is uncharacteristically reticent as she picks up various shells and snaps some avant-garde photos of her feet in the sand, capturing her elaborate, tattooed toes. She peeks up at me occasionally and smiles. Her sunglasses do not completely help with the sun's glare off the sand as she shades her eyes occasionally when she looks out at the sea.

"This sand feels a bit different than it did in Iraq," I say to her.

"You never talk much about the war, Digger."

"What's to say?" I ask rhetorically. "Violence, death, and hotter than hell."

"Y'all had some potential violence going on last night, didn't you?" Venus asks curiously.

"Yeah, that was ugly," I say regretfully. "Solomon was in such a very rare great mood, too. It's like God punished him for smiling or something."

"You handled it unbelievably well. You took charge of that whole scene. Color this redhead impressed!"

"You saw it?" I ask.

"We were shooed out the back, but we could still hear. Babs was freaking out a bit, but Wanda just kept *shushing* everyone. Of course, Babs didn't listen to her. She definitely runs the girls. I think that pisses Wanda off."

"No, it doesn't. Wanda could care less about some false hierarchy," I reply. "You're reading way, way, waaayyy too much into all this and trying to decipher reactions and expressions and all this behind-the-scenes crap. Stop complicating simplicity."

"Yeah?" Venus queries. "It sure seems like they are both vying for queen bitch or something."

"They're not," I say, shaking my head. "Babs has been here the longest. She's the most outgoing and friendly, and the gals gravitate to her. Wanda is just stoic and crabby."

Venus sighs and shakes her head. "She's so frustrating! I tried to get her talking last night, but she just kept trailing off on her own, ignoring me. Clearly, she doesn't like me."

I sigh. "And about this sand!" I say loudly, trying to change the subject.

"Yeah, yeah, yeah," Venus says with a giggle. "I get it. Toes in the sand with me beats boots in the sand with Jihad."

"Something like that, yes."

She laughs. "And you are wearing a lot less clothes today, too, than in the Iraq days," she remarks. "I guess that also makes it much cooler and more comfortable."

"Very," I reply.

"Is that why you're not wearing your cut?" Venus asks. "Too hot?"

"You want me to wear my heavy, leather cut with shorts and sandals?" I ask mockingly.

"Well, you could wear a soft patch."

"That's only in a T-shirt form, not a tank top," I reply. "It may be October, but it's October in Florida. I am on the beach with a pretty girl. Forgive me for wearing a tank top."

"You could go shirtless," she says, "then the tattoo of your patch can be seen on your back."

"So?" I say, not expecting an answer. "Did ya ever think I'm packing my 9mm, baby?" I ask as I point and shoot.

"Are you?" she replies curiously.

"Nope," I say as I reach into the back of my shirt and pull out a gift box, "just this!"

"Oh, shit!" Venus says with shock and panic. "What is it?"

"Ya see . . . uh . . . how this works is that you tear into the paper and discover the contents yourself."

Venus looks at me with an almost fearful look. "What is it, Digger?"

I sigh melodramatically. "Don't worry, my dear, it's not a diamond ring. I'm not down on one knee."

Venus looks at me, embarrassed a bit, unsure what to say. "I know," she says, "but you wish I was down on two, don't you?" She laughs.

I just stare at her with a mildly annoyed look. "*Time for me to make jokes when things get uncomfortable*," I say mockingly in my best Venus voice. "Just open the fucking thing," I say, gently slamming it into her hands. "You're killing the vibe."

Venus slowly and methodically tears the paper. "What's this for?" she asks as she continues unwrapping.

"I don't know," I say flatly. "Because I . . . want to."

Venus finally gets to the box and opens it, displaying an antique mirror with engravings. "It's pretty, really," she says, rubbing the etchings. "I know you, though, and it's symbolic. And me and my slow brain aren't catching on."

"I didn't expect you to," I say comfortingly. "I had to research this, so it's not like it's obvious."

Venus holds the mirror up and blows kisses at herself demonstrably. "Oh, dahling! You are sooooo ravishing!" she says jokingly.

"Okay, Mae West," I say. "First off, many depictions of Venus through art and sculpture over the centuries portray her with a mirror, hence why this symbol is engraved on the back."

"The circle with the cross on the bottom?" Venus says unexpectedly. "The symbol of women?"

"Yes," I say. "That symbol is the *bronze mirror with a handle* that derives from Venus always having a mirror. That's where that all started."

"Oh, cool," Venus says with a smile. "So it's like a mirror engraved on a mirror."

"Exactly," I say. "And then the three birds engraved there are what she considered sacred: a dove, a swan, and a swallow."

"Hmmm . . ." She smirks devilishly. "I know which one you like best."

I stare at her briefly. "Venus, stay with me here. It'll be over soon, I promise."

She loses her smile and looks away. "Sorry," she says softly.

"Anyway," I continue, "the apple and the rose are engraved because they were two of many sacred plants she had, but they were the only two that were engravable. I mean, how the fuck do you engrave benzoin, myrtle, or parsley?"

Venus looks at the mirror and then back up at me. "I don't know what to say," she says in bewilderment. "I mean, clearly you didn't go to Walmart and find this."

"Not hardly," I say. "It was a process."

"Digger," Venus says with a long pause. She looks up at me, then to the mirror, and then out to the ocean. She removes her glasses and waves them in the air a bit. "It's beautiful. I don't know what to say. I'm not good at this stuff. I mean, all I can say is that nobody has ever done something like this for me." She sighs. "I mean, you're just . . . I mean. . . ." Venus struggles for words—any words—but settles on a surrendering "thank you."

"You're welcome," I say passively.

"I'm sorry, Digger, I know I am doing this wrong. It's beautiful, really."

The look on her face has many expressions, but I see a tinge of fear in the mix, it's origin I am uncertain of, though. But I know I must alleviate this awkward and embarrassing feeling for her. "You probably hate it because I didn't engrave the quince or the maidenhair fern, either," I say with a snicker.

Venus laughs. "If the maiden's hair is red, it's probably fake," she says while laughing.

"I'm getting hungry," I say quickly. "There's a place off the pier that has decent onion rings and pulled pork."

"Oh, sounds good," she replies. "But y'all spoiled me with that pig last night. That was freakin' awesome, to say the least."

"Makes you glad not to be Jewish, don't it?" I say.

Venus laughs. "That Babs can pack it in. She ate like three plates last night. It doesn't embarrass her or anything."

"Yeah, that's not something she is prone to—embarrassment, I mean. Several topless barroom dances have shown me that over the years."

"I like her," Venus says, "and she seems to like me. But I wish I got along better with Wanda, though." Venus sighs. "I mean, it's like no matter what I do, she pushes me away. I mean, regardless of how hard I try, how much I give, I can't get her to see anything more in me than she already does."

"Yeah?" I say dryly. "That's got to be a very frustrating feeling."

CHAPTER 20
Family Supper

Solomon / 1955 – Limestone, Florida

"Where are they taking Dad, Mom?"
"Get in the house, Tommy."
"Where are they taking him, Mom?"
"To the doctor, Tommy, now get in the house! Now!"
"Is Dad okay, Mom?"
"Tommy! House! Now!"

October 2019

Solomon never would announce our immense cash influx via his ex-Marine contemporary, but it is the excuse he gives me when he suggests that the club finance all of us— ol' ladies included—to a steak dinner at some new chophouse off the bridge in Tampa. It's just a pretext for Solomon to ride into the city. He never admits it, but he misses living in the city, although he understands the tactical reasoning for moving our clubhouse to where it is now. But the lights, the noise, the crowd, even the smell just emit so much energy.

With all the brothers, and those who have steady ol' ladies, Solomon calls and makes reservations for a party of twenty-seven under the name *J. Martin Eckworthy*, the name of an attorney on an episode of *The Odd Couple* nearly fifty years ago. Sometimes when I forget that Solomon does really have a sense of humor, I recall nights like this. Like the one night he demanded to see a wine list at Denny's, or the night he insisted that the waitress address the lobster he picked from the tank as *Jane Fonda*, or my favorite, when he continually asked the manager to see the military credentials of Colonel Sanders before he would pay the bill.

We will be flying colors, regardless of the fact this steak house is not necessarily a peanut shell-on-the-floor type place. Venus is wearing a burgundy-colored pantsuit with an extremely low-cut shirt, exposing the scenic tattoo featuring a wolf crying along her chest. She said she chose burgundy so she could resemble the color of steak sauce. Zonk is wearing a printed tuxedo shirt under his cut, but he manages to fold a handkerchief into a pointed square, which he tucks into his front pocket.

Prospect was given the night off, or normally he would have to come and watch the bikes in the parking lot. I told him to make certain the bar was stocked and that the air conditioner was set at seventy-five before he leaves for the night. We have a standing policy that prospects wait for one year before we vote on their acceptance into the club, but we discussed at church last week that we are voting on him at the next church meeting. He has been with us since February and has done an excellent job at remaining humble and attentive.

We saddle up and fire the motors. Solomon waits a few seconds, allowing the motors to warm a bit, then raises his hand. We all beep, signifying we are ready. The president leads the pack in almost every club. There are a handful of clubs that have the road captain lead, but most have the road captain ride what they call "sweep," which is last. But Demons Rising has the president leading, and next to him is Tophat. The second row is the other officers, including myself and Preacher. Zonk, the secretary, is in the third row, and then the hierarchy ends. Each member gets in formation in any sequence they can. The prospect always runs in the end. If we are leading a ride with other clubs and citizens, other clubs fall behind us, then the citizens.

Solomon drops his hand, and we roll out of our gate. The night is clear and dry. We find our way onto US 301 and go north to catch the Selmon Expressway. The system works flawlessly between pointing out road hazards, passing traffic while staying in form, and finding the right exit at the right time. Arms raise and traffic flows. Some eyes peer. Others are disengaged, but either way, the ride runs smoothly. Venus does her usual rubbing of my leg, which draws my attention enough to peer into my mirror to see her eyebrows fluttering.

The buildings get taller and denser, and Solomon is smiling. It's only my educated guess, but it's grounded in an evidence-based theory of mine. I think he thrives on the city's energy and misses the old clubhouse. We hit downtown with the unpredictable stoplight patterns, the nearly suicidal pedestrians who challenge every object with tires, and the inexplicable need for some to sell newspapers at every intersection.

Just past Kennedy Boulevard, we capture the attention of a Tampa police car. The car follows us as we head along the bay on Bayshore Boulevard. The car sticks tight but doesn't interfere with our ride. When we do reach our destination—discovered by the scent of steaks grilling—Solomon raises his arm, and we back our bikes into the lot. The Tampa police pull in shortly after and park in-between the white lines in the lot, like regular citizens. The car, the lights atop, and the old-school, blue uniform keep them from pulling that image off, though.

We dismount our bikes, and two uniforms walk slowly toward us.

"Mister Starke," one cop says to Solomon. Solomon's last name matching the most notorious prison in Florida is not without its irony.

"Deputy Fife!" Solomon replies, shaking his hand gallantly.

"I think you know we are not deputies, Mister Starke," one young cop says. He stands about six feet tall, no more than mid-thirties in age, is clean-shaven, with wide ears and a nose that is small, yet crooked.

"Truth is, I have no fucking clue who you are," Solomon says. "Do you need something, or can we go eat?"

"I'm just trying to be polite," the young officer says.

"'A' for effort, young man," Solomon retorts. "Now, one last time, do you need something, or can we go eat?"

"Okay," he says, hostilities down a bit. "I see you and your . . . crew are here to feast. May I recommend the creamed asparagus soup?"

"You may," Solomon says, pointing at him. "Give Andy and Aunt Bea my best." Solomon turns, looks at us, and points at the front door of the steak house. "Grease up, folks!"

We all saunter slowly to the door with Solomon leading the way. Two well-dressed men open the door as the whole cluster of us enter the foyer. The host freezes in his posture and tries to remain diffident. "Reservations?" he asks.

"Yes, twenty-seven for the Eckworthy party," I reply.

"Eckworthy?" he says, repeating the name as if it will make us disappear.

"You can't possibly have two parties with that name, can you?" Walt chimes in.

A well-dressed woman, exuding class and dignity, approaches. She smiles and looks at the host. "We have about a twenty-minute wait. Please feel free to have some crackers and cheese in the lobby."

I glance at my wrist where a watch should be. "If we wanted to eat twenty minutes from now, we would have showed up twenty minutes from now."

The woman smiles boldly. "Seat these kind people in the banquet hall," she says.

"It's not open," the host says.

"It is now," she quickly retorts.

We are briskly escorted to the darkened banquet room. The woman turns on the lights and the ceiling fans. "It will be cool in here in a few seconds, I assure you."

"This fucking meat better be good when it hits my mouth," Babs says. Tophat rolls his eyes and shakes his head.

Venus tries to maneuver the seating where she can sit next to Wanda. I watch as she shuffles herself around chairs, all the while gripping my forearm. Occasionally, she peeks up to see where everyone is sitting. I grab her arm off mine and tug at her slightly. "I know what you're trying to do," I say softly. "We're sitting with Mallet, and Pete, you can talk to Courtney, his ol' lady." Venus looks at me, slightly embarrassed, and gently nods her head.

I see an all-too-familiar face back in the main room of the restaurant peeking out at us. "Oh, shit!" I say to Solomon.

"What?" he says inquiringly.

"Look over your left shoulder," I say quietly. "Isn't that your ex-'Nam cohort, Benjamin Austin?"

Solomon glances over with a surrendered look. "Oh, for the love of all things barbecued!"

"Clearly, he recognizes us," I say. "Is he dumb enough to walk in here and say hello?"

"You want me to say 'no,' don't you?" Solomon replies.

"I do, yes," I answer anxiously.

"Well . . ." Solomon says with a pause.

It was then that Benjamin Austin stood, buttoned his sport coat, and escorted a woman into to the banquet room. "Tommy!" he says buoyantly.

Solomon wears a look of perplexation and says, "Barry?"

Ben laughs aloud. "Very funny, Tommy," he says, looking at his female escort. "Like we didn't just see each other recently," he says with a laugh. "Honey, this is Staff Sergeant Tommy Starke, U.S.M.C."

"Oh!" she says gleefully. "You served with Ben in Vietnam?"

Solomon, through masked, gritted teeth replies, "Yes, Beth Ann, I believe we met once in San Diego long ago."

"Oh, my, yes!" she shrieks. "You were going to come to our wedding."

"Yes, I was, but something came up."

"What brings you here, Tommy?" Benjamin asks.

Solomon stumbles on his words slightly but then quickly replies, "Just out for a good steak with the family. How about you?"

"Oh," Benjamin says overemotionally. "My brother-in-law passed away."

"Oh, geez, I'm sorry, Ben," Solomon says.

"Yep, it appears he got drunk and fell down a flight of stairs."

Solomon expels a heavy sigh. "Again, Ben, I am sorry to hear that."

"Thanks, Tommy. We just came from the funeral. That's my sister, Molly, there," Benjamin says, pointing at this frail, older woman in a wheelchair.

Solomon gives a cursory glance at the table. "Well, again, my condolences, Ben," Solomon says. "I will let you get on with your family. It was great seeing you."

"Um . . . yes," Benjamin says, looking at all of us. "Thanks again."

After an awkward pause, Ben leaves. Solomon looks at all of us and shouts, "Order whatever you want, boys and girls."

The waitresses are both friendly and timid as they serve us. Only once is one waitress a bit rude when she tells Zonk that the iced teas don't have free refills when he asks her for a third during the meal. He quickly snaps back that he sold some blood today, so he can afford all three iced teas.

Babs has to elaborate numerous times that the steak is "hot, tender, and feels good in her mouth" to a waitress who continually blushes. Then she points out the irony about all the times meat *forked* her over the years and how she can now turn the tables on the unsuspecting meat.

Willie bellows "moo" every time he jams a knife into his steak, and Preacher overuses the word "splendid" as he dabs the corners of his mouth with his napkin. Crispy is quiet overall, but he is not shy about ordering several appetizers.

The waitress brings the bill and holds it in her hand, looking at all of us. Solomon takes it from her, opens it, and shows no expression at the $2,460 tab. He puts on his glasses and pulls out a wad of cash, thumbing through the hundred-dollar bills, counting out thirty of those bills and handing them all to the waitress.

A look of relief comes over the staff when they have cash in hand. Their level of graciousness increases as we exit, asking us in a perfunctory way to "come back again."

The sun sinks over the hill, just showing a crust of the golden glow off the still waters of the bay. Solomon has a beaming smile on his face as he saddles up on his bike. All I can think of is that he took pleasure seeing Ben witnessing Solomon paying the tab with a wad of one hundred-dollar bills that were freshly in Ben's hands only days prior.

The engines ignite and the noise rises as we ride out of the parking lot. Onlookers gaze and point as we ride by. The city lights shine, and the energy of the night takes hold.

Ah, family!

CHAPTER 21

I hear tires screeching. I hear a voice scream. I see the glass break. A horn beeps but does so too late. The motorcycle is meshed into the truck's front grill. Blood drips. I see him, motionless, pressed into the windshield. He is gone. Just like that, Willie is gone.

CHAPTER 22
Protocol

Digger / 2004 – Fallujah, Iraq

"At ease, corporal."

"Thank you, sir."

"Have a seat, corporal, I have some news."

"Yes, sir?"

"There's no easy way to say it, Son, but your mom was found dead back in Indiana in her home. I'm sorry, Son, I truly am."

"Oh my God!"

"We are offering you a two-month leave of absence to attend her funeral and tend to her affairs."

"H-h-how did it happen? She is so young."

"Well, reports are sketchy right now, corporal, but . . . what we do know is that your father has been arrested, and they have formally charged him with her murder."

October 2019

I hate that fucking song! It only means one thing, and that is another brother is gone. Two brothers stolen from us in one year is daunting, and I don't care how we lose them, when they are gone, they are gone. Willie's accident was the unfortunate result of a perfect storm. One car hits a pothole, breaking the exhaust off onto the road. Then a truck swerves to miss the broken exhaust on the road and hits the curb, sending him right in Willie's path.

Solomon suggests we cancel our yearly trip to Daytona's Biketober Fest given all that has occurred, but Walt says that is where he and Willie met the club back in 2007, and he really wants to dump Willie's ashes in the ocean on Daytona Beach.

I don't know if I would have minded missing Biketober Fest. Solomon is more and more difficult to deal with that week. First, it's hearing about how *back in the day* they used to race up and down the beaches through the sand with naked chicks on the back, or how you used to be able to camp right there in the sand and have a bonfire all night. And when you did go downtown, every beer tab was picked up by the bar owners, and the party didn't end until it was time for scrambled eggs and bacon.

Then he has a near heart attack whenever he sees a trailer roll in with bikes on the back. He will scream at them, "It's bike week, motherfucker! It's not trailer week!" One night, he actually went around the parking lots looking at the trailers and would go into a rage whenever he saw Florida license plates. I mean, really? Who does this? And every time he saw a Florida plate he would shriek, "They are from Florida, Digger! Who the fuck has to tow their fucking bike when you already live here?" I would always ask why he took the time out to walk around and look at other license plates if it only pissed him off, but, in true Solomon fashion, he would just rant more and louder about how *bugs on your windshield should come from the ride* and how he earned every bug carcass splatted on his bike. If someone came from Alaska, he would be more sympathetic, but he still called them "weak-ass pussies."

Then he follows up with how Daytona Bike Week in March is organic, and that the tradition was born when bikes rolled in from all over the country. But Biketober . . . no . . . Solomon rants how it began with an idea by the Chamber of Commerce and it's rooted in greed, and so on, and so on, and so on. It's then I usually play a Hank Williams song and hand him some bourbon. It's the one-percenter's version of a pacifier.

But laying Willie to rest will most definitely bring a more somber tone to the week. We are all keeping a particularly close eye on Walt. I got a small taste of what they went through together as kids last week when Solomon and he exploded on each other.

Walt, of course, speaks first at Willie's eulogy. He is extremely eloquent, but pithy. He continually refers to Willie as 'our' brother and thanks the club for giving Willie a true sense of family and acceptance, explaining, very rudimentarily, how that was something neither of them had prior to patching in with Demons Rising. Walt focuses in on the past three or four weeks when we all noticed an autonomous uprising in Willie. Walt asks us all not to mourn, but to celebrate. Walt is clearly grieving but keeps a smile on his face, steeped in gratitude, when we bring out Willie's cut in a frame and hang it alongside Pancake Dave's.

Since 1972, no Demons Rising, in the original Florida chapter, has been killed in a motorcycle accident. Many over the years died from natural causes, three were murdered, and one—the very first patch holder to die—did so from an accident in 1982. His name was Hillbilly Mike. Solomon told me that Mike climbed on the roof at the old clubhouse in Tampa in an attempt to wrangle our old TV antenna and simply slipped and fell onto the driveway, split his head open, and died instantly. His is the first cut framed on the memorial wall. It's back when the vast majority of the guys wore old, blue denim. I believe it happened around Labor Day because Hal, Tophat, and Solomon seemed to work a rum and coke into their drink rotation that weekend when we were out on the town, and they are the only ones here in 1982.

It seems logical to simply ask why they do that. I guess it's possible that it is only a coincidence. But I don't ask because . . . well . . . it's hard to explain. In our world, we honor the dead, we honor their legacy, and they are never forgotten, but we don't discuss brothers who have passed all too often. The explanation seems cryptic, but it is believed that in day-to-day life, it's best to let them rest in peace. We have an annual Memorial Run where we visit every gravesite of every member of this chapter. Next year, we will visit Daytona and pay homage to Willie.

The clubhouse empties one by one. Most of the club and their ol' ladies are going into the nearby town of Ruskin to grab some food at Denny's. We are all going to Daytona tomorrow for a final goodbye to Willie.

Walt seems to be the last to leave. He stands stoically with his hands parked behind his back, staring up at Willie's framed cut with his photo below.

"Digger?" Venus says from the front door. "You want the rest of them to wait for you?"

I peek out the window and see my brothers saddled up and raring to go. "Wave 'em on, sweetie," I say. "We will go in a few minutes."

Venus waves her hands a few times and screams, "We will meet y'all there later."

I walk over to Walt, slap his back, and give him a sideways hug. "You're a great brother, Walt," I say, "not just to us, but to Willie. Y'all may not have been blessed with much early on, but he was truly blessed to have you."

Walt catches his breath and nods. "I promised him. . . ." Walt sighs again. "I promised him that I'd always take care of him, Digger. I told him I would never let him down, and I feel like I did."

"Walt—"

"I know, I know," he says, interrupting me. "Intellectually, I *get it*, but I failed to protect him from Dad and from Mom, and I feel like I failed here."

I squeeze Walt a bit tighter. "You gave Willie hope, Walt. You reminded him someone did love him, and you then shared him with us. You know we all loved him, but best of all, he knew it, too."

Walt sighs and then smiles, but stays fixated on Willie's picture. "Thank you, Brother. I really mean that."

Solomon comes out of the meeting room and closes the door. He grabs his flask and takes a swig. He offers it to both Walt and I, but we both decline.

"You ready, Solomon?" I ask. "We're about ready to go."

Solomon shakes his head slightly. "No, you go. Walt and I have things to discuss still." Walt looks up at Solomon with a confused look.

"Talk to him at Denny's, Solomon. We are hungry," I reply.

Solomon shakes his head again. "No, just him and I, Digger."

I pause a bit, still hoping I am not fully understanding what Solomon means. "What about?" I ask Solomon because I am not sure what to say.

"That's none of your business, Digger," he replies.

"None of my business?" I say with incredulity.

"Yes!" Solomon says, growing angrier. "None of your business."

"Solomon!"

"Digger," he says forcefully, "get the fuck out!"

Venus moves the door slightly, causing it to squeak, catching Solomon's attention. Solomon looks at her and waves his hand at her to leave. Venus scurries out the door without a word.

"This is not the time or place and you know that," I say.

"First off, don't tell me what I fucking do and do not know," he shouts as he jams his finger at me. "Secondly, this is our house, so it's the perfect place. And as for time, Mister Carte-fucking-Blanche, it's been a week!"

"The man just buried his brother today," I say sedately.

"So-did-I!" Solomon shouts, pounding his fist in his palm with every syllable. "Now get out!"

"No!"

"No?" Solomon says disbelievingly. "Did I make that optional, Mister Sergeant-at-Arms? Get the fuck out! Now! You're the one who pulled that bullshit *one week* rule out of your ass last week! Well, it's been a week, so go now before I pick your ass up and throw you the fuck out!"

"I can't believe you're doing this," I say. "This cannot be happening."

"Oh, it's happening!" Solomon says as his eyes grow large and change from blue to green. "Your only choice is, do you walk out, or do I throw you the fuck out! I'm the goddamn president here, not you!

You don't fucking tell me what I am and what I am not going to do!" Solomon screams uncontrollably.

"After what happened, after what he's been through, you're gonna. . . ." I halt my words, unsure of what to say. *What am I supposed to say?*

"Gonna what, Digger?" Solomon asks almost mockingly. "You really do struggle finishing a point sometimes. Could it be it's because you're thinking with your bullshit emotions and not your brain? Use your brain, Digger," Solomon says, pointing at his skull. "It's more reliable. It's what men do. We think. We act. And we don't let bitch-ass tears cloud that! You're not on a movie set, Digger. You're in Demons Rising's clubhouse, wearing their patch with honor and distinction, and what comes with that is an adherence to tradition. Now, this is your last fucking chance. Get out now, or as God is my witness, Digger— *as-God-is-my-motherfucking witness*—I will most definitely take you outside, kicking and screaming! And do not . . . *do not* . . . make the mistake of thinking that I can't do it! There is nothing I won't do to protect the integrity and future of this club!"

The standoff seems like it lasts for hours, but it was merely seconds. I don't look at Walt, I look at Solomon, but I see past him and into a window of years gone by for me. Every challenge that I have ever been dealt is being reconfigured in my mind, making me second-guess everything. I am almost forty years old. I know life. I know what it is. I don't want to confuse hubris with confidence. I don't have faith Solomon is right here, but I have less faith in thinking I am. Would a cowardly man walk out, or would a brave man walk out? Would a cowardly man stay, or would a brave man stay? Which one am I, and which one do I think I am?

My problem is that the only man I would ask those questions of is the man at the center of this colossal dysfunction. In my heart, I know what Solomon is doing is wrong.

I turn and look at the memorial wall for a second or two. I hear Dave's voice, and I hear Willie's voice. Their words are inaudible and meaningless, but I hear them. I look over where Venus was. And then, I walk out the door. I kick some dirt as I walk down the driveway. Venus sits on my bike with a look of confusion and panic on her face.

I hate funerals. I really do. I don't think I have ever had any other experience than bad at any of them. People are gone; life changes. And worst of all, life starts to look more and more like reality. That's what scares me.

CHAPTER 23
An Honest Assessment

Babs / 1981 – Daytona Beach, Florida

"You can't just be this party girl forever, Babs."

"I'm enjoying life, and that's what matters."

"You must want more out of life than being used by guys."

"How do guys 'use' me, Tracy?"

"Oh, come on, Babs! Be real! They get you drunk, they get you high, and then they fuck you."

"I like getting drunk, I like getting high, and I like getting laid. So walk me through how I am being used."

"Oh, bullshit, Babs, grow up! You know what I mean. They're using you. It's obvious."

"So the man supplies the Vodka, the coke, the pot, the dick, and usually the bed, and they are the ones using me?"

"So you don't care about self-respect?"

"Au contraire, I respect myself immensely. I enjoy all of it—a lot—so where is the lack of self-respect coming from?"

"That's bullshit, Babs! Do you think the guys see it that way? They see you as an easy mark, that's all. They don't respect you as a woman."

"What is it with you so-called modern feminists? You think I, as a woman, should base my self-respect on a man's interpretation of me? It's like, if a man enjoys himself with you, we as women are selling ourselves short. That's empowerment? I run me, Tracy. What some man sees is irrelevant to me but clearly important to you. You're the one with the self-respect problem."

"Babs, there's got to be more to life than bikers, booze, coke, and sex."

"Well, Tracy, I sure as hell hope not."

October 2019

Thus far, it's been an uneventful time in Daytona. We are staying at an older motel, but it is on the beach. A friend of Solomon's owns it, and has owned it since the 1960s. We have two to a room, and if you are with a girl, then it's four to a room. This will be the first year that I bring Venus with me, so it will be the first year I don't have to share a room with Solomon. And that probably is a good idea anyhow, considering what occurred two days ago. He and I have not spoken outside of any necessities, and neither have he and Walt. In fact, Solomon has kept to himself pretty much. He is bunking with J.J. for the week.

Anyone sleeping on the bottom tier rolls their bikes into the room with them so, to a casual observer, it looks as though there are not actually thirty of us staying here. Solomon insists that we buy out the entire motel during the weeks we come to Daytona.

Venus and I ride to Daytona ourselves. I was up extremely late the night before and so was she. She didn't say much to me all night. I know her. She was bursting at the seams, wanting to ask me about what happened with Walt and Solomon, but she did not do so.

I am more of an early riser, and Venus tends to sleep later. Therefore, I take this opportunity to walk down toward the beach. I can see it was a late night for most of my brothers. I walk by the pool area and note of several bathing suits and shorts wadded up in various piles. I also see a canoe in the pool. I don't know where they found a canoe, or why they decided to float it in a pool no bigger than the average living room, but they did so, nonetheless.

I see Babs sitting on a bench along the shore, tossing crackers to the seagulls while rocking her head to some country music. She steals an occasional sip from her coffee, as she then gets frustrated with the encroaching birds and shoos them away from her.

"Hi, Doll Face," I say to her. I bend down and give her a kiss.

"How does Tophat's dick taste?" she asks with a boisterous laugh.

"Oh, geez," I say, as I spit repeatedly and wipe my mouth. "I know you're kidding, but goddamn, girl, why do you do that to me?"

"It amuses me," she says with a smile. "Where's Venus?"

"Oh," I say, peering back up at the motel, "she's snoozing still." I give the layout a cursory glance. "Where's Tophat?"

"He is making some breakfast. The man loves to cook outside."

Just at that point, I hear Tophat shout from the balcony, "Babs! How much bacon do you want?"

"Have we fucking met?" she shrieks to him. "You've known me over thirty-five years, what do you think? *A lot!*" she screams again, answering her own question.

"Temper, temper now," I say with a smile.

"I'm very even-keeled."

"Is this the same even keel that broke that girl's eye socket in Jacksonville two years ago because she rolled her eyes at you?"

Babs gives me a sarcastic smirk. "Fittingly, she didn't roll them again, did she?"

"Well, I think they spun round and round a few hundred times after that, but no, not at you."

"Yep, spent three days in Duvall County Jail before Tophat and the guys made that bitch drop the charges," Babs says. She looks up at Tophat, who still stares out the window, and she gives him the finger. She then looks back at me. "You'd never know that I absolutely love that man with every ounce of my being, would you?"

I laugh. "Believe it or not, yes, I can tell." I grab a cracker and throw a few chunks to the awaiting birds. "I guess I forgot you two have been together so long."

"Yep," is all she says. She pauses and tosses a few crackers to the birds.

"Just curious, I don't care, but what kept y'all from marrying?"

"Ya know," Babs says then pauses, "nothing specific. It's just that...." Babs hesitates and thinks. "Like I told Tophat, if I marry him, then I become Missus Deborah Jones, and I don't want to be her. I just love being Babs Barros, Greek goddess to the Holy Land!" She laughs.

"What y'all have definitely works," I reply.

Babs continues to bop her head back and forth lightly to the music and sips her coffee. "My favorite thing about him is that he accepts me, and I don't mean in that idiotic romantic way we women hyperbolize at times. For example, the other night when we all went to the strip club."

"Yeah," I say attentively.

"I mean, he knew what I was going to do; he knows how I am. Me, high, in a room full of swinging dicks in my face. What's a girl to do?" She laughs. "But he knows I'm going to have my fun, raise hell, but I come home to him. I don't sneak off in the parking lot with one of these guys. We girls just want to be girls, ya know?"

"I do," I say.

"He makes me brush my teeth, though, when I come home," Babs says with a burst of laughter. "But I understand."

I just laugh and shake my head. "Babs!" I say, with mock disappointment. "What are mommy and I gonna do with you?"

"I learned a long time ago, Digger, not to let life pass you by." She tosses a few more crackers and sips her coffee. "Do you know the play *Our Town*?"

"I think so, from high school maybe. George and Emily from some Podunk town, etcetera."

"Well, yes, but the play is quite deep. It's a carpe diem message, and one part always struck me. We saw it in seventh grade," Babs says, resituating herself so she can face me. "Emily's mom talked about wanting to go to Paris someday. And then a few scenes later, she made

French toast for Emily's dad and he liked it, but she talked about France and all that. Then she stares out the window for a long time. You can just tell she's pondering life and what's out there, etcetera. And one or two scenes later, there's a graveyard scene and Emily's mom is dead! Oh, God, I just started crying and crying. When all my other ditzy friends were crying at George and Emily's kiss on the ladder because it was just so *bu-tee-ful*," she says rolling her eyes, "I cried because I really kept thinking that this woman was going to go to France and fulfill her dream, but instead, she dies. I know it sounds ridiculous, but it made a real impact on me. I was only thirteen, but I knew I was never going to be that woman. That is why I don't ever let one drop of life go unappreciated."

"Damn, Babs, that's actually pretty cool. I like that about you," I say. "I really do."

Babs takes my hand and pats it a few times. "And life with Tophat has not had one boring day, and not one day that I regret—not one." She sighs slightly. "I really do love that guy, Digger. I don't get shmaltzy too often, but I do love him and love him more every day. I don't know what I would do without him."

"Babs!" Tophat yells. "Come on! It's getting cold!"

"Would you shut the fuck up!" she screams. "I'm trying to tell your brother here how crazy in love I am with you!" She looks over at me and shakes her head. "Asshole!" she says. "He just kills the vibe."

I laugh. "I said that to Venus the other day. She kills the vibe sometimes, too," I say.

Babs looks at me and smiles but says nothing at first. Then she blurts out, "You really like her, don't you?"

I just smirk. "Why? Does she talk about me?"

"Yes!" Babs says cheekily. "We talked in the girls' room after study hall right before math class!"

"Okay, okay, I get it," I say. "But you know what I mean."

"Yeah, she does." Babs looks up at the sky and shades the sun from her. "You know me, Digger, and you know I'm a straight shooter. If I don't like someone, I would say so—not cruelly, but I would be honest, nonetheless."

"I do," I reply.

"I really do like her," Babs says, nodding her head slightly.

"Next word is 'but,'" I say.

"But . . ." Babs smiles. "She tries too hard and overthinks things. She attempts to impress us all with her knowledge of biker vernacular and the lay of the land in our world. Here comes another 'but,'" she says. "But I don't think it's to outdo or impress us. I think she fears not fitting in. It's like she tries extra hard when she feels unaccepted but ignores areas where she is already accepted. It seems those areas where she's accepted don't appeal to her, only the ones where she feels out of place. I just try to get her to relax and have fun. That's one reason why I was so happy you encouraged her to go to the stripper show that time. I just told her, *'Put your face on the mirror, then when you're done, jam your face in one of these guys' crotch.'*"

"Oh, good," I say sardonically. "What every guy likes to hear about his ol' lady."

"Oh, lighten up, Pat Robertson!" she says jokingly. "I was trying to get her to get outside herself a bit and let loose."

"I know what you mean, Babs. And I do appreciate it, actually. You're good for her."

"I can only do so much, Digger," Babs says. "I don't see any real substance to her, no core; it's all just fluff. I'm sorry, just how I see it."

I just nod my head.

"It doesn't mean I'm right. I'm not an *ol' lady trainer*. It's probably one of the very few arguments Tophat and I have ever had, besides him using a soup spoon to eat cereal. God, I hate that!" Babs says with a frustrated tone. "But anyway, the only other time we argued is when he asked me to help with some of the ol' ladies and get them to assimilate a bit. It's not what I do," Babs says, throwing her hands out. "That's their ol' man's job, not mine. I am just me, party girl, not some leader of the pack. Most of the gals flock to me because I've been here the longest, but if anyone wants that job of leader of the ol' ladies, they can have it because it's available."

"No, I get it, Babs. I just mean stuff like you're doing now. Maybe if she sees a woman with nothing to prove, it'll rub off a bit."

"It just comes with time," Babs says. "And the other problem is that ol' ladies come and go, and I've learned not to get too close because just when you do, they're gone. Or the guy brings another chick to an event and you know you can't tell his ol' lady that he did, but yet you're friends with his ol' lady."

"I guess you gals have it tough, too," I say as understandingly as I can.

"Kind of," she says. "We get attached to people, too. We cry when one of your brothers dies." Babs begins to weep. "We loved Willie," she says, wiping some newly forming tears. "We loved Pancake Dave. I've been here for all of them. I remember way back when Hillbilly Mike fell off the porch."

"Oh?" I say with a tinge of surprise. "I heard it was the roof."

"No," Babs says, dabbing some tears still. "I was there the day it happened. There used to be this widow's walk on the north side of the old clubhouse overlooking the back of the house. It was rotted out anyway, so the club saw no reason to repair it after Hillbilly Mike died. So they just ripped it down and painted over it."

"Really?" I say perplexed. "I heard it was the roof. In fact, I was told, specifically, that he was adjusting the TV antenna."

Babs shakes her head. "No," she says. "It was definitely the porch. I remember hearing the commotion, running outside, and seeing the whole railing broken off and dangling from the side of the house, then Tophat telling me to get back in the house. It was a day of chaos and I was high as hell, but I do remember that part. Mike landed on the privacy fence separating the two properties. He was hurting but alive, but I think it was too late to save him. They loaded him up in the van and took him to Tampa General, but he died on the way."

"Was that where the TV antenna was?" I ask.

"No," she says incredulously. "It was 1982; cable was all the rage. These guys couldn't live without fucking football and *skin-o-max*!"

"Well . . . stories grow and change over time, I guess."

"Yeah. Like I said, I was high, and that whole day was shrouded in controversy, so who really knows?"

I look at Babs with total puzzlement. "Controversy?" I say probingly.

"You know . . . I mean . . . you know . . . them discovering Mike"—Babs stops after noticing the look on my face, replete with confusion—"and you and I are gonna dance!" she says, turning the volume up high on her iPod. She mouths the lyrics and dances with me theatrically.

"Digger!" Tophat yells from the balcony. "If you dance with my ol' lady for more than two minutes, she becomes yours, and that means YOU go to her mom's on Thanksgiving!"

I spin Babs around and then away from me. "Sorry, sweetness. You may be hot stuff, but nobody is hot enough to make me face that."

"I'd break you anyway, little boy," she says with a villainous grin.

"You probably would, you crazy broad." I wrap my arm around her as we walk.

Babs stretches her neck up and kisses me.

"Thanks, sweetie," I say.

"Do you taste Tophat's dick?" she asks with a laugh.

"Oh, gross! Goddammit! Would you quit fucking doing that!"

Babs laughs.

CHAPTER 24
Belated Birthday

Tophat / 1986 – Riverview, Florida

"Let's kill Travis, today."

"Interesting idea. But why?"

"Because he isn't as happy as he should be. He's had a tough road, and it's time that he dies."

"What happens then?"

"We introduce a whole new man into my life."

"And what will his name be?"

"Umm . . . how about . . . 'Tophat' because you smiled when I bought you that badass hat you wear."

"And Tophat will be happier?"

"Yes! He's got a Greek goddess for an ol' lady, brothers who love him, and a brand-new hog!"

"That's a damn good life."

"Seriously though, Tophat, it's time to cut off that shitbag mom and sister of yours and embrace some joy."

"I can't argue that point, Babs. You're right."

"I can't stand being polite to them anymore."

"You split my sister's lip open last Thanksgiving. How's that polite?"

"That makes my point. I can't sit by and watch anyone treat you poorly. It's not what you do when you care about someone. Nobody mistreats my ol' man!"

"I do love you, Babs."

"Then say goodbye to Travis."

"Okay . . . goodbye, Travis."

October 2019

The clickety-clack of her high heels across the pavement only accentuates her long, quasi-tanned legs, overshadowed only by her royal-blue, silk dress tailored snugly on her curvaceous body. Her long, flowing, auburn hair highlighted by enigmatic, green eyes catches the attention of every person as she opens the door to the Harley Dealership in Bradenton.

The manager, Scott, bypasses two of his sales staff to greet the new customer. "Good morning!" he says cheerfully. "How may we help you?"

The woman stops in her tracks and looks at Scott. "Hello," she says graciously. "This may sound silly, but I am trying to find an old friend of mine who rides a Harley. I know he lives in the Bay Area, so I am looking to see if anyone knows him at the local dealerships. He's a hard man to track down."

"Oh, I don't think you sound silly at all. What is your friend's name?" Scott asks.

"His name is Digger Garcia," she replies.

"Digger?" Scott says surprisingly. He then peers over at the beer tap. "He's not by the beer, so I am going to have to say, *nope*!" Scott then laughs.

"At least I know we're talking about the same guy," she says with a smile. "So he's a customer?"

Scott looks at a few of his staff members and balks. "He . . . uh. . . ." Scott fumbles for words.

"I heard he's a Demons Rising as well. Do they come in here a lot? Do you know where I can find any of them?" she asks.

"I'll tell you what," Scott says. "Leave me your card, and I will pass it on to Digger if I see him. How's that?"

The woman smiles, understanding Scott's reasoning. "Sure, fair enough." She rifles through her purse, pulls out a scrap of paper, and begins writing on it. "Please let him know Tina Deveraux stopped by, and that I will be at the Tampa Marriot in Westshore. This is my cell number, and tell him I'll be in town for two more days. And if you would, please let him know that it's important."

Scott takes the paper from Tina. "I sure will, Miss Deveraux." He then smiles and gives her a 'thumbs-up.'

"Thank you," she says as she walks out the front door.

"I bet Digger knocked some tagalong up on one of his road trips," Scott says, laughing.

"Yeah," one of the salesmen says mockingly, "that's the figure of a pregnant woman."

Scott immediately looks through his contacts and hits 'send.'

"What the fuck?" I say, as I look at my phone. "The dealership is calling me." I push the answer button and shake my head in frustration. "Yeah," is all I say.

"Digger? Scott from Manatee River Harley."

"Hey, Scott, we're in Daytona right now, so what's up?"

"You had a long-legged beauty in here looking for you," Scott says. "Her name is Tina Deveraux. She gave me her number and wants you to get a hold of her as soon as you can."

The pronouncement of her name stuns me into silence.

"Digger? You there?" Scott asks.

"Um . . . yeah." I pause again. "Uh . . . why was she looking for me there?"

"She just said she was taking a chance checking the Harley dealers," Scott replies. "So I take it you know her."

"Yep, she's an old friend from Indiana. I haven't seen or heard from her in fifteen years."

"Okay, pal, well, here's her number. . . ."

"Oh, shit, you look like you just saw a ghost," Big T says.

"My old high school girlfriend is in town looking for me."

Big T gets a look of supportive confusion on his face. "When did you see her last?"

I sigh, pause, and contemplate. "It had to be 2004 or so when I came home on leave."

"Nothing since?" Big T asks.

"No." I shake my head. "She got lost in herself and we grew apart. We were childhood sweethearts all the way through high school and a year or so after."

"Any idea what she wants?" he asks.

"I don't know what I would have that she could want."

"Maybe she's wanting ol' Digger's love stick again!" Big T says with a laugh.

"I don't know," I say with a faint smile. "Eighth step maybe?"

Big T shakes his head at me slightly in a look of confusion.

Tophat seems to read the look of consternation on my face and steps toward Big T and me. "You okay?" he asks me.

I explain the situation to him the best that I can and elucidate to both that my curiosity of her visit is rooted in just that—curiosity. Tina and I grew up together in Elkhart, Indiana, and we were together from age fourteen up until we turned twenty. I expound that I have thought about her over the years, that she was the girl I lost my virginity to and danced with at the senior prom, but that I haven't been pining away for her in some sort of quixotic fashion.

"I'm letting Solomon know that I'm riding back now," I say.

"I'm going with you, Bro," Tophat says. "That way, we can keep each other focused."

"I'm going, too," Big T says.

"I guess I can use the company."

"Let's grab our shit and find a ride back for the girls," Tophat says.

"What are you going to tell Venus?" Big T asks.

I laugh and shake my head in mild disgust. "I'll tell her I'm on some secret biker gang mission; she'll be thrilled . . . and aroused."

Big T looks at me, confused once more. "I'll take her or Babs back for you, Bro," he says. "You two go on."

"Are you sure?" I ask.

"Of course," is all Big T says.

"Prospect!" Tophat yells. "I'll have him take Babs back. It'll be good training for him," Tophat says to me.

"What can I do for you, Tophat?" Prospect asks.

"You're taking my ol' lady back to the clubhouse tomorrow. Digger and I have to go now," Tophat replies. "Go get her for me."

Prospect scurries away, does as he is told, and returns with Babs. Babs, sizing up the situation quickly, asks, "All right, what's up? All okay?"

"Yeah," Tophat says. "Digger and I have to go back, so you're riding back with Prospect and Venus is going with Big T."

"I know she's down by the beach, so please let her know for me?" I say to Babs. "I don't have time to explain to her."

"And Babs," Tophat says. He sighs. "Please don't grab Prospect by the balls on the way, and don't lift up your shirt and press your tits on his back, okay? He's still in the crockpot, cooking slowly. No need to scare him off now," I say to Babs while looking at Prospect.

"Fine!" she says brusquely. "But let him know that every time I see a green pickup—"

"Yeah, I know." Tophat sighs perceptibly. "You flash your tits at him."

"As long as we all understand each other," Babs says with a grin.

"Why green pickups?" I ask.

"Who the fuck knows," Tophat says, shrugging his shoulders. "Trying to discover what makes her tick will drive me to a clock tower with a high-powered rifle. She's done that since I've known her."

I let Solomon know, and he just responds with a tacit nod and cursory "ride safe." Prospect packs our bikes, we back the bikes out, fire up the motors, and take off quickly.

Me in the saddle has always proved to be my most inspirational moments where I can think and talk with myself. I think of when I first met Tina during a snowball fight in the neighborhood. I had no idea who she was, but our friendship grew, as did our time together. I run so many scenarios through my mind.

"I'm joining the Marines after graduation, Tina. I think it'll be a great start."

"You know I will always stick by you, Digger. I'll wait for you."

"You were accepted to Notre Dame, Tina. You might outgrow me."

"I've loved you since I was fourteen. I could never just outgrow you."

"I'm paralyzed with fear, Digger. God isn't listening to me. He gave up on me."

"What are you talking about, Tina? You're not making sense."

"I'm not going to Notre Dame. Not yet. Please don't join the Marines."

"I don't know what's going on with you. I don't even recognize you anymore."

"I just have to sit by and watch the wheels roll on by me. I'm just cold."

"I'm taking you to the ER. Something is definitely wrong with you."

"Dammit, Tina! I found your rig again—needle, spoon, the whole thing!"

"You don't understand. I can't function. I can't do anything. Just once more!"

"You're going to die, Tina!"

"Stop it!"

"I can't deal with this, Tina. I can't watch you die. I'm just waiting for the call."

"So you're just going to abandon me? That's loyalty? That's commitment?"

"Those are just words. Words versus this is no match. Words lose!"

I couldn't save her. That monster was too big, too strong, and too fearless to be scared off by me. I can't imagine what she wants. I have a girl now, and I love her very much. I don't like complications. I don't like challenges that don't make sense. Things are happening in some theatrical sense where the script is written, but I am unaware of the final chapter.

We ride straight from Daytona with only one quick gas stop, where I take the opportunity to text Tina and let her know that I will meet her along the Bayshore walkway at noon sharp. I don't wait for a reply because it's part of the script that I still don't know, but I do feel my phone vibrate in my pocket about twenty minutes later.

As our ride progresses and we near the Tampa area, I realize that I am doing something I tend to do: overthink things. My last recollection is that Tina is still back in Indiana, and I am here at one of the ten most popular destinations in the world for vacation. Tina didn't convey a sense of urgency to Scott. Chances are that she is here, soaking up the sun, and decided to look up her old high school boyfriend and say *hello*. I smile to myself as I feel myself relax.

As we approach the exit for US 301, I give a wave to Tophat so he can go on to the clubhouse while I ride into Bayshore and see Tina. I'm actually looking forward to seeing her. I have thought about her and pondered how she was, and whether or not she was all right. I pull off into the parking lot along the Riverwalk and spot her by a bench. The rumble of the motorcycle causes her to turn quickly, and she smiles as soon as she sees me. She runs to me, gives me a full embrace, looks me up and down, and starts crying.

"I can't believe it's you, Digger. I just can't believe it!" she says energetically.

"Ditto," I say gleefully. "You look fantastic." I take both her hands and rub her palms, taking note of a diamond and a wedding band. I tug on it and smile. "Congrats, Tina. I'm glad you found someone."

"Oh, Digger, he is more than just 'someone,'" she says as she sits on the bench. "He led me to the Lord, and I walk hand in hand with Him in life now. I've been clean—really truly clean—since 2011. I couldn't be happier."

"Ditto again, Tina," I say, tapping her knee. "That makes me very happy."

"I went on methadone in 2004 and it helped a little bit, but I kept relapsing, and that stuff is just as hard to kick as heroin." She sighs and wipes away her tears. "But I met Jack one day when he came to speak at a rehab I was in. We talked, and he spoke of Jesus to me so eloquently, it just grew from there."

"That's great, Tina, it really is," I say. "It's the ultimate irony, then, that you're sitting next to a guy wearing a Demons Rising's patch, huh?"

"Yes," she laughs. "We certainly went in opposite directions." She laughs. "I'm sure you're curious why I looked you up."

"Eighth step?" I say, laughing.

"Well," she says, still dabbing her tears, "you may be being facetious, but the truth is, even though I have been sober since 2011, Jack and I discussed the fact that I never went through the whole twelve steps properly. So, in a sense, yes, seeking amends is part of the eighth step for me."

"You know, I said that to one of my brothers, and then I just started overthinking everything." I laugh. "I can't be any happier for you, Tina, and I appreciate you thinking enough of me to make me a part of your recovery."

"This was a no-brainer, Digger," Tina says. "I ran you through your paces. I lied, I bullied you, I completely brought chaos to you, and you were nothing but good to me. I have to make amends with you on everything."

I smile. "So what do you need from me to make it complete? Do I just say all is forgiven and such?"

Tina stops wiping her tears and looks at me somberly. "My dear, sweet man, I wish it was just that easy."

"And why isn't it?" I ask curiously.

"Because part of the process of making amends is coming clean about everything and making restitution, and there are some things I can't make restitution for."

I, again, laugh slightly. "You're overthinking it, Tina. I tend to do that, too. Just say what you got to say. It'll be all right."

She sighs and looks me straight in the eye. She sighs once more and pauses. "I have to be right with you, right with the Lord."

"I'm all ears, kiddo, just spill it," I say with a smile.

"Digger," Tina says solemnly, "you are the father of a fifteen-year-old boy."

CHAPTER 25
Overthinking

Mallet / 2006 – St. Petersburg, Florida

"You're a hell of a fucking scrapper, aren't you?"
"It's the Irish in me."
"We appreciated your help."
"My pleasure. The name's Richie."
"Richie, I'm Hal, Demons Rising, Florida. This is Walt, Willie, Casper, J.J., and Solomon."
"It's a pleasure, gents. Let me buy you boys a shot."
"No, we will buy one for you."
"Thanks."
"Most of the time, citizens respect this patch, but you always have those small few—"
"Yeah, they just gotta test ya."
"You need some ice for that swollen, mallet-like hand of yours, Richie?"
"For this? Nah! I don't even like ice in my whiskey."

October 2019

I'm supposed to say something here, I know I am. I've seen situations like this; I've read about them. I'm expected to express my inner emotions. I don't want the reactions to take point on this verbal deluge, but somebody needs to step up and say something—heart, brain, gut, send a message to the tongue, and hurry. I'm just staring at Tina, and I can see the discomfort in her eyes with my own eyes.

"How?" I ask. I quickly wave my hands at her and shake my head profusely. "You know what I mean, Tina."

"It was one of the last few times we slept together, Digger. We were broken up and all that, but there was always that leftover passion that steered us back to bed. I am sure it was probably the very last time when you were home on leave. Then you were off to Iraq."

"You could have told me when I was away. Why did you keep it from me? Moreover, why did you tell me now?"

Tina gets a great look of dread on her face. "That's when I went on the methadone, Digger. I was all messed up when he was born. I was going to tell you then, but that's when—"

"What?" I ask, missing the obvious.

"Your mom died, and your father . . .," Tina says, fumbling through her words. "I saw no point in bringing you into this. I had a chance to adopt him out to a good Christian family."

"So where is he now?" I ask, still laden with apprehension and confusion.

"He lives in a Chicago suburb. His name is Gregory Charles. I haven't seen him since he was born, but it's an open adoption and his parents have been good about communicating from time to time. They apparently told him about us—"

"Us?" I interject bitterly. "Don't say that like I was included in any of these decisions, Tina."

"No, of course not," she says guiltily. "I'm sorry." She begins crying again. Tina wipes her tears with a tissue and continues. "I just mean, he knows he's adopted, and they were truthful: his father was a war hero, and his mom was a junkie."

"Why are you telling me?" I ask.

"That's an unfair question, Digger," she says, still wiping tears. "I have no right to continue this lie to you. There's nothing you need to do here. I just can't live this lie anymore."

I slowly sit beside her and put my arm around her. "I understand," I say docilely. "I do."

"His parents are willing to allow us to meet him. I'm not sure if I'm going to, but I just wanted you to know that you do have that option."

"I have nothing to offer him, Tina."

"I do have his most recent picture," she says, thumbing through her phone. "They say he is a good boy, Digger—honor roll, team sports, Boy Scouts—all that stuff that helps a boy be a man. Do you want to see a picture of him?"

"No," I say abruptly. "No, I don't."

Tina ceases looking through her phone and perches some semblance of a smile. "I understand, Digger."

"I have nothing to say here, Tina. I don't mean anger prevents it, just . . . I have nothing," I say. I wipe away a few of her remaining tears. "Look, here's my number. Let's just—"

"I'll stay in touch. I'll let this land, and when it does, you let me know if you want or need anything," Tina says.

"Okay." I stand back up. "Tina, I . . . I am happy you're all better."

"Thank you," she says as she kisses my cheek. "One day at a time."

She pulls away and looks at me with distant eyes, seeing memories of what was and what she thought would be. She turns away, takes two steps, and stops. "Digger?" she says, still facing away from me.

"Yeah?"

"Do you have someone who makes you happy?"

I intuitively smile somewhat. "Yeah, I do."

I see her nod her head. "I'm glad." She wipes her tears again. "Digger?"

"Yeah?"

"A girl never forgets the first man she ever loved."

And with that, she was gone, leaving me to my thoughts and overriding internal energy that zaps my strength. I once more assess what I am supposed to think and feel right now, but my only thought is to get on my bike and go. My thoughts can get lost in that for a while.

I give Mallet a call to see if he wants to go with me. As a nomad, he is under no obligation to attend Biketober, so he stays back in Tampa before he rides out to our chapter in Kansas this week.

"What!" is all he screams in the phone when I call.

"Whoa!" I say. "It's me. What the hell is wrong?"

"What's wrong?" he says with growing hostility. "What's wrong? Some fucking redneck drunk just literally ran me over while I was getting my mail. I mean, just like ten minutes ago! I'm getting mail out of the box, Bro, and POW! This fucking asshole just drives right fucking into me, sending my ass over Teakettle in the back of his pickup."

"Holy shit! Are you okay?"

"Aw . . . fuck. My neck is all fucked up, my elbow is bent in all different directions, I think a rib or two are broken, and my coconut is bleeding bad."

"I'll be right there," I say with obvious anxiety.

"Nah, don't worry," he says in a more calming tone. "This chick, Janet that I hook up with is taking me right now."

"I'll meet you there at the ER at least."

"Seriously, Digger, don't worry about it, and don't say anything to anyone. I'll be fine. A few stitches, a neck brace, and a little plaster of Paris around my elbow, and I'll be back in the saddle with sixty Vicodin."

"All right, you're a big boy. But at least call me when you get back from the hospital and tell me how you are."

"You know I will. Thanks, Bro."

I hear a text come through and it's from Venus, saying Big T just dropped her off at my house. I send her one back that only says, *Jack is coming to my place tonight, and he will not be bringing Jill.*

Venus missed my subtle hint that I just want to get drunk alone tonight because she replied, *OK, I'll make these pork chops for us that u have in the fridge. Want applesauce 2, Peter Brady? LOL.* I grab my flask from my bike and take a big swig, then another . . . then another, and then one last gulp. I order my mind to go blank. I put in my earbuds, crank up Lynyrd, and take off for home.

Red lights are an option, stop signs have a question mark at the end, and I create my own lane along the dotted, yellow line all the way home. Yeah, I'm in Demons Rising, motherfucker, and to answer your question, yes! Yes, I can do whatever the hell I want. Do you want to tell me otherwise right about now? Does anyone really want to call me out on that right this second?

I roll into my driveway, check my phone quickly to see if Mallet called, and then I march into my house. Looking ever so out of place in domesticity, Venus is brushing some sort of sauce on the pork chops. She smiles and kisses me. She licks her lips a few times and says, "I see you already found Jack." She then moves a few canisters and pulls out a fresh bottle for me. "Here ya go," she says, taking the top off for me. "A big gulp for Big Daddy!" I freeze up, motionless, and look at her. It only takes me a few seconds to realize her descriptive of me was mere coincidence, but not before she notices.

"You okay?" she asks.

I take one swig, then two, then three, four . . . five. I bring the bottle down to my side and wipe my mouth. I kiss her. She kisses me back and pulls me into the bedroom. "This way, Jack," she says. "Jill is going to show you something special on that hill, and it ain't a pail of fucking water."

The phone's ring wakes me. I look up through sandy-covered eyes reflecting off the sun's glow. Venus lies next to me, arm draped over my chest and snoring lightly. I fumble for the phone and answer.

"Yeah," I say with a scratchy voice as I wipe my eyes.

"Hey," Mallet says softly.

I sit up and wipe my eyes again. "Hey, still in one piece?"

"Yeah, that," he says with a yawn. "Janet is taking me to the ER now."

"Now? I thought you went already."

Mallet yawns once more. "No, she's taking me now."

"Mallet!" I say boisterously. "We talked last night around six or so. You were on your way then. What happened?"

"Oh!" Mallet says, recollecting the conversation with me. "Yeah, that . . . um . . . as soon as we hung up, Janet's neighbor Monty came over and had a bottle of Jim Beam and was getting a bonfire going, so I went over there."

"You what? I thought you were all banged up."

"Yeah, I just slapped some gauze on the head, duct taped it on there, and just didn't overexert the other stuff."

I burst into a very spirited laughter to the point that I wipe tears from my eyes.

Mallet, unaware of the humor, says quizzically, "What?"

"You don't see the humor here?" I say disbelievingly.

Mallet chuckles but still seems unaware of the root of my laughter. "No."

"Let me review the facts," I say, still laughing. "You are, literally, run over by a fucking truck, your neck may be broken, your head is gushing blood, your elbow is looking like a circus act, and all it took was some whiskey and a bonfire to make you forget?"

Mallet then starts laughing. "Don't forget the duct tape, Bro!" His laughter begins to grow.

"Oh my God," I say. "That is the funniest fucking thing I have ever heard." I laugh so hard I drop the phone. Venus looks at me inquiringly, wanting to be part of the laughter. "You are one tough piece of iron, Mallet. Damn, I needed that laugh. Thanks a lot."

"Glad my near-death experience could help, Digger," he says with a snort. "I better get to the hospital, I guess."

"Let me know how you make out there, provided you don't pass a liquor store on the way, that is."

Mallet laughs. "We are demons!" He laughs again.

"And we are rising!" I reply. I lie back down, tuck my arms under my head, and smile. "Talk about not overthinking things," I say aloud to myself. "That's how it's done, I guess."

CHAPTER 26
Winners Write History Books

Solomon / 1980 – Tampa, Florida

"Solomon."

"Who?"

"Solomon. Don't you know your Bible stories?"

"I'm from the South in the 1950s, just like you. We went to Sunday school together, remember?"

"Then you know who I am talking about?"

"What about him?"

"That's a perfect nickname for you, Tommy."

"Well, my mom did play mind games with men, but I'm not rich or Jewish."

"But you're the oldest and the wisest, with a tinge of brutality. It's a perfect name for you."

"I'm not the oldest, Hal is. He's nearly forty; I am only thirty."

"But he's not a charter member. He's not president. That's you. Our wise, old man. The king."

"And what nickname do we give you, Joe?"

"Well . . . I'll be thirty in a few months. I can then be 'Old Joe.'"

"Thirty! What the fuck? Did you ever think it would happen, Joe?"

"I know. Where did the time go, old friend?"

October 2019

I share the humorous anecdote about Mallet with Venus. She appreciates the irony, but throughout my story, she appears to be anticipatory on sharing something with me.

"When you left Daytona yesterday, I heard some news," she says excitedly. "Breeding Warriors had their Jacksonville chapter shut down by Kindred Brotherhood, a support club for Rebellious Youth."

"Yeah, I know," I say flatly.

"How could you?" Venus asks sullenly. "It was all the buzz seconds after you left."

I emit a perfunctory laugh. "I knew about that last week, Venus."

"No, I heard it started from a fight at Daytona and it grew from there."

"That's not correct, Venus. It's been in the works for over a week."

Venus looks at me blankly and says nothing at first. "But do you know why?" she asks.

"Yes, they had a former Pensacola cop in their club."

Venus stares a bit, sits down, and stirs her coffee.

"Are you upset about something?" I query.

She sighs. "No, Digger, not really. It's just that you always have to flaunt it in my face how connected you are and how *un*connected I am."

"What are you talking about?" I ask with sincere confusion.

"Never mind," she says, waving her hand at me.

"Just for the record, you're making absolutely no sense."

She turns and glares at me indignantly. "You couldn't just admit that I knew something you didn't, could you?"

"What is this, a contest? I thought we were on the same side."

Venus rolls her eyes and shakes her head. "Yep, whatever," she says, waving her hand at me again.

"What the fuck is wrong with you?" I ask in frustration.

"Everything, I guess, according to you."

"According to me?" I say dubiously as I point to myself. "When did I say that?"

"I'm just going to go," she says while grabbing her things.

I know I'm angry, I do, but the energy from that anger that makes me explode from this nonsense is swimming upstream against the absolute mystification and bewilderment that I am experiencing. I hold my tongue because I simply do not believe she is going to leave. Logic dictates that her anger be rooted in reality, but as she grabs more and more of her things, that seems less likely.

"I'll just see you later at the clubhouse, I guess," she says, slamming the door.

I march over to the door, open it back up, and shout, "No . . . no you will not! I don't need this shit right now."

Venus stops and pirouettes. "So it's all about you?"

"How dare you?" I scream. "Everything I fucking do I do with you in mind, and you have the balls to say I am only thinking of myself?"

Venus appears as if she is going to say something. I see her flinch once or twice, but she just turns, gets in her car, and disappears. She leaves me here in utter disbelief, replaying everything that was said, trying to see how she had the reaction that she displayed. I know I've had enough today. Times like this call for my brain to disengage from the angst and saddle up, ride, and think. I'm going to the only place on this earth where life makes sense, where I make sense, where I fit in, where I am accepted.

I roll in and see Prospect near the front door, looking out at the unidentified motorcycle.

"Hi, Digger," he says with zeal as he recognizes me.

Identified! I think to myself. "Hi, Prospect."

"Shot of Jack and a beer?" he asks.

"In that order, yes."

"You got it," he retorts. "Fire is just starting. You gonna just stay out here?"

I look and see Solomon alone, stoking the fire with a big stick. "Yeah, thanks," I say.

"Oh, and Prospect?" I say again. He stops, turns, and looks at me. "If Venus stops by, don't let her in unless she is stoned or drunk. I don't want her driving out of here like that. But if she is sober, send her down the road."

"Roger that!" Prospect scampers back into the clubhouse.

I meander my way to the fire and can tell Solomon sees me in his peripheral vision.

"Digger," he says, without looking at me.

"Hi, Solomon," I reply. I pull a rock closer to the fire and haul out my flask. I take a good, vigorous swig. I hand it to him, and he accepts. He tips the bottom up and finishes off the remaining.

"Where's Venus?" he asks.

"She's . . . uh . . . being a bitch tonight, so I left. I told Prospect to send her away if she shows up."

Solomon's countenance shows a look of unstated surprise. "Oh, okay," he says as he rolls a joint. He lights it, takes several hits off it, and hands it to me. I nod in unspoken thanks and take it. "I also heard your old high school flame was in town, searching for you. What did she want?"

I take two more hits of the joint and exhale demonstrably. "Well," I say, smiling, looking at the joint ironically. "She's in recovery, working the steps, and wanted to cover step eight with me and make amends."

"Oh," he says unenthusiastically. "So another chick you were nice to and who shit all over you, huh?"

I resituate myself on the rock and clear my throat. "Not exactly, no."

"It sure seems that way. The nicer you are to this chick you're with now, the worse she treats you," Solomon says.

I hand Solomon a nickel from my pocket. "Is this still the cost, Lucy?"

Solomon laughs. "It's only three cents since I already gave you two."

I just nod my head, looking at the fire.

"Sounds like you need a night of peace and quiet," Solomon says.

"Yep, I do." I poke at the fire. A pause takes hold, and I look at Solomon out of the corner of my eye. I smile a bit and then peek back at the fire. "Solomon," I say contemplatively, "tell me about the other three charter members."

Solomon sits still a bit, looks up at me, and says nothing at first. "Those were some crazy days, Digger. It was the '70s, and this country was still in dismay from the '60s. What is it you want to know?"

"I know you, I knew Old Joe, but I only know Hillbilly Mike, Klaus, and Picker from stories and such."

Solomon yawns, stretches, and, in true Solomon fashion, pauses before speaking. "On the very first day Jimmy Carter was inaugurated in 1977, he pardoned every single man who dodged the draft and allowed them all to return to Canada. They came over in droves and have been hiding out there for years."

I wait to see if Solomon follows up, but he does not. "Yeah, well, Carter was voted out the year I was born."

"Are you doing a term paper on Demons Rising's origin, Digger?" Solomon asks sarcastically.

I just smile and shake my head.

"Well," Solomon says as he stretches. "Me and Old Joe have been riding all our lives and met lots of people in '72. Back in those days, if you rode with more than two people at a time, you were considered a club and you damn well better back it up. Hence, we knew we had to get a club off the ground quick before some of the other one-percent clubs swooped in and knocked us down. There was Klaus, and old Air Force vet from the war. Then there was Hillbilly Mike. He said he just got back from the Army, which is why his hair was so damn short. We were hoping the fifth guy would be a Coast Guard brat so we could have all five branches covered, but no such luck," Solomon says with a laugh. "But we did find Picker, and he was a good fit." Solomon takes out his flask and takes a drink. "I'm the last of the charters since Old Joe died in 2014."

"Yeah, I know." I reach for the flask. "Picker died of diabetes, if I'm not mistaken, Klaus of a heart attack, and Hillbilly Mike fell off the roof, right?"

"Yep," Solomon says. "I couldn't have started this club without all of them in some way, even Mike."

"Why 'even Mike'?" I inquire.

Solomon sighs a bit. "You're real curious about all this, aren't you?"

"Of course," I reply with a smirk.

Solomon laughs. "Well then, since you're not a cat, I'll share something with you." Solomon takes another drink and wipes his mouth. "As it turned out, we discovered Hillbilly Mike was never in the Army. He was actually in Canada from 1966 to 1971."

"Holy shit!" I pause and shake my head. "I never knew that. That's unreal. That had to upset you all a lot."

"Yeah, it sure did, Digger. It sure did."

"So how did he slip off the roof?"

Solomon stays silent and then laughs a bit. "You don't listen too well, Digger, do you?"

"Meaning?"

"I just got through telling you that the draft dodgers were in Canada until 1977."

At first, no bells go off, but just like one who catches a subtle joke or a passive insult, I understood. For some reason, though, I asked the obvious question anyhow. "How did he get back in the country in 1972 then?"

Solomon chuckles slightly. "Now there's the $64,000 question, Digger." Solomon laughs again. "There were ways to do so back then, but none of them meant good news for us."

Unsure what to say, I just sit, poke at the fire, and take a sip or two of bourbon.

"Do you really think I believed you were doing some sort of club history search?" Solomon asks rhetorically. "I knew you were asking about Mike, so that's why I told you about Jimmy Carter's pardon before this conversation even started. You seem to forget that I'm not stupid. My instincts are what kept me alive all these years."

"I know you're not stupid."

"Really?" Solomon says sardonically, "because you skirted around the real question you wanted to ask, which was how did Hillbilly Mike die that day. Just ask, Digger. You may not always get the answer you want—or an answer at all—but be a fucking man and just ask."

Unsure again of what to say, I sit stoically for a moment. Solomon says nothing, either; he just sits, smokes, and drinks.

"Why is his patch on our wall if he died while not in good standing, then? It makes us look like we built our empire on a lie."

"Fair question," Solomon replies, "but also the last one I am answering about this, got it?" I nod my head slightly. "The last thing we needed was an investigation into an accidental falling death of a man who was just stripped of his patch. Not to mention, 1982 was a whole different time in our world. Biker wars flourished, everybody was cutthroat, and to have it appear that we had, shall we say, an enigmatic creature in our midst whose character was in question active in our club would look bad." Solomon looks at me to see if I fully understand. "And as for the second part of your question, you tell me one—just one—empire in all of history that wasn't propped up on some lies."

I see no point in quizzing Solomon anymore, both because I know he will not answer, and perhaps he is right, in a way, that what occurred nearly forty years ago means little now.

"I don't know what created this interest in Hillbilly Mike, Digger, nor do I care really, but he fell off the roof fixing the TV antenna and died, got it?"

"Yep," I retort quickly.

"Only due to grace and my respect for you, Digger, did I even give you this much info." Solomon saying that he has respect for me pleases me. I still seem to seek his approval.

"The truth is, anything that happened before you got your patch is, in all reality, not your business. Things that occurred when you weren't a member you need not be privy to, unless modern day situations make that necessary. For instance, if we vote in our prospect"—Solomon pauses and looks confused—"what is his name, anyway?"

"'Mud' if he doesn't get here with my bourbon and beer soon," I say, looking at the clubhouse. "But for now, he goes by the handle *Scooby*."

Solomon grows a look of disbelief on his face. "You are kidding, right?"

"No, why?"

"I don't know," Solomon says, sighing. "A grown man infatuated with a cartoon character is just weird."

"That's nothing," I say with a laugh. "Once, on a trip to Alexandria Bay in Upstate New York, we stopped at this place called the Dinosaur Barbecue in Rochester, and there was this guy who painted his Harley like Fred Flintstone. True story! The gas tank had the blue tie and everything. His license plate even said *Bedrock*."

"What the fuck?" Solomon says, shaking his head. "There's a guy with more than a few screws loose."

I laugh, pleased that our tension from the incident with Walt has waned.

"Anyway," Solomon says, resituating himself a bit. "If *Scooby* . . . do get his patch. . . ." Solomon pauses, throws his arms out, and places an exaggerated smile like some vaudevillian comic.

I just reply with, "Bada bing!"

"But if he does, he need not be privy to your trip to West Virginia. Unless it becomes a current matter or problem, he does not have to be filled in on that. Do you understand what I mean?"

I nod slightly.

Solomon appears to read my reaction and looks at me crossly. "You haven't mentioned West Virginia. Are you okay with what went down?"

I sigh heavily, thinking about that day, replaying the events in detail in my head, the regrets of what I didn't say, and what I saw. "I mean . . . yeah, I'm okay."

"What did I say no less than five minutes ago, Digger?" Solomon asks. "Just spill it."

I take a swig of the bourbon and stare into the fire, watching the occasional pop and absorbing the energy it gives off. I may be just flush with Tina's news, Venus's tantrum, and this conversation that Solomon and I just had where he called me out a bit, because that leads me to overthink things at times. "Do you think, sometimes, it is an advantage not to have a conscience? You know, evil is easier than having a conscience."

"That's not accurate, Digger," Solomon says. "True evil people have a conscience."

I snap my head at Solomon quickly from the curiosity of his statement. "That makes no sense."

Solomon resituates himself on the ground. He stretches his leg and rubs his thumbs in his sore knees. He looks up at me, emotionless, spiritless, and does so with a placid expression. "People with no conscience, Digger, can take a life, watch the person die, and still lay his or her," he says with a pause and what I thought would be a snicker, but none came forth, "head on a pillow at night and sleep. Do we agree?"

I sigh. "Yeah, that's my whole point."

"But are they evil?"

"Yes," I say quickly, forgetting Solomon's preference to dance around his point to accentuate it more when it is revealed.

"But think about it, Digger. What does that person have to fear? What dilemma does he face? To raise your hand, pull a trigger, watch as the target clutches their body and falls to the ground, a sociopath feels nothing, so the ease by which he does it is nil."

I continue to look at Solomon. Like a game of chess near a poolside gazebo, I study him, I read his expression, anticipating, examining, scrutinizing, and believing I can hold back the inevitable checkmate.

"A man with a conscience, Digger, a man who sees another man as he sees himself— someone's son, someone's father—a man who can see that in another man, by definition, has a conscience. And to then take that gun, raise it up, pull that trigger, well, Digger, that is evil. A man who takes what he knows and can override those innate instincts and still pull that trigger . . . that, my brother, is evil. When you can set aside your conscience and have the ability to ignore your decency and proceed with murder, that is the essence of evil. I am sorry, Digger, but you and me, we are evil. Our souls are too late to save. That is why we wear this patch," he says, tugging at his cut, "because we are all that we have in this world. The next world won't be kind to us."

"I don't like that," I say. "Why should I feel guilty? He took my brother in the most cowardly and sick way. He deserved to forfeit his life."

"Nobody says otherwise, Digger. But there's a difference—a huge difference—between supporting a decision and being the one to carry it out."

I look at Solomon and sigh, then gaze up at the night sky. "Sometimes I just don't make sense; I don't mean my words, I just mean me."

"Stop searching for answers," Solomon interjects. "In this world, there are angels and monsters, and it's damn near impossible to be an angel." Solomon sits up a bit and glares at me. "The world, Digger, will remember all your bad and forget any of your good."

I glimpse at Solomon blankly and nod my head slightly. "We are demons," I say softly.

Solomon smiles. "And we are rising."

CHAPTER 27
What Happens In Vegas

Crispy / 2018 – Balm, Florida

"What was the vote count?"

"That doesn't matter. Digger won. Whether it was sixteen to one, or nine to eight, it doesn't matter."

"Yeah, actually it does. I've been in this club for well over ten years; he's been here about five."

"And that means nothing."

"It used to!"

"No, it never did. It's an election, not a union job bid."

"I need to get out of here for a while. I need to go roll craps in Vegas or something."

"Yeah? That sounds like another word for tantrum."

"Bullshit, Solomon, it's just me wanting to clear my head a bit."

"Then go."

"I am."

"But Crispy?"

"What?"

"Go be a man and congratulate our new sergeant-at-arms before you run off. He's still your brother."

October 2019

I hear a knock. Assuming it's Venus, I bounce out of bed and go to the door. I see Mallet through the window. I'm disappointed somewhat, but always pleased to see my brother. I open the door and give him a hug. "Hey, Brother," I say. "Come on in."

Mallet comes in and goes to the kitchen. "Got coffee?"

"I'll make some," I say, scooping the bottom of the can.

"Digger, the West Virginia State Police called me. They wanted to talk about Torch."

I sit, stunned, with the scoop still in my hand and say nothing. I catch myself and continue what I am doing. "Okay," I say calmly, as I scoop out coffee. "What did they say?"

"They didn't get to say much," Mallet says. "I let them talk for about a minute, and then I referred them to our lawyer. I thought at first they were following up on that bullshit gun charge that got dropped, so I listened for a minute. But then it hit me. They were from *West* Virginia, so I knew what they wanted. I take it you haven't heard from them."

I pick up my phone and make certain I didn't miss a call and see none, nor any from Venus. I shake my head as I rub my thumb through the call logs. "Nope, nothing," I say. "Let's not worry; they have nothing. They probably just did some old-fashioned detective work and found out Torch was trying to start up Black Shadow again and such. Let 'em be. Any response on our part would be bad."

"Yep, I know," Mallet replies, "but we have to let the club know."

"Absolutely." No sooner do I speak, my phone rings. The call is from Venus. I try to show indifference to Mallet as I say, "It's only Venus." I hit decline and let it go to voicemail, but no voicemail message seems to come.

"What are you going to do today?" Mallet asks.

A feeling of determination comes over me. Suddenly, I feel invigorated. "Ya know . . . I'm just going to ride. What about you?"

"I'm going to swing by Solomon's place, let him know about all this, then I'm heading back to Virginia, picking up Roy-Boy, and we're going to our Kansas chapter."

"Okay, good." I nod my head a few times. "Give Roy-Boy my best, and tell him he still owes me a bottle . . . and a squirrel's tail." I laugh.

"A squirrel's tail?" Mallet replies.

"Yeah." I laugh again. "He'll know what I mean. It was a stupid bet we had one year in Sturgis." I grip Mallet's hand. "Ride safe."

"Always do," he replies.

"You may as well send Crispy back, too."

"Yeah." Mallet sighs slightly. "Word is he's doing good. He's got a better attitude."

"It's overdue." I chuckle slightly.

I decide to check out for a few days, take my bike to the Keys, and give Castro the finger. I continually check my phone, telling myself I am on the lookout for a call from a West Virginia area code or a call labeled *private*, as many law enforcement phone calls are. But I know I am checking for Venus. Even part of my motivation for running off to the Keys is so I can tell her I went without her when the time arises.

I throw a few things into my saddlebags, grab some cash, and take off south. I then cross over and go inland on US 27 until I hit *Route 1* near Homestead. That way, my tires won't even graze the Interstate. I plan to turn a five-hour ride into a ten-hour ride at least, because my goal is to ride.

I have often wondered, does life ever even out? Does it ever settle down as we are supposed to with each dribble of sand in our own internal life clock? Why don't the rules of life mirror actual life? As we age, we are supposed to be moving slower, be more tempered in our actions, and some of the lumps we take early on are supposed to dissipate. One of the biggest injustices of life is that the lessons we learn from bad experiences happen when we are not at a level of maturity to understand their significance. It's like the fire truck arriving after the house is burned, or the rain falling after the crops die. When we are finally mature enough to appreciate things is when those things are already gone. Time is the great equalizer for certain. Nobody, regardless of wealth, power, looks, influence, or even an intangible like luck, can stop the drumbeat of time from stealing from you every second of every day, whether awake or asleep. He who invents the pause button will be a rich man.

By the time I hit Homestead, I stop to grab some vittles in the form of beer. I check my phone and see that Venus did call but left no voicemail. I am now ten hours into my ride, and still no call from Venus where she leaves a voicemail.

I continue *racing the rain, riding the wind, and chasing the sunset.* I'm overthinking again.

Two more hours pass, and I watch as the last sliver of red drops below the calming waters of the Gulf. The small town here is all abuzz with an eclectic mix of people. I find a watering hole inhabited by those same diverse people. I expect that beer is still the universal rallying cry for all.

As I sit at the bar, looking at the surroundings, I feel a slight brush on my shoulder. I snap my head around and spy an incredibly attractive brunette with curly hair, a leather halter, and sporting a red bandana. Her eyes are brown with small, golden specks in them. Although she presents as a run-of-the-mill biker girl, she appears to ooze opulence in some way, whether it be the professional application of her makeup, her Prada boots, or her dangling, diamond earrings.

"Hey there, Demons Rising!" she says cheerfully. "Small world! And long time no see!"

I fully turn my body to engage her head-on. "Longer for me, sweetness, because I know, for a fact, I would remember you," I say, grinning.

"Actually, I meant I only met one of your brothers from Florida once. We spent a whole week together in the Four Seasons in Vegas last January," she says, still smiling and rubbing my leg. "Is Christopher Paul one of your guys?"

"You met him in Vegas?" I ask without answering her.

"Yes!" she says enthusiastically. "We had a ball up until that day."

"What day?"

"Oh, he must have told you," she says, slapping me on the arm. "I think he blames me because I have tried calling him since, but he doesn't answer. You must know him. Chris was his real name, but he said you all called him *Crispy*."

"Uh-huh," I say in a non-committing fashion. "I am shocked he didn't mention you. If I spent a week with the likes of you, I would be bragging about it all over the country."

"Yeah, but like I said, once the law busted in, the fun was over," she says, laughing.

"Oh, that was you?" I ask, hoping to keep her talking. "Something about you had a warrant out of state. . . ."

She looks at me, baffled, but still smiling. "Is that what he told you?" She chuckles. "He's probably embarrassed. No, he was part of a raid with counterfeit poker chips and laundering them for some guys he met at the casino. Apparently, the feds have been keeping an eye on this operation for a while, and they caught him with his pants down." She begins giggling uncontrollably. "I mean that in both ways!"

"The feds?" I ask, not hiding my shock well.

"Yepper," she says, stepping back. "I'm guessing the *Female Body Inspectors* because they pawed this over and over and over," she says, showing off her body to me demonstrably. "They cut me loose in an hour, but they shipped him off to the Federal Detention Center about an hour away. Is he still there?"

"Uh . . . no, he's in. . . ." I stop and grow very anxious, realizing Crispy is in Virginia and Mallet is about to send him back to Florida. "Look, sweetie, it was great meeting you. What's your name? I will tell him to give you a call."

"Sure thing," she says. "Tell him *Bubbles* says hello and to call me."

"Do you have a last name?" I ask as I walk away.

"How many gals named Bubbles can he possibly know?" She smiles and waves goodbye to me.

I walk quickly and text Mallet just as fast, as I am walking outside: *Don't send Crispy back yet!* As soon as I get outside to call Mallet, the phone rings. It's Mallet.

"Hey! Don't let Crispy go!" I say in a panic.

"Yeah, I just read that," Mallet replies. "Sorry, but he took off about ten minutes ago."

CHAPTER 28
It's Time To Open Your Eyes

Venus / 2011 – Oneco, Florida

"This job you were offered . . . how do you plan on getting to all these places in town?"

"The job comes with a car, Clark."

"A car?"

"Yes."

"And I suppose it comes with a company credit card, too?"

"Well . . . yes. I need it for expenses and such."

"And your own phone, right?"

"Yes."

"Well, Mary Ellen, ain't that fucking special! Who did you fuck to get that job?"

"Nobody! I work hard there."

"Yeah, yeah, yeah! Whatever! There's no scenario by which you will be taking any kind of job that gives you a car, a phone, and a credit card. Not fucking happening! Got it?"

"Clark, this is ridiculous. We can use the money."

"Bullshit! This is an excuse for you to whore around without me being able to check up on you, isn't it? Isn't it?"

"No."

"You tell them 'no,' Mary Ellen! Absolutely not!"

"Okay."

"Now give me your phone, take a shower, and wash that makeup off. I'll be in there in a minute."

"Okay."

October 2019

"The feds," I say to myself softly, "just fucking great." I call Solomon since he wholeheartedly objects to text messages. He answers. "Hey, Digger."

"Hey, Solomon. Has the cable installer been there today, or is that next week?"

Solomon pauses for a second. "Not today. We may just go with the dish."

"Okay, see you soon," I say as I hang up.

Being in a high-profile, one-percent motorcycle club creates a level of caution that often spills over into paranoia. But the fact that the government possesses the vast ability to monitor virtually every communication, by every citizen, does lend one to proceed with vigilance. Demons Rising has a standard template we use when we need to speak over the phone but wish to do so where any monitoring is more unlikely. We have burner phones that we use and keep at the clubhouse. They are activated but never used because once they are used, we toss them in the ocean. I give Solomon time to get to the clubhouse, and if I can manage to find a pay phone in this day and age, I will call him in one hour. With the ever-disappearing pay phones, we will sometimes buy a burner phone off a homeless person. They are usually receptive to the idea and extremely unlikely to report it to the law.

I do manage to find a pay phone within the hour and dump a fistful of change in. The call costs four dollars for every three minutes. The phone only rings once.

"What's going on, Digger?" Solomon answers pensively.

"Long story short, I'm in the Keys—"

"What the fuck you doing there?" Solomon interrupts.

"Uh . . . just riding," I say, somewhat rattled. "This is important, Solomon."

"Okay, go on," he replies.

"Anyway, in a total fortuitous coincidence—"

"Fortuitous?"

"Yeah . . . uh . . . it means accidental or unplanned. You know what I mean."

Solomon sighs heavily. "Then just fucking say 'a chance meeting.'"

"Okay. I really need to get this out, you cra—nky old bastard!"

"Okay, go on," he replies again.

"This chick walks up to me, recognizing the patch from when she met Crispy in Vegas last year. Remember him running off after the election?"

"Yep, yep, I do," Solomon says. "Fucker stole my town!"

"Remember how we busted his balls for being gone so long?" I ask but not wanting an answer. "This chick named Bubbles says she was with him until one night, the feds kicked in their door and took them."

"Holy fuck, you have got to be kidding?" Solomon shrieks. "What charge?"

"Apparently, there has been a counterfeit poker chip/laundering ring going on, and Crispy got caught in the middle."

"Hmmm . . ." Solomon pauses briefly. "That fucking scumbag. This explains why the fuzz from West Virginia called Mallet."

"Yes, it does."

"He"—Solomon pauses—"'he,' as in Crispy, didn't have anything to do with that shit in West Virginia, right?"

"No."

"Is he still in Virginia?" Solomon asks.

I sigh. "No," I say with another sigh. "I missed him by ten minutes."

"Well, we will cook up the fatted calf for his return, eat it, and then beat him with the bones."

I shake my head as if Solomon can see me. "I'm betting this skank calls or texts him and says, 'Guess who I just saw'? No, Crispy is in the wind."

"He's crying to some shitbag F.B.I. prick probably," Solomon says bitterly.

"We just swept the clubhouse. There's no recordings anywhere, but he's still such a loose cannon and unpredictable."

"Yeah . . . well . . . it doesn't mean he can't do some damage," Solomon says.

"Like why Mallet got clipped on that bullshit gun charge," I say. "I asked Crispy what he did to prevent it, and he said something about two rookie sheriffs panicking because they had two Demons Rising guys."

"They wouldn't be wearing their cut doing recon on Torch," Solomon intervenes.

"Exactly my point! So why harass two guys on a Harley unless someone called you beforehand? And why did he tell me the cops knew they were Demons Rising members when he knew they didn't, at least not at first. Plus, he said they got accosted coming out of a minimart, but Mallet said they were pulled over by the cops."

"Fucking sellout pile of shit!" Solomon says angrily. "Bad vibe from that fucker in the past couple of years. The feds could cut my fucking balls off with a rusty razor before I'd tell them what was in my mother's meatloaf recipe!" Solomon continues ranting.

"I'm thankful about one thing, Solomon."

"And that is what?"

"Crispy was in Vegas during that problem with our former prospect."

"Yeah . . . well . . . thank Yahweh for small favors."

"Who?" I ask curiously.

"See?" Solomon says mockingly. "You don't like it, do you! Now get your ass back here, Digger." Solomon then hangs up.

My attempt to free my brain from clutter is now cancelled. I find myself saddling up and heading north, but this time, it must be balls to the wall on the Interstate. I don't like being in a hurry; it just means something is important.

My phone dings once more, and I see it's a text from Venus. I open it and spy a selfie of her nude, lying on my bed. The caption reads *cum over and then cum in.* Maybe she's done being angry, but I'm not sure I am. And her using her sexual prowess is clearly a manipulation. Ever wonder why *man* is the first three letters in that word? "Dear God!" I say, shaking my head, "I'm starting to sound like Solomon."

I sigh and contemplate my response. I must craft it in a way where I seem indifferent, because that doesn't come naturally to me. Indifference is a hollow and cold trait. I am passionate about what toppings are on my pizza, on the ever-arguable topic of *Ginger or Maryann.* Indifference is not a genetic marker in me. I decide to use the fact that I am in the Keys to my advantage. I move my fingers with great alacrity and spell out, *I see you made yourself cum-4-table. But after your unceremonious egress yesterday, I jumped on the bike and took off to the Keys. But I'm heading back now. Be back in about six hours.*

I grow a self-satisfying smile. I managed to be sexual, indifferent, and passive-aggressive, all the while making her regret not being in the Keys with me. I am, without a doubt, learning from Solomon. I fill up—both the gas tank and myself—and then release the clutch and go.

It nears midnight when I roll into my driveway. Venus's car is still here, but I am confident she is on her thirty-seventh wink at this point, lightly snoring with a dab of drool on her cheek. I unlock my door, deactivate the alarm, and slide off my boots. I hear the TV in my bedroom, but I hear nothing from Venus. I peer inside and, as predicted, drool and all, she is sleeping.

As I strip my clothes off, she starts to wake. Her eyes flicker as they acclimate to the light from the TV. "Hey," is all she says with a scratchy voice.

"'Hey' to you, too," I reply. "I'm just going to shower and come to bed. Go to sleep."

"No, I'll wait for you," she replies as she lifts her head off the pillow.

I quickly shower, brush my teeth, and then, for some inexplicable reason, take about ten gulps of milk. I walk back into the bedroom, and

Venus is asleep once again. However, my climbing into bed prompts her to wake once more. She rolls over and drapes her arm over me. "The Keys, huh?" she says quietly.

"Yep."

"You saw my pic. See what you missed?" she says.

I look over at her. "Had a great ride. See what you missed?"

"Yeah," she yawns. "Next time for sure."

"I see you called."

"Yeah." She readjusts her head on my chest.

"What did you want?" I ask. "You didn't leave a voicemail."

"Yeah." She yawns again. "I know. Sorry."

"About what?"

"Not leaving a voicemail." Venus pauses. "I just wanted to talk."

"About what?" I query again.

"I don't know," she replies. "Just to say 'hi.'"

"Uh-huh. And you didn't want to say 'hi' yesterday after you left here?"

Venus resituates herself slightly and breathes heavily, as if she is exhausted. "Yeah, I know."

"You know what?"

"That I didn't say *hi* after I left yesterday," Venus says with eyes closed.

"Okay," I say curtly, "it's time for nice, sweet ol' Digger to be more direct." I sit up more, leaning my back against the pillow. "Let's not ignore the elephant in the room. What was wrong with you yesterday?"

Venus rolls over a bit more. "Do you want an apology or something?" she asks with a sigh. "I was having a bad day."

"I don't necessarily want an apology, although I deserve one. I just want to know what was wrong with you."

"Just a shitty day, I guess," she says, still not opening her eyes. "Can we drop it, please?"

"After you answer one more question."

Venus nods her head slightly.

"Why is it you take crap from people who treat you like crap, but poke at those who treat you well?"

"No, I don't," Venus answers.

"Yeah, yeah you do, Venus. You do it all the time."

"I don't mean to if I do," she says passively.

"Look, Venus," I say, looking straight on, even with her eyes still closed. "Don't do that to me. If you're upset about something, then you can either talk to me about it, sit quietly and I'll give you secondary support, or you can leave. But there's no choice that includes unloading on me because you feel it's safe to do so."

She stretches her neck upward and kisses me. "Okay," she says softly. "I don't want you to think that, really. That's not my intention."

I bend my head down and kiss her lips softly. "I'm going to just let it go tonight. I see you're tired." I lay my head on the pillow and reach for the TV remote. "I don't want to live my life without you, Venus, but I will if I have to. Do not devalue what I have to offer you by taking it for granted, because it's not."

She nods her head slightly, then grabs my hand and kisses my fingers.

"There's a difference between not being able to survive without something in your life versus not wanting to live without it, got it?" I ask rhetorically.

She nods and smiles again. I bend down, kiss her cheek, and then whisper in her ear, "It's not like you're my phone charger or something."

She smiles slightly and nods her head. "I understand," she says softly, never opening her eyes.

CHAPTER 29
Betrayal

Walt and Willie / 2007 – Casper, Wyoming

"I thought it was just going to be you and me riding around the country."

"And we have done lots of that, Willie. We have experienced what so many others only dream about or pretend to have done."

"But I love doing this, Walt. Just two brothers riding the wind throughout the land. I mean, here we are in Wyoming, for no other reason than just because. I love travelling the country."

"Yeah, but we have a chance to obtain more brothers and learn about what a real family is supposed to be and share our love of riding with them."

"I know, but these guys are hardcore. I've seen them on TV."

"So? We are not sissies of any kind, Willie. We can hang with these guys like the best of them."

"It would be nice to have a family . . . I mean . . . not that you're not. You know what I mean."

"I do. And you and I, Willie, will always be brothers and look out for each other."

"You've always looked out for me, Walt. I trust you on this."

"It's not a cult. We can walk away at any time if we don't fit in."

"I know."

"You know I always said I'd take care of you, and I am now. I wouldn't say this was good for you if I didn't really believe it."

"Okay, Walt. Let's go back to Florida."

"Instead of just me looking out for you, you will have more brothers looking out for you."

"I want that, Walt, but I'll need your help."

"Little brother, I will always watch out for you. I promise."

October 2019

"We are demons!" Solomon screams.

"And we are rising!" we all bellow in unison.

"Quorum?" I ask.

"I count fifteen members," says Zonk.

"Our club secretary says fifteen. We have a quorum, agreed?" Tophat asks.

In unison, we all yell "agreed."

"I make a motion that we wave the treasurer's report tonight. We have business to discuss of the utmost importance," Solomon says.

"Second," I say.

"All in favor?" Tophat yells.

"Aye!" we shout in unison.

"Digger?" Solomon says, as he waves his arm to the crowd. "Fill 'em in on the details."

I stand up and look every brother in the eye at least once as I speak. "All of you know about Crispy. And as you all are aware, he's in the wind, most likely in the hands of the feds, somewhere in hiding. I am damn near positive that the chick I ran into at the Keys gave him a heads-up. She admitted she had been trying to get ahold of him since their troubles in Vegas, and he had not been responsive. I guarantee she used this opportunity to call or text him to say she saw me. Crispy may be one big pile of worthless, rat-bastard shit, but he's not stupid. He would know the jig is up at that point."

"Digger?" Big T says. "Do we know the damage he has done?"

"We are certain he is the one who called the cops on Mallet in Virginia and also put the West Virginia cops on the trail of Mallet over Torch. Ever since our . . . *problem* . . . with our first prospect, we have had this place professionally swept for bugs weekly and found none. Crispy knew we were doing so, which is probably the only reason he didn't plant any for the feds. We are fortunate that he was in Vegas that night with the past prospect, and he was not involved in the meeting with Benjamin Austin—nor did he ever ask for an update—so he is not privy to either pieces of that information."

"Will it help to track down this chick you ran into? What was her name?" J.J. asks.

"That's an issue," I say regrettably. "She went by the handle *Bubbles*, and when I asked for her last name, she just made a joke about it. Rather than push her and tip her off, I walked away, desperate to contact Mallet to have him hold Crispy there in Virginia. And as Maxwell Smart used to declare, 'missed it by that much,'" I say, with thumb and forefinger nearly touching. "He left ten minutes prior."

"I feel . . . helpless is all I can think of," Zonk says.

"We essentially are, Zonk," I say pessimistically. "This isn't a movie where we run across him in Sturgis or Laconia someday. He's gone in a way that would make Houdini jealous."

Although everyone is aware of what Crispy did, the outrage is quieted as it battles with disappointment, confusion, and fear—the fear being born of the outright betrayal of a man we once called *brother*.

"That brings me to another point," I say lamentably. "I think all of us, me included, took note of Crispy in the past year as being isolated, combative, thinking only of himself, etcetera. When we see behavior like this in a brother, we need to check on him. He could be disconnecting for a host of reasons. When a brother is like that, he is ripe and susceptible to falling apart. We must approach him and remind him he is still family, and family sticks together until one member sticks it to the others." I pause my words, looking around, trying to judge the words and the delivery in everyone's reactions. Heads nod, and I see disappointment and hate in all of them for Crispy.

"On another topic," Solomon chimes in, breaking the tension, "a more upbeat topic, Demons Rising has always had a twelve-month minimum prospect time before we vote, but I'm suggesting we wave that for our newest prospect. He's been here since February. October is swirling the bowl now, meaning he's had a solid eight months and has shown himself to be keen, shrewd, loyal, and attentive. What do you all think?"

"Are you making a motion?" Zonk asks.

"Yes," Solomon responds.

"Then I second it," Zonk says.

"All in favor?" Tophat queries.

"Aye!" we yell in unison.

"Bring him in and see if he answers the questions right," Solomon says.

I open the meeting room door and yell, "Prospect! You're wanted in here right now." Prospect dutifully enters and looks around the room.

"I'll cut to the chase, Prospect. We don't want you as a prospect anymore. Give us your stuff," I say.

Prospect looks stunned as he considers at the stoicism in our faces. He puts his hand up, as if he is about to speak, and then stops. He scans the room once more and says sharply, "No! If you want my bottom rocker off me, you'll all have to take it."

"Oh, really?" Solomon says, standing and facing him.

"Yes," he replies respectfully.

Solomon begins laughing loudly, followed by the rest of us. "I guess you don't want your center patch and top rocker then?"

Prospect nearly collapses in relief that morphs into laughter. "Are you serious?"

"Yeah, we are serious," Solomon says. "You've done a good job; we've been watching and paying attention. You just have two questions to answer and that's it."

Prospect, still beaming with excitement, says, "give 'em to me."

"Club motto?" Hal asks.

Prospect stands perfectly still, as if he is reciting the Boy Scout oath. He clears his throat. "Stand tall, ride free, never look back," he says boldly.

Hal nods his head.

"That was the easy one," Solomon says. "Riddle me this, Prospect: why do we always say 'We are demons' followed by 'and we are rising'?"

"Well . . .," Prospect pauses, unsure exactly what to say. "I mean, it seems obvious." He pauses once more. None of us speak. "Y'all are demons and you are rising."

Solomon's stoic look begins to give way to a smile. "'*You all*' is the right answer," Solomon says as he hugs him. "You may now say 'we all'!"

We all cheer loudly and share laughter and hugs as Tophat presents our newest brother, Scooby, with his top rocker and center patch.

"Wanda will be here later to sew it on for you," Preacher says.

"Truth is, Scooby," Solomon says, "for years, we had all sorts of hazing and shit when we welcomed a new brother. But times are changing, and we are either just more solemn or just old. But the band will be here in less than an hour, as will the food and the strippers. We are going all out for you, Brother," Solomon says.

"I will honor this always," Scooby says, holding up his new patch.

"Go have a seat on the other side of the bar, Scooby," I say.

"But not my stool!" Solomon says forcefully. "I'm still the fucking president here."

"You got it, Boss," Scooby says.

The whiskey flows, the music grows, and the thought of Crispy is gone for the night. Venus huddles with the other girls, trying to shoot darts as they make double-entendre jokes about the darts' poking ability. Scooby's glass never seems to empty, and two of the strippers continually goad him to the bedroom. "Wanna snack, Scooby?" one says with a giggle. "A special Scooby snack, perhaps? I'll dress up like Daphne if you do me *doggy*-style, Rooby Rooby Roo!" They both chortle. "Get it?" she asks. "Because Scooby was a dog," she says, with a genuine look of curiosity on her face.

"Um . . . yeah . . . I get it," Scooby says loudly. "I'm all yours, I swear it. But let me hang with my brothers for a little while longer."

Laughs and echoes of congrats fill the room all night. Venus occasionally comes by me to relay some mundane gossip and to give me a kiss.

Preacher sits to the left of Scooby, so I grab the stool on the other side of him. Walt is taking a shift behind the bar, and I give him the sign to give me some shots. Walt, Scooby, Preacher, and I lift our glasses. "To brothers!" I say.

"Both fallen and standing," Walt adds.

Walt's comment touches me, and I don't know what to say other than "absolutely," and I say it with verve.

Scooby slams his shot glass down and shakes his head like a wet dog. "Damn!" he says. "Good stuff!" Scooby grabs Walt's hand and grips it tightly. "Only one thing could have made this patch more special tonight, and that is if I had the honor of calling Willie brother like you all did."

"Yeah," Walt says passively. "He was a great kid. I miss him a lot."

"We all do," I say. We pause a bit as the mawkish atmosphere takes hold. I spin my finger about the room, signaling for one more round. Scooby grabs his glass and turns around in his stool. "To Willie and to Pancake Dave!" he shouts.

Everyone screams "Huzzah!" but for some unknown reason, Venus shouts "Here! Here!" She is clearly mortified and walks toward me quickly. "Oh, shit, I'm sorry," she says to Walt. "I feel like an asshole."

"Why?" I ask.

"I yelled '*here here*.'"

Walt just shakes his head as if all is good. "No biggie," he says.

"Yeah," I reply. "It means the same thing."

"I look like a fucking moron now," she continues.

"No," I say with a grin. "You look like a hot redhead with nice jugs." We laugh.

Venus smiles somewhat but is still tense.

"Relax," I say. "Nobody but you noticed."

She nods her head reflexively, walks toward the pool table, and pushes a few balls into the corner as she sips her drink. I refocus my attention on my brothers.

"I got to ask," I say to Scooby as I set my glass down on the bar. "Who gave you that nickname?"

"My adoptive father," Scooby says. "Oh, I don't mean to call him that. He was, for all intents and purposes, my father. I was in a foster home until I was about six and the Camerons adopted me."

"Oh, I didn't know that about you," I say.

"Yeah, Mom was a pillhead and in and out of rehabs, and my dad was in prison up until I was twelve. I saw my mom when I was about eleven and met my dad shortly afterward. The Camerons are good people and kept my bio mom in the loop, and my bio dad asked if he could meet me when he got out of prison." Scooby asks Walt for a beer and another shot. The band entrance into the main gate alerts us all to the monitor.

"Your party is beginning," I say to Scooby.

Scooby gives me a routine thumbs-up.

"How was it meeting your dad after all that time?" I ask. "You know . . . I mean . . . it sounds like your family was stable at that point, so did the introduction of your biological parents disrupt you?"

Scooby holds his beer mug still and appears to ponder my question. "No," he says. "My bio dad was all right. He had good boundaries and such. He came to my Little League games, my scout meetings, and all that, but he didn't interfere with how the Camerons raised me. He would sit in the bleachers with my parents, and they'd actually talk in a friendly way." Scooby grows a peculiar look on his face, distant but pleasing. "This will sound weird, but I liked having two dads around. It was really like having one *dad* and one *father*, because there is a difference. One gave me my past, and one gave me my future. Both those things are needed by all of us. It was like having"—Scooby looks at the bar—"two shots of whiskey instead of just one!" He laughs. "I'm not trying to make light of it. I'm just saying that having my bio mom and dad in the background meant a lot to me, I guess."

"Sounds like bio dad was giving what he could, given the situation," I say.

"Exactly," Scooby says. "He really did."

CHAPTER 30
An Unfixable Mistake

Scooby / 1969 – Montour Falls, New York

"Okay, I'll pick Philip."
"Well then I guess I will take Bryce."
"Geez. Okay, I guess I will take... Julie."
"Oh, gosh, okay then, that leaves me with Rhonda."
"That just leaves the orphan. I don't want him, you take him."
"No way! I don't want him either."
"Kids! Stuart gets to play, too."
"Okay, Miss Bradley. Stuart can be all time pitcher."
"I don't want to be all time pitcher. I want to be able to kick the ball, too."
"It's either that or nothing, Stuart."
"Yeah, it's that or nothing. Nobody wants to pick you."

October 2019

I wake to the sensation of Venus's hot breath in my ear with a subtle snore with every other exhale. I take note that the sun still appears to be struggling, making its way above the East. I am assuming the dawn will eke into Venus's psyche very slowly this morning, given the vodka she drank last night at Scooby's patch party. The atmosphere quickly turned negative for her when she felt embarrassed about what she called her *reverse huzzah* moment. Sometimes she frustrates me beyond reason, other times she makes me confused, and there are times like this. Perhaps I am just tired or worn out as of late, or perhaps it's the fact I'm staring at her as she sleeps peacefully. But then there's times like this when the confusion and frustration lead me to commiserate what led up to her taking an innocuous situation like shouting out a different word than the crowd, and transforming that innocuous act into a binge of vodka. I smile at her and kiss her forehead. "You are *'morning beautiful,'*" I say to her, knowing she can't hear me.

I gently remove her arm from my chest and slowly climb out of bed. I fumble for a coffee pod and make a cup of coffee. I laugh, knowing that Solomon would be irate at a coffeemaker he sees as some sort of *conspiracy by France to weaken the American resolve.* The fact that it's an American company that makes the product is lost on him. I am not sure how France came into the mix. Nevertheless, I hold my cup up and toast him.

I hear the bathroom door close, and I notice Venus is out of bed. I grab a second mug and prepare coffee for her. She saunters out of the bathroom with a slow gait and a constant rubbing of her face with both palms.

"Hey there, naked man," she says with a yawn. She shakes her head and says in exasperation, "I'm too tired to even make a *cream in my coffee* joke; just gimmie." She reaches out for the mug that is in my hand. She takes a long gulp of brew and sighs. "Did you take advantage of a drunk girl last night?" she asks.

"Twice!" I say enthusiastically with an animated smile, holding up two fingers. "I'm almost forty. I was quite proud of myself."

Venus smiles and drinks more coffee. "I'd love an Egg McMuffin and a hash brown."

"You want McDonald's?" I ask.

"Yep," she says, taking another gulp. "Sex and McDonald's; nothing beats it."

"In that order, correct?" I quip.

"Hmmm . . .," Venus says with a grin. "Let me taste the Egg McMuffin first."

I just smile and shake my head. "If you're up to it, let's just grab the bike and hit the open road and . . . *The Open Road*," I say.

"Seriously?" she says. "You want to go back there?"

"Yes. I need to go back there and replace something good with what I saw there," I say. "And, of course, we will stop and get pancakes in Dave's honor."

"Yeah, sounds good," she says, sipping more coffee. "The club going to go?"

"No, I thought it could be just you and me. We'll have a few beers, then go into Arcadia and have some lunch at that barbecue place."

"Pancakes, beer, and barbecue?" Venus says. "You want to make it *to* forty, Digger?"

"Only if I'm with you," I say, at once regretting the ill-timed and overly maudlin comment.

Venus ignores my comment. "Wanda said last night she and Preacher were hooking up with Big T and one of his girls, and they were taking a run up to Crystal River for some event."

"Yeah? So?"

"Let's get a few more and go with them," Venus replies.

"I want to go to Arcadia, and with just you," I reply.

"Okay," she says placidly. "But then let's see if we can get everyone to go. It'll be fun."

"Then you arrange it, Venus. I don't care." I walk away and go to the living room.

Venus grabs her phone and begins sending a plethora of texts. Every now and then, she smiles and looks up at me.

After a few minutes of progress, she stands up. "I'm going to jump in the shower and get dressed. Wanda and Preacher, Babs and Tophat, the new guy—"

"New guy has a name," I say piquantly.

Venus, undressing, stops mid-motion. "Sorry," she says uncomfortably. "Scooby, Candi, and Hal want to go. Hal is bringing his nephew. He's got a '77 Ironhead that I want to see."

"Scooby is bringing Candi?" I inquire.

"Yeah!" Venus says excitedly. "How about that?"

I can't tell whether her zeal is from genuine surprise or the fact that she knew something about the club before I did. I don't bother confirming any of the details Venus made regarding the ride. I get ready and pull my bike out of the garage. Venus swings open the door, blows a kiss at me, and jumps on the back.

We meet the others at a diner just off State Route 64 and eat. I do enjoy the time with my brothers. I laugh, mingle, and cogitate about what I am feeling. I am pleased overall, despite my initial plan to be alone with Venus.

Our ride east is filled with smiles, hand signals, and the occasional sight of Babs's boobs flashing the traffic heading west. Venus strives to balance Wanda's eye-rolling reaction to Babs's playfulness with her own version of disgust and impishness, trying to appease both entities. She does so by keeping her shirt on, even when Babs attempts to goad Venus into flashing as well. But instead, Venus uses overt gesticulations of her arms in the wind and makes funny faces at Babs.

Scooby seems to have a look of self-satisfaction on his face, as do I, knowing he will always remember this ride as his first as a patch holder. I make sure that he sees me give him a thumbs-up along the way.

I spot our destination and look over at Tophat. He makes a motion that we pull into the parking lot. As we park, we all, instinctively, look over at the exact spot where Pancake Dave fell. We walk in slowly and solemnly, occasionally patting each other on the back. The citizens move away and allow us to pass—some who were there, and some who knew what happened. They give us a respectful nod as we walk inside.

I motion to Venus to keep walking and that I have to stop and resituate my pocket holster. I carry a snub nose .38, but it often comes loose in the pocket in my cut and becomes uncomfortable. An old man approaches me as I continue to fix the positioning of my gun. He appears to make purposeful eye contact with me, as if he is seeking me out intentionally. The man must be in his eighties, small, withered frame, and several teeth missing. He is dressed in a tattered, old pair of denim overalls with a blue-and-white checkered shirt underneath. He is straight out of a *Hee Haw* skit. The memory of Dave's murder, the fact I am a member in the most high-profile motorcycle club in America, and the fact I am not young and bulletproof any longer, keeps my instincts on high alert.

As the man closes in on me, he extends his hand out toward me. "Howdy, young man," he says gleefully. "Can I grab a moment of your daylight?"

"Sure," I say placidly as I greet his hand with mine. I continue to look at his beltline, both his hands, the woods behind me, and the citizens in the parking lot.

"I'm an old man, served in Korea, I did. That's a promise," he says.

"Thank you," I say docilely. "I am a vet as well. Marines, two tours, Fallujah. What is it I can do for you?" I ask, still with much skepticism in me grown from the reality of who I am and where I am, both in locale and in the world philosophically. I continue to grow my peripheral vision.

"I want your forgiveness," the old man says.

"That depends," I say with a stoic countenance. "Elaborate."

The old man is visibly shaken at my response. I believe he was expecting some sort of solid reassurance.

"I'm sorry about your partner," he says, "your fellow member," he explains.

"Okay" is the only word that I offer him.

The old man clears his throat. I finally release my hand from his. "My name is Chester; people 'round here call me Chet," he says nervously.

"Chet," I again say with a mix of indifference and power. "I'm Digger. I appreciate your respect, but I want to get to the forgiveness part real quicklike," I say with growing impatience. "I have friends waiting inside."

"Fair enough," he says. "I was here when the guy in your club was shot."

I nod my head, saying nothing.

"I saw something and I . . . I . . . didn't say anything. I kept quiet and I shouldn't have."

"Okay, let's start with what you saw," I say, "then we will work from there." I am trying not to feel guilty about purposely intimidating a man nearly ninety years old, but I think of Solomon's point of protecting the club, first and foremost.

"I was walking in the woods just that way," he says, pointing behind the bar, "and I saw this guy with a rifle like I saw in the news and on war shows. High power stuff, big clip, and all that. It wasn't no hunting gun, for sure."

"Go on," I say, breaking his pause.

"He saw me, pointed the gun at me, and said to me, 'You don't see me, I don't see you.' Then he moved closer toward the bushes, just behind there," he says, pointing at brush less than a hundred yards away.

"And you were doing what?" I ask.

"Well." He laughs. "I am . . . uh . . . not supposed to be hunting this time of year." He laughs more.

I offer a fake and mocked laugh alongside his. "Forgiveness is bonded with truth," I say. "Try once . . . just once more." I pause for effect. "But only once."

"Oh, okay," Chet says with a tone of surrender. "I may know about some chemistry labs in the woods, and they throw this old war vet a few bucks to run them up food and such occasionally."

"Yes, expanding knowledge," I say acerbically. I grab Chet by the collar, gently but with a sense of importance. "Fuck you and your Korean War service," I say, tightening my grip. "I don't care if you are bringing chicken salad sandwiches to meth cookers, okay? Now, one last time, what, exactly, did you see?"

Venus peeks her head out of the door, looks at me, and waves her hand. I motion, forcefully, for her to go back inside.

Chet sighs. "I saw, in detail, the guy who shot your member. I didn't tell the cops. I know you guys, and if you ever found out I sat on info like this. . . ." He stops his words. "I have a family."

I loosen my grip slightly and then shove him back away, gently. "Yeah, okay," I say. "I know what you saw: five feet six, buzzed, blond hair, stocky build, Nazi symbol tattooed on his knuckles. Thanks," I say sarcastically. "We got the memo."

"Ya did?" Chet says with a laugh. "Then I'd fire the memo person you have because I'm talking damn near total opposite."

I look curiously. "Okay," I say. "Explain."

"The fella I saw was a foot taller, super-dark hair, weird ponytail, and no tattoos on his arms or hands or anything that I could see. His skin was too white. He looked like a Northerner," he says with a laugh.

"You're sure?" I ask.

"Very," Chet says. "I've seen him around, I think. He's a cooker in Hardee County. They have their own chemistry labs in the woods, ya know. I can't think of his name."

"But you are sure of that description, and you are sure he was the one in the bushes?" I ask.

"Damn sure!" Chet says. "Weird-looking guy. Had this odd burn or birthmark, scar, or something. Zigzag thingy," he says, pointing at his forehead above his eye. "Weird, orange color, shaped like a carrot. Yep," he says with a laugh. *"Like a zigzagged carrot."*

CHAPTER 31
There's No 'I' In Team

Digger / 2010 – Sarasota, Florida

"Is that your Shovelhead?"
"Yep. Bought it new in 1966."
"Wow! Now that's loyalty."
"It's what it's all about."
"Agreed. My name is Digger."
"Hi, Digger. The name's Solomon, president, Demons Rising, Florida."
"It's a pleasure."
"Tophat! Come meet Digger. He's a Jarhead, too."
"Yeah? Nice to meet you. Tophat, vice-president, Demons Rising, Florida, and U.S.M.C., 1975 to 1979."
"Digger, Tophat and the boys are going back to our clubhouse in Tampa. You're welcome to tag along and have a beer."
"I'd be honored."
"Saddle up, then."

October 2019

"This guy sounds ancient, and he seems like a lifelong tweaker. How can you be sure he is legit?" Solomon asks.

"Under any other circumstance, I would say you are probably right," I reply to Solomon. "But he described that lame fuck Brett, who came to our clubhouse that day, right down to the most minute detail."

Solomon just nods and has a solemn look of contemplation on his face.

"Especially that weird-ass scar or birthmark, whatever it is," I say, "but he described that mark of the beast to a tee. I remember being drawn to it, too, when I was sizing him up. He even used the term I did in calling it a *zigzagged carrot*."

"Yeah, point taken," Solomon says.

I sigh heavily and get flustered as I look at Solomon. "That means I—"

"Don't fucking say it, Digger," Solomon interjects tersely. "I can't begin to count how many ways what you're about to say is totally wrong, so don't say it. Got it?"

I cease and look away from Solomon. I breathe deeply a few times but temper my words.

"Got it?" Solomon says louder, apparently wanting an answer.

I sigh again deeply and nod my head slightly. "I understand what you're saying," I reply.

"No," he says, pointing his finger at me. "No, you don't. I said you did nothing wrong, and then I asked if you understand that to be correct."

"But I shot and killed an innocent man."

"No," Solomon says sharply. "He may have been the wrong man for that specific target, but innocent?" Solomon says derisively. "He was no saint, Digger. He was some wannabe neo-Nazi who was the reason for that bullshit club to start, which set off the whole chain of events. If not for him, Pancake Dave would be here today. Don't you dare call that guy innocent." Solomon calms himself and puts his hand on my shoulder. "Now, you didn't tell me. I said you did nothing wrong, and then I asked if you understand that to be correct."

I nod again. "I do. I know you're right."

"That's better."

"Okay, now what?" I ask.

"You tell me," Solomon replies.

"I'll start with the pragmatic stuff. He will be very easy to find. Chet said he was a meth cooker in Hardee County. I know his name. I can find him and his cook shack in a matter of hours."

"Okay," Solomon says as he seems to wait for more information from me. "Then what?"

"Then what?" I say almost mockingly. "I go and kill the cowardly turdball. Is that straightforward enough for you?"

"Too much so," he says. "That's the obvious conclusion, but give me the steps up to that conclusion."

"What is this?" I ask incredulously, "a fucking 'how to' seminar?"

Solomon, unphased, bores in more. "What's next, Digger?"

I decompress some, close my eyes, and think. "I verify his location—"

"You said that already," Solomon interjects.

"I don't know what you want me to say?" I say heatedly. "I kill the fucker!"

"Have you informed the club?" he asks.

"I didn't say anything to anyone," I reply. "Once Chet talked to me, I went in, had a beer, and then came here."

"Dave was a Demons Rising brother, meaning we all have to be in on it."

"But they are," I say with an authoritative tone. "We voted that the killer of Pancake Dave meets *Hell's Fire*."

"You're trying to nuance this," Solomon says. "You don't go alone, and you don't make this about you righting some mythical wrong about killing Torch."

"I'm not!" I say loudly but with obvious tentativeness.

"Which one?" Solomon asks. "You're not going alone, or you're not making this about you righting some mythical wrong?"

"The latter," I reply.

Solomon shakes his head. "I'm not going to debate that point with you, Digger, so I'll just hit you with the obvious." Solomon faces me head-on and points directly at me. "You do not go alone. It's not pragmatic, and your way is not a collaborative effort. Our brotherhood is a collaboration, so the answer is no."

"Hey! Alex Trebek!" I shout as I wag my finger at him. "I did not phrase that in the form of a question!"

"Oh, I see," Solomon roars. "So you're going it alone, Mister Lone Wolf? Oh, thank you, Digger! You are our hero."

"No, I will not be alone!" I say with boldness. "I will be there with Dave! His spirit! His energy! He will be with me!"

Solomon rolls his eyes and mockingly applauds. "Oh, bravo, Digger," he says as he continues to clap. "Lights! Camera! Action!"

Solomon's words both anger me and deflate my self-made rage. "This is my responsibility, Solomon," I reply in a calmer tone.

"You still don't get it, do you, Digger?" Solomon asks. "It's *our* responsibility; we're a brotherhood. That's got to mean something more than a clever cliché on a bumper sticker."

My moral high ground just became flooded with the flush of truth. I am used to edging around things I don't like and using nuances to bring about truth. But when real truth charges in, I am defenseless. I lose my energy to the force of legitimacy, bringing about my defeat.

"Okay," I say faintly. I pause in an attempt to find one sentence, phrase, or even a word that will give me some footing in Solomon's counterargument. "I don't go alone."

Solomon smiles and slaps me on the shoulder. "Now we're getting somewhere," he says. "In my many nightmare scenarios, one is where I picture a tombstone someday with Demons Rising's name on it, and the dates are 1972 to . . . some obscure end date. But conversations like this with you, Digger, give me confidence that is one nightmare that will go by the wayside and into the chasm of the unfulfilled."

I step back and give Solomon a look of exaggerated confusion. "Deep . . . deep thought from a man who once ranted that Mister Whipple was some sort of control freak who needed a severe beatdown."

"Wait," Solomon says, tossing his hand in my face. "The man grew irate because some lonely housewives squeezed toilet paper. Are you going to tell me that he didn't just need the shit beat out of him? Is that the argument you're going to make, Digger?"

I combine a smile with a look of false shock and dismay. "Me argue with you?" I say. "What's the point?"

"Yeah, be a smart-ass, Digger," Solomon says. "But you know as well as I do that Mister Whipple was a complete, fucking asshole. It was toilet paper, for Christ's sake! Just lousy, fucking toilet paper!"

CHAPTER 32
Righting the Wrong

Pancake Dave / 1999 – Tampa, Florida

"Just one more question, Dave. The first one was easy; the second is trickier."

"Okay."

"Now, number two: why do we yell 'we are demons' and follow up with 'we are rising'?"

"You said the second one would be hard, Joe. That's not hard. Don't give me an easy one on purpose because you think I'm not smart enough to get it."

"Old Joe is right, Dave. That's the second question."

"No, I think you just think I'm some dumb retard, so you're giving me an easy one."

"If it's so fucking easy, then answer it!"

"Okay. You all do it because you are demons and you are rising and getting stronger."

"You got it!"

"See? I told you that you gave me an easy one."

"No! Do you know how many prospects had two months added to their prospect time because they said 'we' are demons before they actually were? It's not about brains, Dave, it's about respect of the club and earning your patch. That came so naturally to you that you didn't even have to think about it. You may now say 'we'!"

"Oh my God, I can't believe I am now one of you!"

"Just hit that quart of bourbon and get ready!"

"What's next?"

"Same thing we do to all new brothers: we drag you by rope through the yard behind my bike!"

"Let's do it!"

"You are definitely one of us now!"

October 2019

The ride is quiet. Neither Solomon nor I make so much as a peep. I turn the radio on. I hum a few familiar tunes over and over in my head as I stare out the window.

In an effort to remain inconspicuous in public, Solomon manages to curtail his normal Tourette-laced, road rage tirades. However, I can see the angst on his face as drivers are going too slow, too fast, driving too close to the car ahead of them, too far behind them, passing too many cars, not passing when they should, etcetera. He even manages to get angry at a car with spinning hubcaps because it is "*distracting.*" And every now and then, he does yell "fucking yankee!" when a car from New York or Massachusetts drives by us. For some reason, those two states bother him the most. I know, with the exception of his three years in Vietnam, he has always lived here in Florida, the epitome of a *Florida Cracker*. But the people from those two states really irk him more than the others. I used to think it was because New York and Massachusetts were two of only three states that do not have a Demons Rising chapter, but recently, Mallet helped get a chapter started near Cambridge. For two straight weeks afterward, Solomon would occasionally yell "take that, you Harvard fucks!" as if the Ivy League institution took any formal position on our new chapter.

"Tweakers always have dogs near their cook shacks," Solomon says. "Have you planned for that?"

I tap my pocket a few times and nod my head. "I have a pound of raw burger with enough Diazepam to knock them out in under a minute."

Solomon looks at me, perplexed. "You have raw burger in your pocket?" he queries.

"Of course," I say. "One dog might want it rare and one might want it medium-well, and I am not cooking two special orders for dogs I don't even know."

Solomon shakes his head and looks at the road. "Always the smartass," he says. "Now let's go over this again—"

"No," I say as I hold my hand up at him. "We've been through it enough. I know what to do, and I trust you do, too."

Solomon says nothing, and he doesn't appear to look any angrier than he customarily does.

The sun is setting over the flatlands of Hardee County. We drive by a bar in the village of *Ona* called Charlotte's Web. I want an ice-cold beer so bad. Solomon grew up in the town of Limestone, about ten miles from where we are. When I mentioned that I found our target only ten miles from his hometown, he didn't flinch. Solomon has discussed growing up in Limestone only once, and that is when he claims he saw Greg Allman ride by on an old Panhead in 1973. Whether it's true or not, I will never know. Always with that poker face of his.

We pull down an old logging road as the darkness creeps in to swallow the sun. Just as in some dime-store noir, we synchronize our watches. Solomon just stares at me and nods slightly, giving me a look of confidence. I exit the van and begin a light jog through the woods. I palm my .44 snub nose as I meander through trees and brush, slowing my march as to maintain quiet. I am operating by pure instinct at this point. When gathering intel, it isn't as though I obtain a Google map from that intel. But I trust my instincts from my Boy Scout days, to my Marine training, and just my good, old-fashioned intuition.

I slow my steps to a near halt as I spy a rudimentary structure that has no business being in the middle of the brush and trees. Surprisingly, I don't hear or see any dogs. I move quietly toward the shack, trying to hear more details, such as the amount of voices, dogs, and maybe any motorized equipment. Thus far, I hear none of the above. All I hear is some unrecognizable music being played at a level too high for my tastes. But, I confess, I do love his music. That music is on the side of Demons Rising, as it will keep him distracted.

I walk a step at a time and nearly make myself flush with the outside wall. I feel like I am better prepared this time; my thoughts are fewer and my actions have increased. I look down at my watch once more, gauging my time. I place my ear flush with the wall and can finally detect a voice. I identify a man singing along with his music, various glass clanking, and some occasional steps along the floor.

I hear Solomon's voice in my head, asking me, "What's next?" Good question. Do I kick the door open and scream as I wave my revolver at him? Oh, wouldn't that look pretty damn cool? So theatrical. I notice my breathing is getting heavier, and the beads of sweat on my forehead have nothing to do with an October evening in Florida. I feel my own heartbeat as I slowly reach for the makeshift door handle and push it ever so slowly. I note that it doesn't make noise and it's not locked, which invites me to push it more until it is fully open. I hug the revolver up against my chest and walk in sideways with my eyesight fixed straight ahead. I peek around the wall and see Brett, the man who came to our clubhouse, bebopping his head to and fro to his music as he clangs canisters together. I see two burners going at a high flame.

No theatrics. I walk slowly behind him. He is still turned away from me. I take note that he is alone as of now. That does not mean that someone did not step out to take a piss, get some air, etcetera. I see Brett is gowned in an apron of sorts and has a mask tied behind his head. I find it remarkable, in a way, that he manages to keep beat to music and sing it at a low tone as he is cooking methamphetamine. The whole scene appears incongruous to how it's supposed to be.

I slowly point my revolver at his back. I wait, hoping his internal senses will alarm him to the fact he has someone standing ten feet behind him, but it doesn't appear to be so. I finally kick a table to draw his attention. He snaps his head back around and takes note of me; his eyes grow wide. He rips off his mask and takes a step back. He says nothing at first, nor do I. I hold my revolver up, pointing straight at him.

Finally, he speaks. "What do you want?" is all he says with fear, but not panic.

"We will start with money," I say. "I know you have a bunch, so give it all to me and do so now," I say calmly but sternly, with my revolver still pointing at him.

"Cash?" he asks. His question perplexes me.

I shake my head in confusion and say, "Of course. That was a stupid question."

"I don't know what I'm supposed to say. I mean . . . I'm not sure what to do here," Brett says. "I mean . . . please don't hurt me. I have a lot of cash here. A lot!" he says with emphasis.

"Good, good," I reply. "Give me a number that convinces me you're not holding out on me."

"Look, dude, I have about fifteen thousand here. It's yours—all of it," he says.

"I'll take that now, thank you," I say. However, my nerves increase because if he has that much cash on site, then this is not only the cook shack, but the storefront, too. And that means Brett and I won't be alone for long. And yes, he's scared, but he's expecting people and expecting them soon. His countenance seems to have a mix of abject terror blended with a smidgen of confidence.

Brett points to an old bureau, seeking permission to walk to it.

"Okay," I say, "but keep one hand tucked in your back waistband, and if you so much as scratch your ass, you'll be filled with lead." *Damn, that sounded cool*, I think to myself, *like an old Cagney movie.*

Brett complies, opens the drawer, and pulls out a cardboard box. I see cash in it as he tips the box toward me.

"Jam it all in that bag," I say, "and be quick."

"Okay, okay," he says as he crams the cash in the bag. "Then we're cool, right?" he asks with a bit more relaxation but still visibly scared.

I don't answer him. He fills the bag and slides it over to me. "You want product?" he asks. "I have a whole batch done and wrapped; it's yours, too."

I shake my head. "No, just the cash. I have to walk back to my limo. I don't want illegal contraband, right, Brett?" I ask.

"Oh, you . . . you remember my name?" he replies.

"Do you take that as a compliment, Brett?"

Brett, unsure how to answer, just shakes his head. "We're cool now, right?"

I reach in my pocket, still holding my revolver at Brett. I pull out a picture of Dave. I flip it over and show Brett. "You see him?" He doesn't answer. "Answer me!" I scream.

"Yes," is all he says in response.

"Do you know his name?"

"No," Brett replies nervously.

"Well, my friend, I'm going to tell you," I say with a stentorian boom. "His name is . . . was Delbert Alvin Van Eagan. Those initials spell out 'Dave.' That's what we called him. We loved him."

"Please, dude, I under—"

"Shut up!" I scream at Brett, hurling my body, creating the revolver to shake. "I'm talking!" I say, pointing at myself. "You fucking listen!"

"I'm sorry," is all he says, as he looks to the door behind me, hoping and praying someone walks in.

"Dave had an ol' lady named Candi. He had a daughter named Rachel. Dave liked the music of Crosby, Stills, and Nash, he liked pizza with extra cheese and heavy crust, he smoked Lucky Strike cigarettes, he liked to fish, and he was great at horseshoes!" I continue the verbal onslaught. "Look at him!" I screech, shaking the picture at Brett. "He was our brother, and we loved him unconditionally. He belonged to our family! He wore a Demons Rising patch with pride every day! Under what theory do you think you can take a family member away from us and still live?"

"Hold on, hold on, dude," Brett pleads. "I was not even there that day."

"Oh, I think you were," I say with more equanimity and less furor, but with no less passion. "I think you saw us when you were all snorting crank in the men's room. You knew who Demons Rising were, and you knew the hell you were going to face, so you rushed out the back like the cheese-eating, shitbag, rat bastard you are." I pause momentarily and catch my breath. I refocus my energy to remain calm, but an anger-filled calm that allows me to control the situation. "I thought I counted six when y'all came out of the bathroom. Then when we were outside, I counted five. You scurried away."

Brett stays stoic and calm but still shakes in fear. He continues to look at the door behind me. Even in the middle of my soliloquy, I peek at my watch. But I continue.

"You ran," I say, waving the revolver at him. "And later, when your crew went off on you for rabbiting out of there, for acting like a coward, you wanted to save face, right?"

Brett shakes his head slightly.

"It wasn't a real question!" I shout. "You knew in this country, bumfuck area that word would spread quickly, so you decided to look like a badass, sneak back down here, and just shoot anyone with a Demons Rising patch. Didn't matter who, right? Well, Brett, guess who you killed?" I ask, waving Dave's picture again. "You killed him! Our brother! And then you knew you had to make sure your so-called club would scatter and run in all directions so your cowardice would never be discovered, so you could still have some gravitas in this area as some big-time meth dealer, so you pointed us to Torch. You kill any Demons Rising member, we kill a Black Shadow, and then all the turmoil clouds the fact that you punked out, and you go on doing what you're doing, right?"

Brett stands still, saying nothing.

"That you can answer!" I shout.

Brett gulps and shakes and still remains silent. He appears to try to do so but says nothing.

"That's all this Black Shadow bullshit was, right? A way to spread meth around and have some credibility. I think you convinced Torch that Black Shadow was about fulfilling some sick Nazi crap, and he took it and ran with it. But you knew what it was—a cover to deal this crap." I stop and wave my revolver at him. "How am I doing so far?"

Before he answers, the door opens, a man looks at me, eyes opened wide in fear, and I turn and shoot two times, dropping the man to the ground. Brett makes a run to the back of the room, so I turn to him and shoot three more times in his back. Brett stops, grabs his spine, and falls. He didn't turn and look at me, he didn't scream; he just fell. I quickly focus back to the first man as he lies on the ground, short of breath, dying. "Damn," I say quietly to myself, and to the dying man. "You are what the experts call *collateral damage*." I kneel a bit and stare at him once more, then stand straight up, looking down at him. I reach down and touch his cheek for reasons unbeknownst to me. The man is going to die; it's clear and convincing. But what is also clear and convincing is that he is just a customer, not one of Brett's crew. "I'm sorry," I say to him, staring into his withered, old, tired eyes. "I really am."

I grab the money, look at my watch, and make sure Brett is dead. Instincts, not common sense, make me look around the whole room. I knock over every container filled with any substance that I can and then step back. I grab a fistful of paper and start a fire. I toss it on some stuff I know must be combustible and watch it burn quickly. When I see that the flames will soon dominate, I grab the money, throw the gun in the flames, and run. I run with hell fire at my heels toward the road.

Among the multiple advantages of wearing this Demons Rising patch, such as never paying a cover charge, citizens clearing out of your way because they know you're important, girls throwing themselves at you, no bar tabs, never having to wait for a table, etc., there is most importantly the fact that it gives me the utmost confidence that Solomon, my brother, will be exactly where he said he would be at the exact time he said. It's called faith. It's called trust. It's called brotherhood.

As I near the road, I see the van. I see Solomon.

CHAPTER 33
Love Hurts

Venus / 2018 – Tip Top Tavern: Bradenton, Florida

"Mary Ellen? That's your name? Really? Do you get many jokes about Walton's Mountain?"

"Yep, but usually they're staring at my tits when they say 'mountain.' Kinda like you just did."

"I did not!"

"Oh, yes! Yes, you did. Now what's your name, and don't say 'Peter' or 'Dick' because I don't want you accusing me of staring at your crotch for those reasons."

"Oh! Wow! I think I love you. My name is Digger."

"Aren't you going to say, 'learn it because you'll be screaming it later'?"

"Uh . . . I'm just about done with this beer. Want to go for a ride?"

"Yep, Mister Badass Demons Rising man. I have lots of vodka and lots of coke at my place, and no, I do not mean cola."

"This is usually the part where I wake up alone. You are what dreams are made of."

"That's funny, because my ol' man says I am more of a toxic nightmare."
"He who let you squirm away is a stupid man."
"He's in jail right now, waiting for hell to freeze over so I can bail him out."
"Oh . . . is that where you got the black eye?"
"Hey! Biker Guy! Do you want to save me or party with me?"
"I guess the latter. Jump on and hold on tight."
"Hmmm . . . I think I might just say the same thing to you later."

November 2019

The clubhouse is abuzz on a Saturday night. We no longer have a prospect, but since Scooby is considered a probationary member, he still does some of the work the prospects do.

The November air this evening is a bit crisper than normal, but still quite comfortable, but the mere fact that we are two weeks from Thanksgiving makes a bonfire even more desirable. Scooby does just that and gets the fire roaring. It's been a chaotic few months, to say the least. With all that has happened, we cancelled our annual Halloween party and our annual trip to Sturgis, and we didn't go to New Orleans like we usually do the first week in November.

"Y'all need anything else?" Scooby asks. "If not, I'm taking Candi down to Bradenton to eat and hit that Ride Hard Saloon for a beer or two."

"We're good," Solomon says.

Scooby turns and sees Candi walking toward them. He waves her back and says with a smile, "Let's go, Candi."

Candi returns the smile. "Hi, fellas," she says to me, Solomon, Tophat, and J.J. We all nod and smile back.

"Candi and Scooby," J.J. says. "Well, I'm glad she's got a brother looking out for her now."

"Yep," I say, tossing chunks of wood in the fire. "She's a good kid; she was good to Pancake Dave for sure."

"You guys hanging here for the night?" Tophat asks.

"I will be," says Solomon. "I'm going to be cooking flapjacks and bacon in the morning if any of y'all want to roll in here about seven or eight."

"Yes!" Scooby yells from a distance. "I heard that, Solomon, and I'll stop in about six or so and help you."

Solomon gives Scooby a thumbs-up.

"I'm staying for a while," I say. "I'm sure Venus is going to go with Babs and the girls to that bar in Homosassa tonight."

Tophat smiles and laughs slightly. "A night off from Babs!" he says. "I think I'll go back inside, drink myself stupid, and then ride back home." Tophat then sighs.

"Then I'll wait for the Citrus County Sheriff to call me about Babs getting in trouble."

I chuckle and continue throwing debris into the flames.

"I'm going to go with you, Tophat," J.J. says. "I'm calling it an early night, too."

"I'll hang here with Solomon for a while," I say. "Y'all know he hates being alone."

"What I hate is a guy from Indiana using the term 'y'all,'" Solomon says.

"And what's a guy from Indiana supposed to say?" I inquire.

"I dunno," Solomon says. *"Damn that goat looks sexy in the moonlight?"*

Just then, we hear the cackling of the girls encroaching in on us.

"Howdy, boys!" Babs says with her trademark booming tongue. "We are heading to Ybor City to that place that makes those badass B.L.T.s."

"And Babs will substitute the *L* and the *T* for extra *B*," Tophat says as he laughs.

"What can I say?" Babs retorts. "I've always had an affinity for greasy pigs!"

"*Oink!*" Tophat shouts thunderously and with pride.

"I thought Wanda said we were going to that bar in Homosassa?" Venus says.

"She might be, girl. I don't know," Babs replies.

"I might just stay here with Digger then. I'm not hungry."

"I'll go with Babs and them," Cricket says. "I don't feel like driving way up to Homosassa anyway."

"What do you *feel like*, Cricket?" Solomon asks devilishly as he flickers his eyebrows up and down. "Tell your weird, old Uncle Solomon, who has boundary issues, what you feel like!"

"Heaven," she says to him. "Pure heaven!"

Venus looks down at me and mouths, "See? I told you. He likes everyone but me."

I respond by putting my hand up, telling her to stop.

Wanda and Maggie begin walking toward the fire. "If we're going to go, let's go. I'm hungry," Wanda says.

"You're going to Ybor, too?" Venus asks.

Wanda nods without looking at her.

Venus looks down at me again. "I guess I'm going to go with them. Do you mind?"

"Quit asking me that, Venus."

"Let's go, girls!" Babs shouts. She bends down and gives Tophat a kiss. "Love you, Hon."

"Love you, too," Tophat replies. "Be careful, Babs."

Venus bends down and kisses me as well. "I'll swing by your place later?"

"Yep," I reply pithily.

Venus hurries to catch up with the crowd. Tophat and J.J. go into the clubhouse.

"Aw," Solomon says mockingly. "She didn't say she loves you."

"She said she loved me once."

"Did your heart go pitter-patter?" Solomon asks with a grin as he pokes the fire.

"It was in a text message," I say, chuckling.

"Ah!" he says dryly. "There's a *Lifetime* movie in the making there for sure."

"I'm certain she loves me in her own way."

"No," Solomon says. "She loves power and being a part of it and living vicariously through it. She doesn't care about you. She just cares about the doors you open for her, the parties you get her into, the clubhouses, the connection to the underbelly of life. You're just the portal to all that, and that's all you are. You are nothing else to her. That's not something lacking in you, Digger, it's something lacking in her."

"That's not all she is," I say placidly. "She's not that shallow."

"Oh no?" he asks sarcastically. "She's half-filled, kiddie pool shallow."

I sigh in frustration, and in a veiled, desperate attempt to defend her, I say, "She always says that you don't like her."

"Well, she is right. I don't. Not one damn bit."

His bold admission surprises me some. "Why not?" I ask.

"Look, I'm going to tell you this for your own good," Solomon retorts.

I sigh and shake my head. "Here we go," I say as I sigh once more. "I look back at the best times in my life, and none of them were for my own good."

"Humor me," Solomon says. "Now listen, Digger, you're barking up the wrong tree here. You're trying to make this chick out to be something she's not."

"How so?" I ask unenthusiastically.

"You can turn a housewife into a whore, but you can't turn a whore into a housewife," Solomon says calmly.

I don't get a chance to even so much as eke out a word when Solomon interjects, "Before you say a word, let me finish."

I don't know what it is—the moment, the curiosity of what his thinking is, the respect he's earned from me—but for some reason, I want to hear him out.

"This is just how we talk, Digger," he says, swinging his finger back and forth to him and then to me. "And I don't just mean you and I. I mean us as a collective bunch in this subculture biker life we live. We are not on Oprah, and we are not hypersensitive crybabies. People all too often measure your views simply by the nature of your communication style."

I sit and listen, mildly angry at him, but the trust that he has earned from me leads to confidence in his overall wisdom, even if articulation of that wisdom is not his strong suit.

"The thing is, Digger, when a woman gets that title affixed to her, most of the time—I'm not even saying some or half, but most of the time—it's not her fault. She is broken in some way. Something in her life went horribly wrong, or it's just a steady drumbeat of negativity, or probably a combination of both. Let me tell you this. I hear so many so-called experts on families clamor about how the problem today is kids don't go to church on Sundays, eat supper with their parents, do chores, and learn right from wrong from good, solid parents, etcetera, etcetera."

"You think they're wrong?" I ask curiously.

"On the contrary, Digger. I think they are one hundred percent right. But them thundering about it high upon their milkcrate—"

"You mean soapbox," I interject.

"I mean *shut the hell up* and let me finish," Solomon says. "But by them pontificating from their pulpit about the importance of a strong family and social network as you grow up, they are admitting that such an upbringing has a gargantuan impact on them as adults, right?"

"Right," I say, still not following him completely.

"So it stands to reason that if a kid grows up with the exact opposite, then isn't that just as impactful in a negative way? Doesn't that poisonous upbringing still carry that weight in the adult that they become, only now it's in a destructive way? These self-righteous blowhards can't have it both ways. They can't say how monumentally important family is on shaping your character, but then say it makes no difference if you had a fucked-up family in your childhood when you're a fucked-up adult. I hear them all the time, *'Ah . . . that's no excuse cuz mama didn't love you; you still know right from wrong, you still should know better,'* blah, blah, blah! When someone is a fucked-up individual and they have a fucked-up childhood, we shouldn't be surprised that they are fucked-up adults if you are making the argument that family is the key to shaping character. I mean, either it's important and impactful or it isn't. Pick a lane, assholes."

"Yeah, I think I know what you mean," I say contemplatively.

"And your ol' lady, Digger, is fucked up. She's broken. I don't know why she is or when it happened, but she is. You want her to be something she isn't. You want her to be something she is not capable of being or truly doesn't want to be. Either way, you got an ol' lady who is never *ever* going to care about another human being other than herself. She's never been married and no kids, right?"

I just nod my head.

"Cat? Dog?"

I shake my head, knowing the point he is about to make.

"How did I know that?" Solomon asks with a smirk. "Everything she is, everything she does is so fucking fake and artificial, she doesn't know where reality begins and fantasy ends. And that, my brother, is the way she wants it to be—that she can control or at least thinks she can." Solomon leans into me a bit and hands me the flask with the lid popped open. "And I am certain, Digger, that deep down in your soul, you already knew," Solomon says, crumbling up some scrap papers. "And I say that because people always tell you who they are, but only if you're willing to listen. They speak through words, they speak through actions, and they also speak through *inactions*." Solomon tosses a few bits of wood into the fire. "She doesn't give you back what you give her, and she doesn't intend to. Accept it. You don't want to be angry, hateful, listening to sad country songs, and drowning yourself in bourbon for the rest of your life."

"You mean like you?" I say with a smirk.

Solomon emits a small chuckle. "I know you're being a smart-ass, as usual, Digger, but yes . . . exactly like me."

I smile slightly and take a swig of bourbon.

"She feels safe with Digger, the badass sergeant-at-arms, but not Digger, the guy who loves her. She loves the former and hates the latter. She has no respect for kindness. She responds positively to people who mistreat her."

"That makes no sense," I say sharply.

"Yeah?" Solomon says scornfully. "When she met you, swilling beer at some old, dive biker bar, what do you think she thought when she saw you? That you would be that type of guy who buys her wine, writes her poems, and opens doors for her? That you would be the guy to treat her like a princess? Is that the vibe you give off to women? No!" he says, answering his own rhetorical question. "She thought she was getting a guy who would scream '*no fucking way!*' when she asked if she could go to a strip club or to Ybor City unchaperoned with the girls. She thinks you cannot combine kindness with strength. Venus believes kindness is weakness, and she hates you when you're kind to her," Solomon says flatly but with command. "I know," Solomon says, holding up his hands at me, shaking his head fervently, "it doesn't make sense. But, Digger, something can be true but still not make sense. Like I said, she's broken, and neither you nor anyone else can fix her." Solomon pauses momentarily. "She has no interest in you saving her, so don't. Save yourself before you save the world, Digger."

I stare at Solomon and fight for some words to come forth and follow his words, but none rise to the surface. I sigh heavily and stare into the fire. "I really love her, Solomon," I say, still looking at the fire. "I really do."

Solomon pauses a bit and actually smiles at me slightly. "I know you do, Bro, I honestly do," he says softly. "But Digger, people like her," he sighs, "people like *us*, we got demons in us from years gone by and day by day," he says reflectively and with emphasis. "Day by day, Digger, those demons"—Solomon pauses slightly and sighs—"those *demons* are *rising* in us and they will, someday, consume us entirely."

Solomon and I have had so many different talks out here alone, away from society, two-folded: once by the nature of our chosen life, and the other by the fact that the other members of our own self-made society are not here. I learn so much from this man. He has made me angry, he's made me laugh, he's made me contemplative, he has made me roll my eyes at times, and he has made me understand that I have a purpose in life, even if I go to my grave not knowing that purpose. I learn through all the emotions he sparks, whether he does so intentionally, meaningfully, or sarcastically, but I learn. I absorb the energy he emits through his years of riding the roads and never having the same ride twice. What I most admire about him is the fact he knows who he is. Whether he likes or even respects himself is not relevant because he has answered what we all wish we could do and what we think to ourselves on our deathbed: *Who am I? And why was I here?*

I know he's right, and that flushes an inordinate amount of sadness in me, but I keep it in me. Solomon is a traditionalist, a caveman, if you will, and men don't just hide sadness, we simply don't feel it.

"Yeah, Solomon, you are right," I say passively but with meaning.

"Yeah?" he asks with enthusiasm. "You should have that printed on a fucking shirt." He laughs a bit and hands me the flask once more.

"Look, Digger, if you mention that I said this shit about women at my funeral, I'll come back to haunt you." He laughs slightly. "And I know what I said was hurtful, but I said it because you are the future of this club. You may not have noticed, but I'm old, I'm broken down, I abused drugs and booze my whole life, the only greens I put into my body are in the form of marijuana, and my blood pressure breaks the balloon. And Tophat ain't far behind me. Thirty years from now, you need to be the one sitting here, crushing the hopes and dreams of your prodigy."

I take a long, hearty slug and bottom out the bourbon. I wipe my face, sigh deeply, and hand him back the flask.

"Solomon . . . you do know you're a total pain in the ass, right?" I ask.

Solomon slaps me on the back and smiles. He then takes back the flask and hands me a fresh one. "Yeah, yeah, I know, Digger. I know."

CHAPTER 34

The Fire Goes Out

Solomon / 1970 – Saigon, South Vietnam

"I'm looking for Sergeant Thomas P. Starke."
"Yes, sir! He and his platoon are washing up in the lagoon, sir."
"Sergeant Starke!"
"Yes, sir!"
"I'm Colonel Harold O'Connor. At ease, Son, this is an informal visit. I was going to ask you a question, but after seeing you, there's no need."
"Sir?"
"You must be related to Captain Raymond Starke; you're the spitting image."
"Yes, sir, he was my father."
"Was?"
"Yes, sir. He passed away in 1960."
"I'm sorry to hear that, Sergeant. Your dad and I were great friends. We both were in the Normandy Invasion in '44 and stayed in Germany until '46. He was a brave man."
"Thank you, sir."

"We had a great time in Germany after the Nazis were wiped out. We ripped through Berlin like rabid dogs!"

"Yes, sir."

"Yep, I am sorry he's passed, Son. I liked him very much. He was one crazy S.O.B."

"Yes, sir. I've heard that about him."

November 2019

My phone's ring wakes me. I fumble through the crusted eyes and reach on my nightstand, trying to grab it. I palm it with one hand as I wipe my eyes clean with the other. Venus wakes, too, and starts rubbing my chest.

"Hello," I say with a noted squeak to my voice.

"Digger?" the voice says quietly.

"Yeah," I respond. "Who's this?" I ask, as I turn my phone around to look at the call log.

"It's me," he responds.

I finally clean my eyes enough, focus, and see that it is Scooby. "Are you fucking crazy?" I ask. "It's four a.m."

"I know," he says quietly.

"My ol' lady is twirling her finger in my chest, so I think you need to get to the damn point," I reply.

"Digger, I'm at the clubhouse. I . . . uh . . . came here to get a head start on breakfast and maybe surprise Solomon."

"Yeah?" I say impatiently.

"He's here," Scooby says. "He's by the firepit."

"Who?" I ask.

"Solomon. He's here," Scooby replies.

"Yeah? So?" I say, growing impatient. "He does that sometimes. He's probably up early, too."

"No," Scooby says as his voice begins to crack. "You don't understand." Scooby pauses and then sighs. "The fire is out. Solomon is gone, Digger. He's gone."

CHAPTER 35
Saying Goodbye

Digger / 2005 – Fallujah, Iraq

"Gold bars?"

"Yes. We definitely believe you are officer material, Sergeant Garcia."

"I'm honored, sir, but may I ask why you feel this way?"

"The Marines are steeped in tradition, Sergeant, but we also are in a constant evolutionary challenge that makes us seek out those who can continue tradition with pride but bring about the new values in leadership that match the world today."

"I do find that challenge intriguing, sir."

"We have the confidence that you know those challenges and can bring about solutions in leading in a new era that has left behind some of the old mores, whether good, bad, or indifferent, because leadership—real leadership—requires that we adapt to those changes in culture."

"You are giving me much to consider, sir, but I'm honored either way."

"Leadership today requires respecting the past, respecting the traditions, all the while being able to navigate in a new world with new values *and new surroundings. The culture of the Marines is changing, Sergeant, and we do need to change with it while maintaining pride and respected traditions. Do you think you can do that, Sergeant?"*

November 2019

I hate this fucking song. Since I've been a Demons Rising member, I have buried four brothers . . . three just this year, though. Old Joe died in 2014, and I didn't see him much. He wasn't a fixture here because he was ill when I was patched in. And Old Joe's death was not a surprise. But fast forward to this year, and I lose two brothers—young and without any warning. The fact I didn't expect it made it more difficult.

Nevertheless, Solomon, at his age, his state of mind, and the fact he was not the bastion of health by any measurement, should come as no significant shock, but it does. The realities of age and state of mind aside, I just never—not once—envisioned my life here without him. I am not speaking about the anxiety of worrying he would die someday. I mean I did not see him as not being here. I'm confused. I don't know how I am supposed to keep the Demons Rising name going, keep myself going. Solomon was most certainly grooming me for life without him, but he never told me that he was honestly going to die. He may have joked about it, mentioned it, but he truly failed, and I mean failed miserably, in making me understand that one day I would get a call like I did, and once that call was over, my life without him started all over again.

The stages of grief are supposed to be denial, anger, bargaining, depression, and acceptance. I say bullshit! I am very angry already. I know he's gone; I'm not an idiot. I know when I walk on the clubhouse grounds tonight with hundreds of clubs from all over the world being there, Solomon will not be there. I accept that, but dammit, I am angry! I'm past denial, I don't bargain well with anyone, and depression is something that would enrage Solomon. Shed a tear for Solomon Starke? No. So I'm left with anger, and I am feeling it. Solomon had no fucking right to do this—none! Selfish bastard! Doesn't he know I have to walk onto our clubhouse grounds experiencing something I never had to experience?

The media has turned this into a damn circus. I have ten different news stations banging at my door, wanting interviews. And they all want the same thing: They want a piece of our history that we earned and created, so they can spin it into some cheesy byline. *The founder of one of the most notorious motorcycle gangs dies!* I know they'll be parked outside our front gate, along with Florida State Police and windowless vans with fucking satellite dishes on top, snapping a photo of every face entering. Fuck them! We got word out for everyone to meet a mile down the road at the beginning of an orange grove and to cover their face and license plate. Solomon would never give in to these parasites, either.

Venus has called at least ten times today. I've ignored every call. I just want to be alone. I called Babs and asked if she would take charge of Venus today, get her organized, and make sure she gets a ride here. My back seat is empty today.

As I roll into our clubhouse, the quagmire I predicted comes to fruition. Cameras, people with microphones, all sorts of cops, and windowless vans abound. J.J., Zonk, Big T, and our friend Glen stand as sentries. After closing the gate, they follow me onto our grounds. I ride in, unencumbered, and park my bike. The crowd is outside around a makeshift stage we made yesterday. Venus sees me, smiles, and starts to walk toward me, but stops. I nod to her slightly, and she walks with a bit more swiftness.

"Hi," she says timidly. She kisses me on the lips and steps back. "I'm sorry."

I nod and formulate a slight smile. "I'm glad you made it here," I say. "Now go hang out with the girls, okay?"

She nods. "Absolutely," she says. "You know where to find me if you need me."

"Yes, I do. Thank you."

As Venus walks away, I head to the podium, shake a few hands, and accept a couple of hugs along the way. I walk up the steps; the outside noises dissipate. I whisper to myself, *"I'm going to have my moment with you whether you like it or not."* I walk up to the edge and look out at the sea of faces, all friends in some way, all garnished with respect. To the right of the crowd are the Demons Rising members from all over. My first sentence sets the tone. I know that. I sigh. I close my eyes. I smell the embers.

"Thank you all for coming. Ya know, I purposely had this stage built to where I would be facing the woods in the back because I am not ready to face the clubhouse, nor am I ready to face the firepit where life excelled and grew for me, nurtured by words of wisdom, heartache, anger, humor, and love, all of which typically took place simultaneously." I look down at Scooby and make a drinking motion. He nods his head and runs to the clubhouse.

"I want you to meet my brother Solomon," I say. "I look around here and I see so many faces who have known him for decades, but I still feel the need to introduce you to him because y'all. . . ." I stop and smile slightly. *"You all,"* I say, correcting myself, "do not know the man we know, and even some of us are shielded from the real Solomon. I look out and see some clubs that were, at one time, at war with Demons Rising where punches flew, shots were fired, and blood was shed. Solomon was instrumental in starting the Florida coalition and merging enemies to unite us against the real enemies," I say, pointing to the parasitical citizen mob out in front of our clubhouse.

"But he is more, much more than that. Let me start with the bonfire pit you all see behind me. I cannot tell you how many hours or how many nights I sat there with him, talking about life. Solomon has this theory about good and evil. He always says how his soul is not savable and he is heading to hell someday. I would usually follow up with the customary joke about 'save me a chair if you get there first.'" The crowd shares in a laugh. Scooby brings me a jug of water and a bottle of Jack Daniels. I whisper to him, and he nods and runs off.

"But Solomon, right about many, many things, is totally wrong about him being evil. For reasons I don't wish to speculate or share with anyone, he wants that perception carried forth about him. There are three different anecdotes about Solomon that all intersect into one life lesson. I'll start with a story most, if not all, of the Demons Rising brothers know, and probably some of his older friends from the '60s and those who knew him in Vietnam. Solomon shared a story about a Vietcong attack where he shot and killed a twelve-year-old boy. He and I debated that story and his reaction to the shooting right there," I say, pointing to the firepit. "Solomon excoriated me—and I mean harshly—because I said he had to have felt some sort of sorrow for being forced to kill a boy that young. But if any of you ever tried arguing with Solomon, you all know you have a better chance of Helen Keller finding Waldo than winning an argument with him." I see heads nodding amidst the laughter.

"But there are some things that always struck me about that story that just didn't jive. Solomon specifically said the boy was twelve, not 'about twelve' or 'he looked to be twelve,' but he very explicitly said *twelve years old*. How did he know? Fair question? Did Vietcong carry photo identification? And when he described it to me in detail, he said, and this is a quote, *'I never had to forgive myself because I didn't care, and I still don't. I didn't think about his face, his name, his cry, his eyes. None of it.'* Think about that," I say with emphasis. "Think about his words. Solomon said he didn't think about *his face, his eyes, his cries* . . . really?" I ask rhetorically. "Sounds like awfully detailed descriptions of things *not* to think about. Face? Eyes? Cries? Those are powerful memories to have no memory of. And let us not forget the fact he mentions unambiguously about not *recalling* the boy's name. So he knew it at one time. Again, did the Vietcong have identification? How the hell did he know the boy's name? And before some of you say that could have just been a coincidence, it wasn't. And I can prove it." I take another sip of water. I look down at the crowd and see Venus. She has her arms folded neatly in front of her and is attentively looking at me.

"We all had an inside joke with Solomon about his son's name. His son, for those of you who don't know, is named Xavier Ignacious. Solomon blamed his ex, Sheila, for giving him that name. But I spoke to Sheila yesterday, and she assured me it was Solomon who named him, and she said he was extraordinarily passionate about it. And for those of us that know him well, you know that translates into *angrily about it*. Sheila told me he told her why about three years later." The crowd quiets, some waiting to have the confusion lifted. "Solomon did investigate the name of the boy he killed in Vietnam. He learned his age and his name. His name was *Shee*. Now it's a harder 'shhh' sound, but not quite a 'cha' sound. But the spelling in the boy's native country of his name is *X-I*, hence Xavier Ignacious." I hear the mumbling grow louder as many bodies twist and turn and look at one another and speak. "We all just sort of picked on Solomon about it, but in Solomon's mind, the significance ran deep. That Vietnamese boy never left Solomon. His face, his name, his cry, his eyes never left Solomon's mind."

"The third anecdote linking this is the time of year it happened. When Solomon told me that story, he said it happened in the winter of 1970. The word *winter* escaped me because we instinctively think of cold and snow, even those of us in Florida. But the fact is, after some research and speaking with Sheila, I learned this occurred on December 23rd, 1970, two days before Christmas." I look down at Venus, who gasps. She clutches her cheeks with both hands and shakes her head fervently. The tumblers just fell into place for her. "Solomon despises Christmastime. Oh, he tries, every year, to enjoy it for our sakes, but all Christmas does for him is remind him of seemingly the worst day of his life—a day he has never forgotten or forgiven himself for. Those of us in Demons Rising know all the Scrooge-like Christmas stories, and we all just chalked it up to the fact he is a crabby, old man. But the fact is, he is hurting every year. Just recently, Solomon was as drunk as I ever saw him, and although he was good-humored and cheery, it was an alcohol-fueled jovialness, which was unusual for him overall. He is either angry when he is drunk or very solemn, but never perky and upbeat. He said something to me outside that didn't resonate until today. He said he saw Christmas decorations at a store that day, and I didn't realize what an odd thing it was for him to bring it up out of nowhere. But now I see. Now I understand. The Christmas season had begun in his mind, and he ran to the handlebars and the bottle, like so many of us do."

I take another sip of water and gauge my own performance and reactions. I know I am speaking from the heart and with purpose, but I also know Solomon would not want these stories told. He sees them as a weakness, and he fears other clubs might also see them that way. I learned that with the whole Pancake Dave fiasco when he forced a vote on stories we can tell. But this man loves his brothers and is a good man, and the world, our world, the only world we care about, needs to hear it.

"I have one last story that I think must be told. I contemplated just telling Demons Rising members only, or just those in Demons Rising's inner circle, but I think in this new era of cooperation among the other clubs, we all could learn a bit from the story. I weighed the pros and cons of the age-old rule in every clubhouse, which is *'what happens here, stays here,'* and I think I can still honor that tradition and tell you this story simultaneously.

"Without the details of what led up to it, I will only say that Walt and Solomon nearly knuckled up with each other one night. Tempers cooled for the night, but Solomon reserved the right to confront Walt at a later date. The day of Willie's memorial was the day Solomon picked. Solomon made me leave the room. I was so angry at him, fearing he would clash on the very day Willie was laid to rest, so I never knew what occurred that day between the two of them." I look down at Walt, and he nods his head at me and smiles. I acknowledge his sign to me and then face the crowd once more. "Walt and I talked about this before I came up here because I wanted to make certain he agreed to let me tell, what is essentially, his story. Walt asked that I tell the story directly for him. Therefore, without adding any of my own words and such, I will simply recount what occurred and what was said between the two of them, according to Walt."

"Sit down, Walt," Solomon said with some seriousness in his tone.

"Why?" was all Walt replied.

"Because I said so, that's why. I don't have to explain. Now do it," Solomon said.

Walt sat down at the bar, and Solomon went behind the bar and fidgeted underneath momentarily. Walt looked on curiously and, admittedly, also with some trepidation. Solomon stood back up, holding a sandwich and a glass of milk. Solomon handed the sandwich to Walt and simply said, "Here."

"What is it?" Walt asked as he looked down at the sandwich.

"It's a peanut butter and jelly sandwich," Solomon responded.

Walt looked up at Solomon and glared. "Is this supposed to be funny?" Walt asked bitterly.

Solomon shook his head and said peacefully, "No . . . not at all, Walt."

"Then why are you doing this?" Walt asked with skepticism.

Solomon sighed heavily and tapped his fingers on the bar. "Well, Walt, I just wanted your brother to make you a sandwich for once," Solomon said earnestly.

Walt looked at Solomon, unsure what to say or do. Walt then picked up the sandwich, took a bite, and chewed it slowly.

"It's something that is very much long overdue for you, Walt," Solomon said sympathetically. "Long overdue."

Not another word was spoken as Walt ate the sandwich slowly, occasionally looking up at Solomon. Intermittently, he would sip the milk and then continue eating.

"For those of you who don't know, and without the details, Walt and Willie were also biological brothers, raised in an exceptionally brutal home. Often, their dad would lock Willie in the closet for days with no food or drink, and Walt, just a boy himself, would sneak him in peanut butter and jelly sandwiches." I stop, pause, and take a deep breath. "Walt said to me that he felt it was Solomon's way of apologizing, but I respectfully disagree. Solomon did not believe he was wrong, and in our own world, with our own rules, and our way of life that they don't understand," I say, pointing at the mass of citizenry out by our front gate, "Solomon was right, so an apology was not needed, meaning what Solomon did with Walt and the sandwich he did because he loves his brothers more than he loves himself, and that is the essence of who he is. That is not a man who once described himself as evil because anyone who knows that level of love for family cannot, by definition, be evil."

"Solomon teaches me so many things simply cloaked in his stories, his actions, and his inactions. I have always had this tendency to overthink things. I keep asking myself if this is how it's supposed to be, how it came to be, etcetera. But Solomon teaches me to deal with what is and just leave the *why* to a higher power to reason with. He teaches me to not think about life, just live it. He reminds me that such things as loyalty, justice, faith, honor, sacrifice, commitment, pride, and the concept of family are not just words, and they mean different things to different people. The words that define them stay the same, but what they mean to us and how we live them change exponentially and do so forever. Solomon teaches me that *you'll shed blood for your family, but you don't need blood to be family.*" I stop momentarily to take one last, big gulp of bourbon.

"Solomon despises fear, he despises weakness, but he has a compassion for people and understands how people think. As for me, right now, I am scared. There's a reason we are all out here and not in the clubhouse. We are here because I am scared. I am scared to death to walk in that building and know he won't be there, that his barstool will be empty, his voice deafened, and I am too scared to face that. If you haven't noticed, I am still talking about Solomon in the present tense. I can't say things like 'had' or 'did' or 'was' yet. Tonight, we are relighting the fire," I say, turning and pointing at the lifeless firepit, "and sending the flames so high, they burn Solomon's feet. I will not shed a tear for this man because that would enrage him. I ask that none of you do, either."

I bend down and pick up a bottle of Jack Daniels. "Scooby has handed all of you a shot of whiskey. So, from here on, without tears and without sadness, we keep the legacy of Demons Rising alive forever." I raise my bottle and shout: "To United States Marine Staff Sergeant Thomas Paul *(Solomon)* Starke, founder and president of Demons Rising Motorcycle Club!"

Everyone shouts: "Huzzah!"

I then look slightly to the right of the crowd—where Solomon's original five started out using Solomon's old, dilapidated garage as a clubhouse—that has now swollen into the thousands of Demons Rising members from all over the country here today, and I smile. And as we salute and say goodbye to our founder and the last charter member, I look proudly at the sea of faces.

"Brothers!" I screech, while raising my fist. "We-are-*Demons*!"

With smiles abound, they roar in response, "And-we-are-*Rising*!"

EPILOGUE

January 2020

"Are you Mister Garcia? Gregory's father?"

"Uh . . . yes . . . sort of," I respond with an uncomfortable smile.

"Yes," the man says cordially. "I'm aware of the nature of Gregory's new and extended family."

I nod my head and smile again.

"I'm Abbot Peterson, the troop's chairman."

"Digger," I say, extending my hand. "Digger Garcia."

"Well, Digger, I commend you for coming tonight. I think it showed a lot of character. Gregory is a good boy, he truly is," the chairman says.

"Thanks," I say, not certain why I feel the need to say so.

"Gavin and Shelly Charles have done a wonderful job raising him. They are highly active parents. Gavin sits on the local baseball youth board—he's a trustee for this troop—and Shelly is president of the P.T.A."

I nod my head and smile again. "I'm happy that he's been so fortunate."

"Gregory worked hard on obtaining his Eagle Scout. He chose this quite unique project of incubating abandoned baby birds," the chairman says. "He is truly making it his own. Boys like him make this organization so worthwhile. It instills great values like loyalty, justice, faith, honor, sacrifice, commitment, pride, and the concept of family."

"Yeah," I say faintly. "I was actually an Eagle Scout myself."

"Really?" he says pleasantly. "That's wonderful. Your father must have been pleased as punch for certain."

I reflexively nod my head in tacit agreement. "I would concur he took immense pride in that accomplishment for sure."

"I have no doubt, Mister Garcia," the chairman says. "The Scouts are a wonderful tradition. If not for organizations like this, they would learn their values in the street."

I emit a reflexive laugh and nod my head, looking straight ahead. "I agree." I sigh some and clear my throat. "But I like to think instead of the street, you can learn those values *on the road*."

The chairman grows a bewildered look on his face. "Uh . . . yes," he says and then pauses, not sure what to say. "I . . . uh . . . guess I don't quite follow."

I laugh again slightly. "That's okay." I pause and smile. "I'm just being a smart-ass," I say as I look at the chairman. "My . . . uh . . . dad, he used to always say that to me." I nod my head and smile. "'Digger!' he'd say, 'I know you're just being a smart-ass.' But he always said it with love, Mister Peterson. Always."

"That's a heartwarming story, Mister Garcia," the chairman says with a smile. "Your dad sounds like a wonderful man."

I finally feel a slight tear in my eye but wipe it quickly. "Yes, Mister Peterson," I say as I look out the window. "He most certainly was."

CPSIA information can be obtained
at www.ICGtesting.com
Printed in the USA
LVHW020115090819
627062LV00004BA/21/P